A Dark Omegaverse Novel Book Two

ALL'S FAIR IN PAST AND PRESENT

NICHOL GOLDSTEIN

NIXCOMIX
PUBLISHING

ALL'S FAIR IN PAST AND PRESENT
Published by NixComix Publishing
nixcomix.com

Copyright © 2023 by Nichol Goldstein / NixComix
No portion of this book may be reproduced in any form without permission from the publisher, including but not limited to reproducing, scanning, or distributing, except as permitted by US copyright law.

NixComix Publishing™ is a registered trademark, all rights reserved.

ISBN (print): 979-8-9870103-7-2
ISBN (e-book): 979-8-9870103-6-5

An application to register this book for cataloguing has been submitted to the Library of Congress.

First Edition: October 2023

Cover design by Fiona Jayde Media
Editing by Margaret Bates
Illustrations by Nichol Goldstein

This is a work of fiction. Names, characters, businesses, places, and incidents are the products of the author's imagination or used fictionally, and any resemblance to actual persons, living or dead, business establishments, events or locales is purely coincidental.

To Karen.
In all ways, shapes, and forms, this is for you.

WHOA-HO! A/B/O!

For those of you who read the first book in this series, you may remember the foreword explaining what to expect from the Omegaverse genre. Adding to that will be a small section on male Omegas.

THINGS TO KNOW:

Male Omegas share all the same traits a female Omega would, such as making lubricating slick and going through a periodic heat. Surprise! That includes having a uterus. Yes, friends, male Omegas have a womb squirreled away up their rears that can only be accessed during a heat and are completely capable of carrying and giving birth to children. Do note, we're not diving into the trope called "m-preg" at this time, just know it's something male Omegas are able to do.

For your information, similarly, female Alphas have knots and can impregnate others. Omegaverse is weird, isn't it? I love it so much.

Onward.

CONTENT WARNINGS

Explicit sexual content, abusive relationships, emotional manipulation, drugging/forced heat, graphic violence, stalking, kidnapping.

THE PAST

CHAPTER 1

MAMA

NILES STARED at his mother as if waiting for her to fall from the high, slender rope of a trapeze. His teeth clenched, his eyes rounded, and his child's heart thumped like a rabbit's. She didn't know he was looking, and that was the only reason he could.

It was much darker in his room than it was in the cramped kitchen where she sat like a stone. Niles and Trey's only window faced the faded brick wall of the building next door, its eight stories blocking their view of the summer sunset and keeping Niles hidden in the doorway's blackened shadow. He knew that wasn't what made the biggest difference between their spaces, though. It was the too-bright lightbulbs that hung over his mother's head. Landlady Kira put in the highest voltage possible, the kind that hurt to look at, all because they made it impossible to hide anything from her mean, graying eyes. Tiny cracks in the tiles. Chips on the stovetop. Little indents in the wall from when Niles or Trey knocked into it a little too hard. They were always knocking into something or other, running around, making their mom crazy. But she wasn't crazy just then. She was crying.

Niles peered into the long line of light between the open bedroom door and its badly painted frame, snooping even though he knew he shouldn't. His brother, his biggest protector, was deep asleep in their shared bed a few feet behind him after another hard day at school, leaving Niles to brave the moment alone. He snatched a glance over his shoulder at his brother's relaxed face, jealous of the peaceful dreams he saw there. He wished Trey would wake up to feel the truth of reality instead. The tension of it. The crackle of static in the air. The unlikable thrill you got when you were doing something you weren't supposed to.

Niles hated doing things alone, especially now. He was counting down the days to his brother's abandonment. Trey was going to middle school in the fall, leaving Niles to fend for himself in second grade all alone. Pessimist that he was, he knew it was only a matter of time until the bullies attacked. Once he had no big brother to fight his fights for him, it was an open invitation for the soon-to-be fourth graders to pounce. They were getting ready for it, giving Niles nasty grins when his brother couldn't see. He felt a pit of horrible tightness under his lungs every time he went to school now. It made him want to stay at home, safe under his covers. His mama called the feeling *dread*. Fear, but not the kind you had for what's happening today. It was fear for the things that were coming tomorrow. Dread was exactly what Niles felt right then.

His mother looked exhausted, the blinding lights making her tears track dark marks down her brown skin. One of her hands was tucked deep into her puff of tight black curls, clutching at them so hard her knuckles went pale. She was shaking. The water glass made clinking sounds against her wedding ring as she lifted it to her mouth…then took it down…then lifted…then down again. She never actually took a single sip. Her voice was low and small as she whispered, "I don't want to do this."

Her back to Niles, their social worker leaned over the kitchen table and clasped her hands together. "I know you don't."

His mother glanced up and Niles pulled back, taking shelter farther behind the door. He peered into their small living room and noticed his mom's bed was pulled out from the sofa. It was a mess of unmade blankets and her sneakers were half under the mattress frame. She must have been too tired to put them by the door. It caught Niles's attention in a strange way. Mama was always so bossy about keeping the shoes by the door.

"I'm trying! Can't you tell them I'm trying?" his mother said, hanging her head and shaking it back and forth. "Ever since James died, all I've been trying to do is get us on our feet, but who wants an Omega clogging up their payroll with her heat leaves and mother's hours when they can have a full-time Beta? All I have is my hands, Lou! I don't have degrees or sponsors or, hell, even boyfriends! I've got no one but those two little boys, and I'll be damned if—"

"They're going to take them, Deidre. If you try to fight, you'll lose, and it will make more of a financial mess than you can afford to clean up."

"Why is this happening?" his mother said, her voice a whimper.

"Mrs. Kline."

His mother's face went narrow-eyed with anger even as her mouth pulled up at the corners. "Mrs. Fucking Kline."

"Yes, Mrs. Fucking Kline," the social worker agreed. "She said Trey was eating out of the garbage."

"That's a goddamn lie, and you know it!"

"I know, Dee. I do. But she hates you, she hates your kids, and it doesn't matter how many people I tell about it. She's biased and terrible, and everything she's doing is wrong, wrong, wrong. But all people see is that Niles has less than a week's worth of clothes…"

"That I keep clean and neat and—"

"…and that the boys are skinny…"

"Of course, they're skinny! Have you seen half the kids in their class? They're rail thin, all of them! And my boys are the tallest in their grades!"

"…and they also know you're getting evicted."

Niles's mother froze, her full lips parting slightly. Her lashes seemed to sparkle with the tears puddling in her eyes. "How would they know that?"

The social worker shrugged. "You've got two young kids. Maybe they said something?"

Niles's stomach dropped. *He* had said something. He asked for Jeremy's mom's phone number so they could still be friends if he had to change schools. Jeremy had asked why.

"And you don't have housing lined up, do you, Dee? Where are you going to stay? The car?"

His mother grabbed the cup again, and this time, she did drink. A big gulp that made her throat work.

"It's about to be summer," the social worker said, digging into a bag stashed under her chair and taking out paperwork. "The kids are going to be out of school, and you have no one to keep them with."

"Tessa—" his mother started.

"Has already told you she won't take them again. How are you going to get a job with them around, huh? Ask the kids to sit in the lobby while you do interviews? Make them hang out at the park all by themselves once you actually manage to get on the schedule somewhere?"

His mother's shoulders curled in, as if she was shrinking. She let out the terrible, soft sounds of sniffles and sad hiccups.

"I understand." The social worker tried to take his mother's hand, but she pulled away.

"No, you don't."

There is a pause and a deep sigh as Niles stared at the social worker's back. Her shirt had little flowers printed on it, but that bright kitchen light washed them out until it seemed like there was no color at all.

"You're right, I don't. But you need to make a decision. Do you want a better life for your children? Do you want food in their bellies and clothes on their backs? Because if you do, then you let them go."

That horrible twist of his gut owned Niles as he tried his best to stay quiet.

Mama, please don't let them take us. Fight. Fight and bite and never let us go.

But she did none of those things. Instead, his mother squinted at the white glare shining down from the ceiling, her arms wrapping around herself. "Do you promise not to separate them?"

Niles recoiled, head swimming.

The social worker flipped open her papers and turned one toward his mom with a pen in her hand. "I'll see what I can do."

Stumbling back from the doorway as silently as he could, Niles watched the world get blurry as his tears fell. He wanted to scream, but his voice wouldn't work. He didn't have enough air, no matter how fast he breathed. Sheer panic sent electric fire under his dark skin.

It wasn't just his brother who was leaving him behind. It was everyone.

THE PRESENT

CHAPTER 2
CHANCE MEETING

Niles sighs and peeks at his phone, checking the time as he stands in line at the swanky, pricy coffee shop, its fancy swivel chairs in vintage colors more decorative than useful. He drew the short straw at work today and, lo, was sent off to brave Boston's fluffy snowflakes on a never-ending quest to save the office from the java junk management stocks in their little kitchen. That shit is like waxing your insides with every scalding hot swallow.

He flicks his round, earth-colored eyes to the window and purses his full lips. Niles takes in the gentle fall of snow with all the patience of a woman in a long line with a small bladder, tapping his foot irritably and missing the fall season with his whole heart. It may or may not be exacerbated by the fact that he can no longer get pumpkin spiced anything, but that's a fact he'll tuck away into his heart and admit to no one.

"Excuse me," someone murmurs, and a man reaches over to grab some swizzle sticks perched with their kin to Niles's right. Niles glances at him so casually he doesn't even see him until the man keeps his proximity and stares a little too hard.

"Oh. Excuse me," the man says again. Upon second glance, he's not bad looking. Large. Strong. Blonder and more blue-eyed than Niles likes, but not terrible. Niles takes a quick, shallow breath through his nose to get a sense of this stranger. Despite his size, he's a Beta.

Niles lifts an eyebrow. "You're excused?"

"Sorry, that came out wrong." The man huffs a chuckle and points his nose directly at his shoes. "Um, this might be a bit forward of me—"

Then I suggest you don't do it, Niles thinks mildly.

"—but you don't happen to be an Omega, do you?"

Niles's eyes are like a planet in orbit, rolling around in their fullest circumference. How a Beta could tell what his designation is, he has no idea. It's not like the man could smell it on him. A Beta's senses don't work that way. He's not wrong, though.

It's annoying. Male Omegas are rare in the best of times, but Niles is a true miracle. A tall, black, *gay* male Omega. Looking for one of him is beyond a needle in a haystack. It's a single bubble in an Olympic-sized swimming pool of champagne. It gets him noticed by every Alpha male—even straight ones—just for being the sheer anomaly he is.

"How did you guess?" Niles says, a tiny sarcastic tick of the side of his mouth saying all he'd like to on the matter.

"Sorry," the man continues. "It's just…well…you're really pretty."

Pretty. Oof, he hates that word. "Handsome, you mean?"

The man fumbles his words this time, getting pink in the cheeks. "Yes. Yes, sorry, handsome. All the Omegas I know are stunning."

Well, that was the nicest thing anyone has said to him all day.

"Plus, you know, you smell amazing."

It must be his new cologne. There was a commercial that snagged his brain on a hook: a gorgeous, lithe man swam with an untamed horse in the ocean before transforming into a centaur—an ad spot which was somehow intended to sell perfume, mind you—and, against all odds, it was effective as hell. Niles bought two bottles on day one and now dabs it on himself religiously. That plus his scent blockers are supposed to hide his Omega designation and keep the unwashed males at bay.

"Thanks," Niles says, not exactly unused to people coming on to him so strong. "What can I say? We Omegas have a thing about scents."

The Beta male blushes harder and shifts back and forth from one foot to the other, a shy smile thinning his curled lips. "What do I smell like?"

Ugh. Why do Betas always want to play this game? It's like they expect you to taste test every frigging note in the air, asking things like, "Oh, do I smell like chrysanthemums dipped in chocolate with a droplet of barbecue sauce and a smidge of dirt?" or other weird mixes no one's ever smelled before.

"Next please!" a barista calls from behind the counter, luckily too caught up in her hard day's work to notice Niles's painful encounter.

"That's me!" He raises his hand to half-mast and walks forward, skirting the black strap that keeps everyone in queue. When he pulls a list from his pocket, the barista eyes it narrowly, her scent suddenly reeking of exhaustion. Niles can sympathize.

"Don't worry," he reassures her, "Not only is it a long list, but it also has lots of special 'only one and a half squirts, not two' crap for you to deal with."

The Blond Beta behind him snickers, and Niles smirks in spite of himself.

"But the best part is"—Niles hands the list over—"I don't care if you spit in any of it…except the hazelnut. That one's mine. The rest is fair game." He flashes his best grin and flips his long black-woven-with-blue braids over his shoulder.

The woman behind the counter feigns offense. "I don't spit in things. I only sneeze."

"Admirable. Such restraint should be rewarded," Niles says as seriously as possible, earning chuckles from both the Blond Beta and the barista this time. He's on a roll today.

"I'll get this together, gimme a minute." She considers the list again, grimacing. "Maybe a few minutes."

Niles says his thanks and pulls to the side, slipping his phone from his pocket and thumbing through the passcode, checking his texts. His best friend sent him a message this morning complaining her feet were somehow swelling out of her shoes, and he feels a deep-seated need to harass her about it.

"I'll have hazelnut, too," Blond Beta says to another barista taking his order as he hands over a rewards card and a twenty. When Niles turns to face him, the Beta shrugs with a smile. "They don't have anything pumpkin spiced, so you've got to get your flavor somewhere."

The man's street cred suddenly goes up a notch in Niles's book… until he accidentally drops the cash on the floor, lunges down to get it, and *baffs* his forehead off the counter with a grunt. Niles winces on his behalf, his shoulders pulling up to his ears as he lets out a sympathetic hiss.

Waving the money at the wide-eyed man behind the counter, the Blond Beta manages a proper hand off this time. Face flushed, he touches his forehead with a gingerliness that silently screams, "Well, that hurt!"

After receiving his change with no further injury, he steps up beside Niles, smelling like sheer humiliation woven atop something sharper. It's unlike any Beta Niles has ever smelled before. Not bad, just different.

"Sorry you had to see that," the man mumbles, tucking his change in his pocket.

Niles waves his phone absently. "I saw nothing. Of what speakest thou?"

The Beta's face blooms into a smile while his forehead simultaneously blooms into a bruise. "You're funny."

"And pretty, apparently."

"Handsome," the man corrects, holding up a finger and *tsk*ing him lightly. "I hear it's better to say handsome."

They share a moment of silence as Niles tries and fails to make his best friend laugh via speech bubbles.

"So," Blond Beta says, rocking on his heels. "Would it be offensive if I asked you to sit and drink your coffee with me before you go?"

Startled from his phone, Niles takes in the man's hopeful face and pastes a sympathetic smile on his own. "I've got to get the order back to the office."

Unfazed, the man tries, "How about same time, same place tomorrow?"

The phrase "Take a hint" swirls a spiral through Niles's thoughts, and his smile tightens. "Sorry, I don't think so."

It doesn't seem to change the man's facial expression much, except that he seems more interested. His eyes glimmer brighter, and that sharp piece of his scent raises a tick.

Niles lifts his eyebrows. Is it obnoxious to say he doesn't date Betas? Not anymore at least.

Thankfully, he doesn't have to explore that train of thought, because the barista calls his name, his order assembled in the most precarious way possible, and Niles uses that as an excuse to say his abrupt goodbyes, gather his caffeinated burden, and work his way back out of the shop again.

"Ohhhh, you have become my ultimate best friend," Katelyn says as she shuffles forward, arms out and fingers itching to latch onto her mocha peppermint monstrosity. Her funky dress is somewhere between hipster and bohemian, and her thick, red-rimmed glasses clash well with her dangly, peacock feather earrings.

Niles hands over her order with an exaggerated sigh. "Yes, yes, I know. We all suffer a horrible addiction, and I am your dealer today."

Her lips wrap around the wide, environmentally friendly paper straw in a pink lipped pucker. Eyes sinking closed, she slurps her drink, humming in satisfaction.

"Yo!" Niles calls out to his smallish office. "Come show me the adoration I so rightly deserve!"

There are a few "woots" from the cubes across the floor as people jockey for position and first dibs on their mid-afternoon jolt of energy. There are shoulder pats and thank yous, but most importantly, everyone pays up their seven dollars in exact change. Niles hasn't held this many dollar bills since he last went to a strip club—which he hated, by the way. Too many hormones, pheromones, and G-strings.

"C'mon," Katelyn says after he's relieved of coffee duty. "I want to show you my layout."

Her walk is somewhere between a skuttle and a skip as she leads him to her cube. "Look. What do you think of this color palette?"

Niles checks out her screen, leaning over her chair slightly—a rickety thing that creaks as he settles his weight on the back. Sadly, the office has yet to invest in bringing them out of their 80s vibe into something without that odd shade of orange laced with fuchsia triangle patterns. To make matters worse, Katelyn's cube is covered, wall to wall, with postcards of abstract geometric patterns in blacks, whites, and painful rainbows. The visual clutter is louder than a shrill flute, which suits her personality perfectly.

Niles asks, "Didn't they say they wanted something in the green family?"

"Teal is totally in the green family." Katelyn squints at her own work.

"Lime and forest and hunter are in the green family," he points out.

She pouts. Adjusting her glasses, she hits Control + U to bring up the color panel and tweaks a few dials, ebbing out the blue. "I don't like it," she grumbles.

"Attached to our vision, are we?"

"I had this whole ocean theme in my mind."

"And your landscaping client would want an ocean theme, why?"

She huffs and sucks her drink again. "Because it's pretty."

Niles chuckles. "If you don't want Kevin to come down on you, think *jungle*."

"Jungle," she mutters to herself, her mind obviously whirling down a new creative path. Snapping out of it suddenly, she cocks her hip and nibbles her straw, speaking through her teeth. "So, what's up with Beebee? You find her yet?"

Niles sighs. "No. And I've put posters up all over the Common."

"With pictures?"

"Yeah, her and me together with my phone number at the bottom. You have no idea how many people have either sexted me, tried to sell me something, or attempted to pass off some dirty alleyway corgi for the beauty that is my Pomeranian."

"I love her tail," Katelyn recalls, having been lambasted with pictures of Niles's dog when she first went missing a few days ago.

On cue, he yanks out his phone and shows his lock screen. Bee-bee lights up the camera lens with her adorable doggie tongue lolling out and her little eyes bright and happy. "Who wouldn't love her tail? It's a puff ball! An actual puffball!"

He stares at the picture of his dog with his heart aching. Everyone in his life always leaves him. When he was young, his father was shot, his mother gave up him and his brother to foster care before dying of cancer, and he never saw his brother again after Trey aged out of the system. Not to mention the fact that Niles's best friend up and moved away to be with her Alpha soulmate. And now, even his precious Bee-bee has decided to find greener pastures.

Shamefully, his eyes dampen, and he takes a deep breath.

"Hey," Katelyn says in an absurd growling voice, rubbing his back too hard and too fast. "I know, buddy. You'll find her."

He nods sharply, tucking his phone away. "I hope so." He sniffs back wetness and plucks at his shirt for no reason other than to do it. "What time is it?"

Katelyn lifts her wrist to glance at her paisley-strapped watch. "About three."

"Crap. I've got a meeting with the devil."

"Jannah isn't the devil, Niles. She's just a low-level imp with a gap in her front teeth."

He smirks at that. "She's going to hate the campaign I have to show her."

Katelyn blinks, draining the last of her drink with a hollow slurping sound. "Why?"

Simply, "Because Kevin will like my idea better than hers."

With a slight tic of his eyebrows, Niles winks, blows a platonic kiss, and strides off to pick up his laptop. It's time to put on a show for the office imp.

Said Imp had been truly annoyed and yet, wonder of wonders,

admitted his plan was the better idea. It was a shock to his system, one he celebrated with a glass or two or four of cheap wine last night. Alone.

This morning, Niles's fingers fly over his phone screen as he waits for his own, singular coffee and texts his best friend Ari.

> I love it when I win.

> I wouldn't call it winning. I'd call it doing your job.

> Stingy. I let YOU say you won when you do all your lawyer-y things.

> That's because I'm literally winning.

> Cases, that is.

> Not, like, life in general.

> Don't be a brat, you're totally winning life in general.

She sends over a blushing face.

> So, did your Alpha pass his PT test or did he fail with flying colors?

> He didn't not pass.

> That's a very confusing answer.

> Ha! He actually did GREAT!

Little bubbles flutter on the screen, taking too long as Niles moves a step forward in the trailing morning coffee line. Her text should have come by now; instead, there are more bubbles. And then more. And more.

> If you're about to send some epic tale about either how awesome he is or how awesome you are for cheerleading him, I don't want to hear it.

Those bubbles disappear, and Niles grins at his own prowess. He called it.

There is a long pause where Ari must be sulking and staring at her phone until bubbles start again.

> You're no fun. Who can I regale with my wins and woes, if not you?

Niles sends her a GIF of a superhero standing in the cheesiest pose ever. It's literally captioned "Cheesiest Pose Ever." It gets him little "ha-has" attached to his message.

> When are you coming over?

> When I find Bee-bee.

There is another pause. She's probably debating telling him he'll never see his dog again. If it's been this many days, Bee-bee's either been taken in by people who were happy to obtain a free designer dog, or she strayed too far into the road and…

Ari interrupts his morbid train of thought.

> Hey, you know someone will call you ASAP once they find her. Come over. It's Friday! And it's not like I live eight hours away or anything.

> Traffic dependent.

> Yeah well, there's that.

Ari left Boston proper when she met her Alpha. Her *real* Alpha. She was in a terrible, impossible situation that breaks Niles's heart even now, and it makes complete sense she'd move as far away from the mess that was her life in this city, but she used to be only fifteen minutes away. That was when traffic was stop and go…and then stop some more. Now she's thirty minutes in the dead of night, forty when traffic is light, and ninety or more in commuter traffic. He hates it. He hates it, and he's lonely.

Niiiiiiiiiiiles!

It's like he can hear her whine in his mind. Ari sends over dozens of desperate, teary-eyed faces. Then double-weepy faces. Then skulls.

Yeah, yeah. I'll be there. Are you cooking or Ben?

Ben cooks worse than I do.

Exactly. I'm trying to figure out how much antacid to bring.

…

…

…

That's it, I'm lacing your food with urine.

I'd expect nothing less.

She sends a GIF of a small child with chubby cheeks making an enraged, fury-filled face and shaking a hairbrush at him. He chuckles to himself.

Love you.

Love you back. Go win or something.

To which he sends a purple, devilish face.

Smiling to himself, he approaches the counter and sees the same barista from yesterday. She doesn't seem to recognize him, which makes sense when you're pushing out order after order to random faces every day. But he had made her laugh. Isn't that supposed to count for something?

"Hazelnut," Niles says. "The largest one you've got, please."

"Name?" she asks, barely looking at him.

"Niles."

"Spelled with a 'y' or an 'i?'"

Who the hell spells Niles with a y?

"An 'i.'"

She scrawls something unintelligible, his name evidently, on a cup with a haphazard 'HAZ' below and sets it beside her. "Okay, that will be—"

"Wait," a voice calls from behind Niles, scootching around him and approaching the counter with his hand out, a little rewards card in it. "He can have my discount for the day."

Blinking, Niles realizes it's the Blond Beta, far larger than he should be and smelling eager atop that sharp scent that's all him. "You don't have to do that."

The man seems sheepish with a tiny, baby smile on his face. "I know."

Still, he waves his card in the barista's general direction until she takes it with her eyebrows up, surveying Niles as if asking his thoughts on the matter. Niles shrugs, unsure if he wants to make a scene by turning the man down, and who doesn't want five percent off? It's almost as if you don't have to pay taxes. Massachusetts already has too many taxes.

Niles decides to get his own rewards card.

The barista gives him the new price with a suggestive smile, flicking her eyes at the Blond Beta, who has shoved his hands in his pockets while he stares at his shoes with unbridled fascination.

After handing over his credit card, Niles says the polite thing. "Thank you."

"NowWillYouHaveCoffeeWithMe?" blurts from the man's mouth, the words strung together fast and blurred.

Ah, and here's what Niles was trying to avoid.

Clearing his throat, he says, "Sorry, I have to get back to work."

"I work near here, too," the man says, finally peeking up. "What building are you in?"

Niles isn't quite sure why he answers him. "This one, actually. Up a few floors."

"Do you, um, do you go out for lunch?"

Oh, dear. This poor, unsmooth, awkward, tenacious man.

"I bring myself a lunch bento."

The man's eyebrows pull together. "What's a bento?"

"Jason," the barista interrupts. "Are you going to order, or am I going to marry you both at my counter."

The man, Jason apparently, turns a furious red again and puts his face in his hands. "Jenna, would you just…just…"

She sets Niles's drink on the counter. Behind them, in the winding line of morning coffee-goers, there is a mix of reactions. Some of amusement, some of weight shifting in annoyance at the delay, and some of blissful oblivion, their noses to their screens, lost in some imaginary phone world.

Unfazed, the barista waves Blond Beta Jason off. "Yes, I will get you your hazelnut."

Niles smirks. "But will you stop embarrassing him is the question."

Jason tosses the ceiling a look of "Someone save me," and Niles chuckles at his expense. The man seems harmless. And he's trying very hard. Plus, his constant embarrassment is sort of endearing.

"Miss Jenna," Niles asks, "would it be alright if I brought my bento here for lunch today?"

She echoes Jason. "What's a bento?"

"I can't explain its compartmentalized, portion-controlled wonder."

"That's what the internet is for," someone in line gripes, his boiling point tipped. His business suit is impeccable, his tie politically red as he twirls his fingers in a forward motion. "Can we speed it up?"

Niles shifts the winter jacket draped over his arm so he can hold his hot beverage of choice. "Noon-thirty, maybe?" he asks Jason.

A slow smile spreads on the man's face. "That would be nice."

With that, Niles ducks back through the doorway leading into the vestibule of the skyscraper-tall office building.

"Was it a date?" Ari asks, her eyes wide and glittering as she stirs the pot of beef stew.

There are a great many recipes in this wide world Niles's best friend destroys, but beef stew isn't one of them. Caleb—her first… husband, Niles guesses is the best thing to call him—had left her a litany of things when he died. One of them was a homemade recipe book that was titled *Kitten Can Cook*. It was tucked away in a safe under the bed, and Ari was inconsolable when she found it. It's precious to her. To keep Caleb alive in her heart, she makes use of every gift he gave her, refusing to toss or squirrel it away. Ari is someone who gathers up sad memories and uses them to build her into who she is today, after all. She doesn't run from them, hide from them, or bury them, like Niles does. She just lets herself feel them. He admires her for that. Ben, her Alpha, does too.

Ben sits at the table, his walker by his side, leaning back with his fingers laced over his flat belly. "A date, hmm?"

"It was absolutely not a date. I shoved sushi in my mouth while he ate something panini-ish. It was an amicable eating-meals-in-the-same-space sort of moment."

"So, a date," Ari confirms, taste-testing her own concoction, crying out because it's too hot, and panting to cool her tongue.

Ben snickers, so in love that it's sickening, and tugs her apron strings. Likely intentional, he manages to mostly untie them as he pulls her backwards to sit on the arm of his kitchen chair.

"I wanna go on a date," Ben purrs.

"Audience!" Niles scolds, whapping his hand off the table. "Honestly! Have some compassion!"

At which, a devilish grin splits Ben's face as he nuzzles Niles's best friend. She's too busy sucking air in and out to notice though, waving at her tongue and oblivious to the show her mate's putting on.

"Dew yew tink yull see him agaiwn?" she says, tongue still out of her mouth.

Niles shrugs casually. "He's a Beta."

"So is eighty percent of the world," Ben reminds. "Don't look down on Betas."

Which is difficult sometimes. All three designations work together and share the world, of course, and some of Niles's favorite colleagues are Betas, but there's always an air of condescension when you can no longer pretend you're all the same, and designations actually come into play. Betas hate picking up the extra work when their Alpha colleagues go into rut or Omegas into heat. An Alpha's innate aggression tends to earn them higher paid salaries, no matter whether it's a white or blue collar job, causing deep wells of jealousy and bitterness in the Beta community.

Meanwhile, Omegas are expected to be subservient, even outside their heat—which is absurd, by the way—causing chasmic rifts when Betas say something thoughtless and asinine. Despite popular opinion, Omegas are just as strong as anyone else and are intensely offended should you suggest otherwise...unless it's an Alpha. A special Alpha. *Their* Alpha. One who makes their body weak for their command.

Niles could never be weak for a Beta's command. There's no such thing. They have no special pheromones, no deep, dark, liquid gold voices, no tantalizing scent glands, and no sharp eye-teeth for that perfect, dreamed-of mating bite. They don't even have knots, which is the key draw of an Alpha during sex. Sure, there are toys and, well, attachments to help a Beta fake it, but it's not the same. Niles would know.

It's not like he hasn't been approached by Omega-chasers, the same way his counterparts can have run-ins with Alpha-climbers. Some Betas have relegated the other designations into a fetish or checkbox fantasy, and it's not like every Alpha and Omega refuses that kind of attention. In the end, they're all just people.

"I'm not trying to look down on them, but I'd have to be hardcore into a guy to let something like that go without thinking about it. Plus, he's too mild-mannered."

"But forward," Ben adds. "You said he came straight out and asked if you like guys."

"Like he couldn't tell already. Have you met me? Either way, he didn't make eye contact when he asked. He's too damn meek."

"But brave enough to get your attention," Ari chimes in.

Niles points at the two. "No ganging up on me. I refuse."

"Just hang out with him. You don't have to have sex," Ben says, suggestively nipping up Ari's arm until she stands with a squeak, going back to stir her stew.

"And even if you do have sex,"—Ari has the sense to blow on the ladle this time before taking a taste—"it's not like you have to marry him. Just be casual."

"Casual," Niles muses. "I'm good at casual."

And it's true. He hasn't had a serious boyfriend since high school. That went so wrong, it warded Niles off men completely for a while. Now he has no desire to fall in love, except for that he's so damn lonely.

"I miss my dog," Niles sighs.

"Non sequitur," Ari says.

"Well, I do. I've got no one to come home to at night, and texting you is only so enjoyable, you know."

"What about me?" Ben grumps. "I text you."

"Yeah, but it's usually to ask me questions about *her*." Niles points a glare at his best friend.

"And to have you talk me down from suing half the state for not being ADA compliant."

"Ah, yes. *That*. You're always such a cheerful man."

"You try to be cheerful when the ramp is too steep, you bastard." Though it's said with love.

"But that's why your arms are so buff! Without that little challenge, you'd have super scrawny bi's and tri's."

"Ri-ri? Kill your friend for me?"

Ari snorts over her stew, saying nothing as she adds in some red wine. Some for the stew, some for her glass, but most of it for Niles. He knew he liked her for a reason.

"He's driving," Ben reminds.

"He's staying over," Ari counters.

"He likes the guest bedroom," Niles says of himself, taking the proffered drink in hand and wishing for some expensive cheese to go along with it. "You have my favorite silky pillow."

Ben pouts.

"Ugh," Niles says. "Don't be like that. You can still have sex, Benjamin, just be quiet about it."

"Impossible," the soulmated pair says simultaneously, Ben with a smarmy grin and Ari with a resigned sigh.

Frowning, Niles can't help but agree. They suck at silence. Unfortunately, he knows firsthand.

Maybe he doesn't like the guest bedroom after all.

This is stupid. Niles is stupid. More than stupid. Idiotic. Moronic. Absurd. Dunderheaded. All the thesaurus words.

It's noon-thirty yet again, and Niles slinks into the coffee shop, bento in hand, peering side to side like a cat burglar, ready to spook at the smallest—

"Niles!"

He doesn't *eep*. He swears to God he doesn't *eep*.

Jason is sitting in the sun, the coffee shop window showcasing the gray winter mist alongside the slush and grime of the city streets. Skyscrapers frame the clouds as pedestrians stream by, but the Blond Beta has eyes only for Niles, a good boy smile on his good boy face.

"You came," Jason says.

Truth be told, they hadn't planned to make a second date (though this is not a date!), in fact, they never even talked about speaking again. Yet, here Niles is, heart in his throat as he jerks a thumb behind him.

"I'll get us drinks, yeah?" he says.

That good boy smile gets wider. "Thanks."

Niles is more than happy to turn on his heels and get in line. The barista glances at him with a smirk of recognition, and Niles can't help but think, *Not so forgettable now, am I?*

He already knows it's a mistake to be here, but how cute is it that the guy was waiting for him? Or maybe he comes here all the time, and this is a coincidence. Or maybe it's fate or something. Or maybe Niles is just a dumbass. Perhaps all of the above.

Heading back to the table, two coffees in hand, Niles catches Jason unwinding a heavy scarf from his turtleneck sweater. The Blond Beta sits straight up in the chair with perfect, rigid posture. It's not that he seems bred into prim propriety or anything. He just seems tense and electric.

"DoYouHaveABoyfriend?" Jason blurts out this time, immediately looking like he wants to die, and Niles doesn't know whether to smack him or pat his shoulder in sympathy. "I mean,"—Jason waves his hands back and forth as if trying to wipe his words away—"I recently went through a really bad break up, but…you know…that doesn't mean I can't do better next time! I have hope for the future!"

What the hell is this guy? Niles wonders, clearing his throat.

"I'm sorry! I don't mean to make this awkward!" Jason puts his face in his hands and grunts, thereby making it even more awkward.

Niles takes pity on the now-confirmed Omega-chaser.

"The only relationship I'm in is the one with my dog," Niles says. "However, she has left me at the altar to galavant around the city with God knows who and will likely come back pregnant if she comes back at all." He'd meant that to sound charming, he really did, but his bitterness seeped through.

"Oh no! What's her name?"

Niles takes a sip of his drink and lets the warmth fill his belly. "Bee-bee."

"That's cute. Do you have a picture of her?"

Sitting back in his chair, Niles works his phone out of his pocket and hands it over, the lock screen bright with his cheerful pup on the background wallpaper.

"Wow. That's much cuter than I thought. You seemed like a golden retriever kind of guy."

Niles's eyebrows go up. "Disappointed?"

"Never," Jason replies. Niles is about to say something self-deprecating to change the subject when the man plows on. "I can help you find her. Put up posters and stuff. Where did you lose her?"

"The Common. I had her off-leash and another dog, a big one, pounced. I think it was only playing, but she yipped and streaked away. I followed her little paw prints in the snow for a while, but they got mixed in with other dogs and people and…I dunno. It's been almost a week. I need to start preparing myself for the fact that she's not coming back."

Jason touches the screen to keep it from fading to black, staring intently at the picture like he really cares. It makes Niles tenderhearted despite everything.

He gives himself a moment to take in the other man. Jason's not unattractive, even if he's not Niles's usual type. It's not that he doesn't like white boys, but he does like *toned* boys. Jason is not one. Big as he is, he seems more like a bear, although Niles can't see his shape through his winter clothes well enough to know. He idly wonders what Jason's naked body is like, but more out of curiosity than any sort of erotic desire. The man has high cheekbones, denim-blue eyes, and thin, pink lips that pull into a straight line as he seems to try to memorize Niles's dog.

"She has a white diamond shape before her tail," he notices.

"I almost named her Sparkle, but that was too girlie, even for me."

The man hums and nods before handing the phone back over. "I can help. I live near the Common."

"You must be rich."

He smiles. "I'll keep my eye out for her. Bee-bee, right?"

Niles nods, appreciating the man's kindness enough to offer a little honesty. "Just so you know, I'm not looking for a relationship right now. My best friend went from, well, the absolute worst to the absolute best, and I'm not ready for either of those experiences."

Jason lets out a breathy laugh. "How about something completely mediocre?"

Niles chuckles at the man's insistence. He can't help it. Rubbing his eyes with one hand and letting his flattered grin reign supreme, he offers, "For now, why don't we stick to lunch?"

The man's face is like the sun, the way it beams. "I can do that."

Niles's hands are dug deep into his hoodie's center pocket as he saunters down the aisle, scanning his eyes over this and that, working his way through the pharmacy section of the department store. Ari's most recent concoction wasn't the thing that did him in. No. It was Ben's morning meal of basically raw bacon. Niles needs something to coat his stomach lining and stopper his asshole, or he's going to have a real problem, real fast. This is not the way in which he would prefer to die.

He sighs loudly, not just to himself, but to anyone who's listening, *everyone* who's listening, because he's being followed. Again.

Here we go, he thinks.

Breathing in, Niles can smell various people milling about—someone in aisle twelve spritzing on every perfume known to man and someone in aisle ten oozing with body odor—but there's one scent that's lurked behind him for the past five minutes or so, haunting Niles with whiffs of wintergreen. He glances out of the corner of his eye to see a store clerk's red vest, the dumpy man within watching and waiting for Niles to steal something. Kicking himself, Niles flits from aspirin to adult diapers. He should have known better than to wear his old hoodie in a place like this. He's in the hoity toity part of town. A place where people say all the right things but think all the wrong thoughts in their paranoid, suspicious, little minds. To say he's not in the mood would be an understatement.

Cutting through the recycled air are dangerously smooth words aimed at his stalker. "You must think he smells amazing."

Niles freezes. He knows that voice.

"Because if you're following him around for any reason other than that, you're about to back the fuck off."

Behind him, the racist clerk's scent spikes with adrenaline. "S-sorry!" he chokes out, and Niles can hear his cheap shoes squeaking as he turns tail and hustles away.

Trying to play it as cool as he possibly can, Niles picks up a bottle of pink antacid without turning around, trying to tamp down his urge to vomit.

There's a huff of laughter behind him. "What, no 'Hello to you, too?'"

Niles tries to keep his voice steady, though he feels like his heart is about to jackknife into his stomach. "Hello to you, too."

He inhales slowly and turns to see a man he hasn't seen since high school. A man he still dreams about, both as fantasies and nightmares. A man he never wanted to see again.

Tristan.

He doesn't look the same, but he also does. His black hair is faded perfectly at the sides, the top wild with soft waves. His skin is a beautiful, tanned brown, and his eyes are so tawny they're almost yellow. His jawline is cut for fashion magazines and edged with trim facial hair. His clothes are designer and form-fitted. This is no longer the scrawny teenager who presented so late, the one who Niles thought was a Beta when he fell in love with him, the one whose transition into Alphadom was so destructive, it left a scar on Niles that would never fade.

Niles swallows, a million emotions zipping through his body at full speed. He is thrumming with excitement, fear, curiosity, nostalgia, heartache, and the nearby Alpha must smell it on him. Tristan's position goes from straight-backed and protective to round-shouldered and soft with his hands out in front of him.

"I'm sorry. I just saw that guy following you and—"

"Thank you," Niles manages, trying to rally through his cascade of feelings. "But I'm not worried about people like that." He nods in the direction of the clerk who slithered away.

"Yes, you are," Tristan replies simply, knowing him all too well. That slight contradiction alone is enough to make Niles's Omega ache.

You were ours once, Alpha. You were ours, but you betrayed us. Frightened us. And broke our heart.

Keeping his posture non-threatening, Tristen steps back, giving Niles more space as if trying to ensure he's comfortable. Niles doesn't know if he likes that or not. Part of him wants his Alpha to step closer while another part wants him to disappear completely.

"You look great," Tristan says. Gesturing, he draws his fingers down in a flowing line from his head over his shoulder. "I love your hair. The blue is a nice touch."

"Matches the color of my eyes, don't you think?"

Tristen snorts. "Your *brown* eyes?"

"Whatever do you mean? They're blue as sky."

A smile that could only be considered dopey spreads on Tristan's face as he draws his words into long drawls. "There you are. I was wondering where all that personality went."

Niles's chest gets tight, filling with hope, trepidation, and a million other things.

Tristan's nostrils flare. "Do you want me to walk away?"

No. Yes.

"I don't know" is what falls from Niles's lips.

They study each other for a long moment, neither minding how the other one sizes them up, eyes drifting from faces to chests to toes and back again.

"I'm sorry," Tristan says, his voice gentle. "I know that I did a bad thing. I went...haywire, I guess. I don't know what else to call it. But I'm not like that anymore."

Niles tries to smile. "Why tell me?"

Tristan doesn't try to smile at all. "Because I want to." His ochre eyes drop to the floor. "I've always wanted to."

"We were just stupid kids," Niles says. His hands strangle the throat of the medicine he'd come in to buy, all thoughts of discomfort whisked away by the more present threat of drowning in this moment.

Softly, Tristen corrects, "*I* was a stupid kid. You were—"

"A genius?" Niles cuts in.

Tristan laughs softly.

"A man among men?" Niles tries again. "A paragon of virtue?"

"A beautiful human being," Tristan says. "And you didn't deserve any of it."

The weight of that sentence hits Niles so hard his eyes water.

His once-Alpha seems like he wants to step closer but presses his lips together instead, clearing his throat and brightening his voice. "My sister will be happy to hear you're doing well. She talks about you a lot."

This is much safer territory.

"How is Beth?"

"Good! She has little ones now. She and her husband are living out their happily ever after in New Jersey."

Niles grimaces. "There's no such thing as a happily ever after in New Jersey."

That earns him another chuckle. "I've told her that, like, eighteen million times. She's beyond hearing me at this point. But, hey, she's living the dream, so maybe we've been tricked. Maybe New Jersey is the place to be."

"Take that back, or I will spritz you with holy water."

Tristan holds his hands up again, laughing, and this time some of the tension ebbs away.

"The kids are Holly and Hailey. I'm always calling the wrong name when I want to yell at one of them."

"Are they vicious little monsters?"

"Well, you know my sister."

"Little demons, then." Niles nods sagely.

This time, Tristan does step closer, but slowly. Non-threatening. Gentle. His voice is as sweet as cotton candy when he asks, "How are you, Niles?"

His name coming from that man's mouth is like a drug, even now.

"Tummy troubles." Niles waves the medicine. "Ari's Alpha made breakfast, and I absolutely should have known better."

Tristan smiles again, teeth white and lips kissable. "Ari managed to find a boyfriend?"

"A mate, actually. A *soul*mate if you can believe it."

"Whoa." Soulmates are rare enough to impress damn near every-one, and it seems Tristan is no exception. "Little, scrawny Ari Jacobson?"

"Still scrawny but more badass now. She's a lawyer."

The man seems stunned. "Oh wow! Hey, I was going to figure out how to ask you this anyway, but now I *have* to take you out to dinner. I need to hear how scabby-knees McGee ended up on the passing side of a bar exam!"

Niles gapes. "Are you actually asking me out on a date? Should I be stupefied, horrified, or should I save time and backhand you now?"

Putting his hands in his pockets, Tristan kicks his shoes in little, scuffing trails on the industrial strength linoleum. "Not a date, per se... More like a 'catch up dinner.' You can tell me about Ari and how, against all odds, she became a badass. I can tell you about my new company. I finally got it off the ground."

"You didn't..." Niles starts, his lips pulling into a sly smirk.

"Geriatric Gamers is a thing now."

A bark of laughter bursts from Niles at a disturbing volume. "You've gotta be kidding me!"

"Turns out a lot of Boomers and Gen Xers are willing to shell out cash to learn to play the latest games. We pitch it as a bonding exercise with their kids and grandkids. We've even been teaching them new slang. Do you know how gratifying it is to have an eighty-year-old woman tell me when I'm being cringe?"

"And suss?"

"Hella suss."

"Ohhh, I need you to show me your ad campaigns. Oh my God, what the hell does your logo look like?"

Tristan grins, rocking on his heels. "If you want to see it, you've got to come to 'catch up dinner' with me."

Niles's complexion is too dark for blushing, but that doesn't stop his face from getting hot. He holds up the medicine again. "I don't know. I may be incapacitated. For an hour or for life, depending on how much salmonella I just ate."

His Alpha, somehow always his, lets his expression sink into some-thing akin to hurt. "No worries, I just—"

"—just need to take me out to a place that only serves fully cooked dishes, please and thank you." Niles's eyes are wide as he cinches his full lips shut. He has no idea why he said that.

The glee in Tristan's scent strengthens the man's familiar notes of fall leaves. "Fully cooked, spicy as hell, and sans fish."

"Anyone who eats fish should be beaten with one," Niles agrees, nearly choking on his own spit while wondering what in the hell he's doing.

"Can I give you my number?"

"No." Niles puts down the bottle of medicine he was holding with a *thunk* and pulls out his phone a little too quickly. Trying to be suave for some damn reason, he says, "But I can give you mine."

He doesn't step closer, needing to hold on to some thin shred of his sanity, but Niles takes in as much of Tristan's scent as he can, reveling in the reminder of his favorite season. His favorite smells. What was once his favorite person.

Twiddling his phone to confirm he sent off a practice test, Niles smiles and nods. "Now, if you'll excuse me, I need to buy this pink stuff before I ruin the carpet with vomit and/or other liquid nastiness."

People passing by the aisle stare at him with surprise and disgust, and normally, Niles would be embarrassed by his own lack of a filter, but there's no reason to be embarrassed with Tristan. That man has heard every idiotic thing he's ever had to say.

Making his excuses, he works his way toward the registers, feeling Tristan's smile on his back like a tangible weight. A good one? A bad one? He doesn't know. All he knows is his body is in disarray. His stomach is in his feet, sloshing miserably. His nose is where his elbow should be. His hands are flopping up and down on his shoulders as he walks, and his ass is jangling somewhere up between his ears. With his mind mix-matching body parts, he's too distracted to step aside when an unknown shopper collides with him at top speed, knocking a mountain of things to the ground—chocolates, candy bars, potato chips—a pile of deliciousness Niles can't bear to stomach right now.

He groans, rubbing his face. "Sorry, sorry! I was lost in thought."

"Niles?"

Actually looking this time, he sees Jason ducking down to the floor to pick up the mess Niles made when he slammed into him at full clip.

"Oh, man! I don't know whether to feel better or worse that it's you!" Niles says. "I mean, better because I think you'll forgive me, but worse because I'll have to see your face again after I'm done throwing up on you."

Jason's eyes drop to the chalky concoction held boa-constrictor tight in Niles's hand, and grimaces. "I suggest you drink that now, then."

"I haven't bought it yet," Niles protests weakly.

Jason snags it, cracks the cap open, and hands it back over. "Drink."

"Bossy," Niles manages before downing a good gulp. It does him an immediate favor, quelling the churn in his gut, and he mutters, "I hate you, Benjamin Allein. You're on my shit list if I ever get out of this alive."

Jason eyes him in a funny way, and Niles waves him off. "I'll be alright. I may just have a little food poisoning. Let's get me to the counter before they arrest me for illicit imbibing or something."

"Sure, yeah, okay." Jason loops an arm over his shoulders, a completely unnecessary gesture, one that makes Niles strangely guilty, his conscience flicking him between the eyes.

Did his coffee friend see him with his…he has no idea what to call Tristan. Ex-boyfriend doesn't begin to convey the intensity of it. Former lover? Former obsession?

"Sorry to bother you like this," Niles says as they slide into line behind way too many women with messy buns.

"You saw me slam my head off a countertop in front of an audience. This is nothing."

Niles takes another slug of pink stuff. God, he hates it. If this is what pink tastes like, to hell with that color. He checks around quickly to see if Tristan is anywhere in the vicinity and suddenly wishes him a long shopping experience. He has no desire for Alpha A and Beta B to meet. If Jason is awkward on his own, God knows what would happen if Niles were to mix those two particular oils together.

Not to mention that Tristan would…

Tristan.

What the hell have I gotten myself into?

CHAPTER 3
DESIRE

"Are you drooling right now? Is your nose bleeding? Whatever it is, stop it. I can hear your soul leaving your body."

Ari *SQUEEEE*s on the other end of the phone, and Niles has to block his ear, wincing and putting his best friend on speaker phone so he can get far and away from her auditory onslaught.

"It's like one of my romance novels," she says, her voice tinny as it comes from the blackened screen.

"You hate him," Niles says, point blank. "I hate him."

"Pfft, well obviously not if your Omega was about to implode when you saw him."

Niles whines, flopping back on his overlarge mattress with his sheets in complete disarray, rumpled around his head. He hasn't made his bed in days. Weeks? And he hasn't washed the bedding in even longer. The fabric is an inoffensive gray-blue, and he drags a wadded swath of it over his face to scream.

"If that's how you're going to be about it, then dinner is a horrible idea," Ari says.

"Ya' think?" It comes out muffled, but Ari understands him anyway.

"Second chance romance or not, Tristan comes with too much baggage. And risk. You should just stick with Blond Beta. He seems like a safe choice. At worst, he'll bore you, but at least he won't twist you up in knots."

"Your Alpha's food twisted me up in knots."

She ignores him. "You've said it yourself, you don't like dealing with drama. You're a drama-free kind of Omega."

"Agreed," he mlurfs behind the tangle of fabric.

"Then don't simultaneously date two guys, and you can stay that way."

Niles yanks the sheet away. "I'm not dating anybody!"

She doesn't say words, she just lets out a sly hum. Niles yanks the phone off the bed and takes it off the speaker, ramming it to his ear so he can hiss at her properly.

"I'm not dating! I'm drinking hot beverages during the day and having *one meal* out with an old…friend."

"Old Alpha," Ari says, the smirk obvious in her voice. She gets low pitched, breathy, and dramatic, moaning, "Alpha, Alpha, please. Scent me. Mark me. Claim me, Alpha!"

"Ri-ri?" Something on Ari's side of the phone thumps and bumps and tumbles over, Ben's low voice cursing, "Shit! Fuck! Ow!"

Ari drops the phone, and Niles can hear it *ploof* on the bed. The slow satisfaction of knowing she just lured in her mate only to make him fall all over something is vindicating. She's on her side of the line saying her "Sorrys" and giggling at Ben's misfortune. Niles giggles along with her.

"No running, Benjamin!" he yells over the line.

"Go fuck yourself, Niles!" he calls back pleasantly. The man has a mouth on him, just like his brother.

Ari must pick up the phone again. "So, what does it need to have to qualify as a date? Goo-goo eyes? Alcohol? Interpretive dance? Do you have to sleep with someone?"

"I'm not sleeping with anyone!" Niles groans, his irritation building up in a bubble.

"Well, you better not lead them on. You'll only get yourself in trouble if you do."

"Look, I don't want some Omega in her first relationship giving me instructions on how to manage my love life."

As soon as it leaves his mouth, Niles wishes he could stuff it back in. Ari is silent on the other side of the line and the moment drags, long and terrible. Ben isn't her first relationship at all. It was Caleb. Too intense, all too real, unforgettable Caleb.

"Ari, I'm so sorry. I didn't mean anything by that."

But it's Ben on the phone now, nonplussed. "What the hell did you say to her, Niles?"

"Shit, Ben, I didn't mean it."

"Ri-ri...honey, don't cry."

Niles groans again as he hears her sniffle with a far away, "I'm not crying. My eyes are just leaking!"

"It's the same thing, sweetheart," Ben soothes.

"Put him on speaker!" Ari demands, and Ben must comply, because the audio quality changes to an airy wafting of ambient noise. There is ruffling and thumping as Ari likely picks up whatever Ben knocked down. "Niles, I know you're a big boy and can take care of yourself, but these guys obviously have expectations of you regardless of whether you have any for them and you're stupid if you don't realize it."

Niles knows, at this point in the conversation, his job is to shut his mouth and take his lumps.

"If there's anything I know," Ari continues, "It's that Alphas can go overboard." Ben doesn't deny it. "They get fantasies in their minds about what their Omega will be to them, and their hormones rule supreme. Getting involved with Tristan again in any way, shape, or form is going to give him ideas. Hell, all he had to do was see you in a store, and immediately, he went into protective mode *and* cajoled his way into seeing you again."

She's not wrong.

"Meanwhile, you have this Beta literally throwing himself at you. Omega-chaser or not, he wants to be your teddy bear or something. And you might not be saying yes, but you're sure as hell aren't saying no."

"So, you're calling me a man-whore?" Niles asks, and her pause tells him she's staring a daggered glare at the phone. "I'm just check-ing, you know, since I haven't screwed, kissed, or even held hands with any of them."

"You did with Tristan," she reminds.

Niles breathes in deeply and holds it for a full ten seconds before letting it out in a long *whoosh*. "Not for a long time."

"And never again?" she asks instead of tells.

To that, he has no answers.

"Ari? Does Tristan remind you of Caleb a little bit?"

It's her turn to sigh. "Yeah. Yeah, he does."

And that's a red flag if there ever was one.

———

The week ebbs on without a message from Tristan—something that almost let Niles put his fear behind him. Perhaps his once-Alpha had realized this was just as bad an idea as Niles knew it would be. Maybe, without words, they'd come to some kind of telepathic understanding.

But then Friday comes.

> Hey. It's me. Are you still up for dinner? Tonight would be…

Niles refuses to click into the rest of the message. If he does, it will show as "read" on Tristan's side, but Niles doesn't quite know what to do with it yet. Does he ghost the man? Does he give him the benefit of the doubt? What is it he wants from their meeting? Closure? A rekindling? A friendship?

Mired in this muck of thoughts, Niles prepares to make his way down to the bottom floor for his lunch-and-coffee engagement, walking past Katelyn's cube and tousling her hair. She'd teased it up and wide, so he only helped increase its volume, a fact that is not lost on her as she squeals in delight.

"Want me to bring you back something?" he asks.

"No. But tell that big Beta bear of yours I said 'hello.'"

Niles *pffts*. "He's not mine. I don't see him like that."

Katelyn rolls her hazel eyes so severely she actually swivels her head around. "Yeah. You go out with him every day because you think he's a pain in the ass."

"Gay men are allowed to be friends, Katelyn. Just because you put two of us in a room together doesn't mean we're gonna shag."

There is a ridiculous pause filled with blinking on her part. "What the hell am I supposed to say to that?"

"Absolutely nothing. But to apologize for your lack of tact, you can buy me a new dog."

"Random," she gives him a confused stare until her expression falters. "Oh, Niles. You're giving up on Bee-bee?"

He shrugs. Then nods. Then puts his hands on his hips and says, "I just hope whoever she left me for is treating her like the princess she is. They better learn she prefers chicken to lamb and wet food to dry. Their groomer better be the kind that gives her a little bandanna when she does a good job and looks all pretty. And they better let her sleep at the foot of the bed."

He purses his lips together tightly, sucking the inside of his cheeks and sitting in this moment of misery. Katelyn squints her eyes behind her thick-rimmed glasses before offering, "Those bastards. I can't believe they're stealing your dog."

Yes, Niles prefers that option to the animal control option or the hit-and-run option or the larger predator option.

"We should give them a name," Katelyn says. "Let's call them 'The Asshole Family.' They're rich and cheap and entitled. They drink sparkling water. Their house looks like it's from a magazine, but in that cold, sterile kind of way, and their maid secretly wipes pee on their toilet seats and spits on their toothbrushes."

"Yes. Yes, I like this idea," Niles says, already feeling a little better.

The bubblegum pink smile his office confidante gives him is wide and kind. "Now go hang out with your *friend*. You know he gets all apologetic, even when you're the one who's late."

Which is definitely what happened the other day. Niles had to come back upstairs when he'd realized he'd forgotten his bento box, and by the time he finally got down to the coffee shop, Jason was all, "I'm sorry, I got here too early!" with, like, a million facepalms.

———

Niles comes down to the café to see Jason at the little table they've claimed as their own. The Beta's hands are clasped and worrying at themselves as the he stares out the window, waiting. When Niles slides into the seat opposite, Jason seems as if he's about to dive straight into apologies again, but Niles holds up a hand, fingers splayed.

"Down, boy," he says.

He's met with that Good Boy smile he's grown fond of. Romance or not, this man has begun to take the sting out of Niles's loneliness. His scent has become a safe comfort, his straightforward awkwardness and quirkiness something that sets him apart. His denim-blue eyes are a familiar, welcome sight, reminding Niles of his long-lost brother. For some reason no one in his family could quite understand, Trey had always had the deepest, most denim-blue eyes.

"I got you your drink today. I hope you don't mind." Jason slides a coffee over to Niles and then another. One hot, one not, filled instead to the brim with little square ice cubes. "Both are hazelnut. Wasn't sure if you wanted it cold."

Niles frowns, gesturing at the icicles hanging from the window outside. "You think I want this to occur within my body?"

Jason hangs his head with a self-deprecating smirk and shrugs his meaty shoulders. "Sorry, I…well…you've bought drinks for me, so I figured it was my turn. I just didn't know what you were in the mood for."

"Hot in winter, my friend. Always hot." Niles picks up his Styrofoam-clad drink, happy to note it's cooled off enough not to scald him and takes a swig of sweetness. Well, what's supposed to be sweetness. It's undercut by something sour. He swirls the liquid around in his mouth for a moment before swallowing it down, grimacing all the way. Their cream must have gone bad.

"Is something wrong?" Jason asks, his scent beyond worried for some reason.

Ah, hell. What could he possibly say to those people-pleasing, puppy dog eyes?

"It's just hotter than I thought." Niles makes a big show of blowing on it, and takes another sip, holding his face steady and preparing for another tummy ache. If this man wasn't trying so hard, Niles would spit this mess right the hell out. Instead, he knows pity will keep him drinking.

"I was wondering, would you like to come out with me tonight?" Jason asks, still worrying his hands together. Peeking up sharply, pink-cheeked, he adds, "We can go check for Bee-bee. I've been keeping an eye out on my way home every day, checking out the dog parks."

Why is this man so sweet? Too sweet. But hanging out at night is different somehow. Niles's mind flicks back to Ari's words: *What does it need to qualify as a date?*

"Sorry, I actually..." Niles hesitates. "I have dinner plans for tonight. I ran into an old friend. An old ex, actually. He wants to catch up."

"Oh." Jason visibly deflates. Biting his fingernail and glancing to the side, his scent downshifts, and Niles can tell he's upset, though he does his best to hide it. Instead, he offers a chagrined smile. "I thought you said you weren't interested in a relationship right now."

Niles snorts, taking another sip of the disgusting mix in his cup. "I'm not."

Jason pleads with his eyes. "It's just...I'm enjoying getting to know you. I'd hate for someone to whisk you away and take up all your lunch time."

Ari was right. This man's hopes are higher than a mountain. Even so, Niles can't help how good it feels to flirt and be carefree. Just hang around with someone who seems safe, someone who would bend over backwards for him a little bit. Maybe Niles is leading Jason on, but who knows? Maybe a nice, calm Beta is just what he needs in the end.

"No one's taking away my lunches, don't worry. I've got those earmarked for you."

Jason brightens, a sly smile on his face showing off his dimples. "You sure you don't want to blow off your ex? I promise we'll have a good time. Nothing fancy. Bowling, maybe? Karaoke? I do a mean heavy metal scream."

"Now that would be amazing but no. This is probably something I have to do. Besides, I made a commitment, and I always stick to my commitments."

Which is true.

I guess I'm not ghosting him after all, Niles thinks. He eyes his phone again, pulling his braids over his shoulder and futzing with the frazzled ends. He needs to get them redone soon.

With a rough sigh through his nose, Niles adds, "Anyway, it's a one-time thing."

I don't need him anymore. This is a one and done kind of evening. No instant replays. No second-chance romance.

Just putting that into words makes Niles feel a little better. A little stronger. Yet the million-dollar question remains: can he believe his own words? He wants to. He *plans* to. But even now, he isn't so sure.

"Did I ever tell you about my ex?" Jason asks.

"I haven't had the pleasure." Niles grimaces but more over his drink than the topic.

"He was…so many things. Actually, he was kind of like you. Looked like you, too."

"Have a type, do you?"

"I suppose." Jason chuckles, tapping his fingers against the cup held loosely in his hands. "But I don't think it's a bad thing. It means I know what I want."

Niles nods. He can respect that. Even envy it. He's still trying to figure it all out, and he might be failing slightly, given his present circumstances.

"When we ended, it was…explosive," Jason continues. "It's one of those things where there's no going back."

"No, 'Let's Be Friends?'"

The angled tip of Jason's lips is sad. His shoulders slump, and his eyes dip down so Niles can't see them beyond their lashes. "Unfortunately not."

The man downs a glug of his coffee with no issues, heaving a heavy gust of air when he's done but coming away otherwise unscathed.

Apparently, Niles is the only one who got the spoiled dairy products poured into his lunchtime pick-me-up. He still takes another sip, though, if only to somehow comfort the man across from him, whose sullen scent seems to mellow again when he sees Niles drinking.

"Is it good?"

"It's warm" is Niles's careful reply. "So, what did you do to make lover boy run?"

Jason's gaze gets far away, and he faces the streaked window. The light catches in the icicles hanging from the wide, green awning that shelters a small patio from the weather. The long, frozen drips don't sparkle or glint, but they do fracture the gray sunlight flowing down through the mist of winter cloud cover.

With a quiet voice, Jason asks, "Why do you assume it was my fault? Why does everyone instinctively blame me?"

Niles flinches. "I'm sorry. I shouldn't have said that."

"I made mistakes, but my ex was the real problem toward the end," Jason says. "Always on the verge of leaving. Threatening it every day. Always making me feel like I wasn't good enough, no matter how hard I tried. I'd like to say I didn't get clingy, but that would be a lie. I was so desperate to fix things, so sure I could make it work no matter what his issues were." Morose, he blinks down at his coffee again. "But I just couldn't fix it, you know?"

Niles shifts in his chair, unsure of what to do with this conversation. This man has always been too honest. Too blunt. Too forward. Spilling his story to someone only a shade closer than an acquaintance seems very on-brand for him, yet Niles can't chastise him for it.

Jason seems so vulnerable in this moment, so open and soft that Niles finds himself admitting, "It was like that with my ex, too. I hoped he'd get better, snap out of it, but he didn't. I'm not like you though. I didn't try to fix anything. I tried to withstand it maybe, but I didn't do it for long. He scared me, and I'd had enough of living my life afraid. I told myself he was betraying me. And he was, in a way. He was killing the person I thought he was and giving me something I didn't want in return."

"Then why see him again?"

Taking another disgusting gulp and letting his belly bubble, Niles considers. "I want to believe the best in people. I want to believe they're better than they seem. Sad part is, I'm wrong most of the time." He huffs, slumping in his seat and draping an arm over the back. "This conversation is depressing."

Jason shrugs. "Life is depressing. That's why I want to find someone who can make me laugh. Someone who can commiserate with me when laughing is impossible. Someone to help me keep my head on straight and be the best person I can be."

"You seem pretty good already. In fact, I call you Good Boy in private."

Jason cocks his head with a sarcastic tick to his lips. "And now in public. Any other nicknames I should be aware of?"

The ringing bell of 'Blond Beta' sounds a clear chime in Niles's skull. "Nope. Why? Would you like one?"

A slow smile spreads on Jason's face. "I know what yours is."

Niles's eyebrows creep up in curiosity.

Lifting his Styrofoam coffee cup once more, Jason scuffs it against Niles's in a toast. "It's 'Handsome.'"

***

This restaurant has a thing for the color red. Not a blood red but a deep burgundy that lines the fancy seats and covers the walls in extensive swaths of heavy fabric. It's velvety and rich, making Niles wonder if he can afford this dinner. He wore something nice at least, a button up that fits his figure. He has no idea who he's trying to impress, Tristan or the hostess, who looked bitchy enough to kick him out if he wasn't dressed properly.

The booth they sit in is a crescent shape, curved around a half-circle table with breads and butters and exotic oils set out for them. Whether Niles wants it to be or not, this is definitely a date. If there were any specific criteria to check off, this does it.

Niles sips the wine in his fine stemmed glass, alcohol being another thing that checks off the "date" box and tries not to frown.

"Too much?" Tristan asks, casting his eyes around the restaurant, likely smelling Niles's discomfort.

"A catch-up dinner consists of fast-food diners, Tris, not five-star restaurants."

Tristan hums a little to himself, picking up a whiskey. "You know no one else calls me that? Just you."

"What do they say instead? A string of insults?" Niles asks, defensive after being lured into a place made for kissing. Their little alcove is hidden behind the wings of the high-backed seating, protecting them from the eyes of strangers.

Swirling his glass around and listening to the ice tinkle off the sides, Tristan agrees, "I've gotten my fair share of 'Prick' and 'Dick' and 'Asshole.'"

"Any other genitalia references? Boob? Perhaps a C-word?"

Tristan laughs sharply. "See? And that's why I wanted to come out together."

Niles scowls, tipping up his wine and taking a swig. It's good. Delicious. Somehow that also pisses him off. "I hope you're ready to pay for dinner because I'm having at least four of these."

If it's going to be a date, let it be a goddamn date.

"No worries. It's on the company tonight. I'm calling this a 'consulting dinner.'"

"Oh."

Well, that's a bit better.

"You said you wanted to see my marketing,"—Tristan taps the laptop on the seat beside him—"and I thought it would be nice to get your opinion. You always had an eye for that kind of thing."

"That's what I do now, actually," Niles says. "I make ad campaigns. I don't do the design, but I draft the…vibes, I guess. And the cadence. The audience too. Segmentation is the most important part to make sure you don't blow money on getting your commercials shown during toddler TV time or something."

"You do commercials, too?"

"I storyboard them." Niles smiles to himself, proud to be showing off his prowess. "I'm not involved with casting or filming, though."

Tristan leans in, his near-yellow eyes focused. "It must be cool when you get to see the final product."

"It can be. Sometimes they get it perfect, and it's like my dream came to life. Other times, they get the mood all wrong, but I have no say in reshoots or editing, so I have to make do with what I get. I've gotta tell you though, when they follow my vision to the letter, the ads perform better."

"Not that you're bragging."

Niles has to laugh. "Well, it's not like I can do it in front of anyone at work. That's not the sort of thing you say if you want people to like you."

"So, it was just for my benefit?" Tristan's smile is annoyingly handsome, and Niles empties his drink, immediately signaling their waiter for another.

He feels weird. He's not tipsy, not yet, but he's hot under the collar. It must be the way his old flame is completely focused on him, not to mention the way the Alpha is dressed. Niles is slender, but Tristan is a perfect triangle shape. Broad, firm chest, tapering off to a narrow waist and thin hips. He likely has that V that leads down to his groin now that he's older and fitter. Niles imagines the ridge of his iliac crest would be perfectly lickable as well, a hard, masculine line that begs to be attended to. This is another body Niles would like to see naked, but this time for *completely* erotic reasons.

His face gets heated, and he realizes Tristan has been talking.

"—advertise to kids as much as adults. What if they want to connect with their parents in different ways, and gaming together might be it?"

Catching up, Niles considers. "Slow down a bit. You've set yourself up in an iffy position. With a company name like Geriatric Gamers, you run a risk. You could offend the statistically defensive age group you're trying to market to, *and* you might make kids think your ad doesn't apply to them and tune out."

Tristan's expression falls. "We've been doing alright so far."

Niles holds his hands up, meaning no offense. "I didn't say you weren't, but I do think you could probably do better. Right now, your sense of humor is tickling a very niche market. If you're going edgy with your name, you've got to lean into it hardcore but create different campaigns for the different age groups you're targeting. If you're aiming for tweens and teens, you might be barking up the wrong tree. What teenagers actually say, 'I want more quality time with the old people in my life?' But if you go for the ten-year-olds, you might hit a sweet spot there."

"Like world-build age. We do a bunch of world-building games."

"Perfect. Those kids might want someone to play with who's not on the other side of the world kicking their ass and talking to them through a headset. They haven't hit their anti-adult phase yet. But you can see how the ads for a ten-year-old and a forty-year-old need to be different, right?"

Tristan nods to himself, pulling inward and noodling on the thought, his wheels obviously turning. "You may have just saved me a lot of money."

"Yes and no. It will cost you more up front to make two campaigns but less on the back end because you're not running ad spots that are bound to fail. If you're going to invest money, then better to hit it right the first time." Niles shrugs, his next wine arriving and just as delicious as the first.

"Are you sure you're not in sales? You just sold me on hiring you."

Niles snorts his drink up his nose. It burns like a sonofabitch as he snarfs, launching his napkin to his face and coughing up a lung while Tristan rubs his back, something that feels way too good. Even with his nose on fire, it's almost sensual.

"I'm sorry, what?" Niles manages through his watering eyes and leaking sinuses.

"You alright?" Tristan asks, still petting him.

"Yeah. Yeah, I'm fine." Niles makes one last, rather offensive sniff, and leans back, immediately picking up his wine to try again and earning a smirk from the man who is suddenly much closer beside him.

"You haven't changed at all." Tristan hands over his own, clean napkin to Niles, while moving the wine/snot one to the edge of the table where a server quickly whisks it away.

"What? Yes, I have."

"Don't get me wrong, you've definitely grown. You're more accomplished, sexier—"

Niles almost snorts his wine again.

"—and you seem to have found your place in life. I just mean, underneath it all, you're still the person I remember. The quirky, sassy person I used to do stupid things with."

"We definitely did stupid things."

"Remember when we were throwing rocks into that sketchy creek and hit Ari by mistake?"

Niles grimaces. "She had a welt on her head."

"But she didn't cry. And she didn't tell on us."

"No, she just threw rocks right back."

Tristan laughs. "And remember the time we snuck out at night so we could fool around, and your warden caught us with our tongues down each other's throats?"

No matter how much time passes, Niles is mortified by that event. His foster care provider—he refuses to offer her a warmer title than that—was always catching them in the act. He'll remember forever the day when she sat him down to explain that Omega males can *indeed* get pregnant, a fact that was lost on Niles until then. But she told him, as long as his partner wasn't an Alpha, then there was no chance of their seed taking.

"That's why she was so glad when we thought you were a Beta. But…then you presented."

"Then, I presented," Tristan agrees, sighing through his nose and knocking back the rest of his drink. "And then I went absolutely insane."

Niles faces away. He's not sure he wants to have this conversation.

"The doctors explained it to me after," Tristan said. "Presenting at seventeen is too late. I'd built up so much…potency, they called it, that everything in me dived over the deep end. I was obsessive, possessive, and cruel. I was violent. I was everything I'd never been before." He catches Niles's chin between tender fingers and connects their gazes. "And I'm sorry. I couldn't control it. It's not an excuse, but it's the truth."

The sincerity rolls off Tristan's skin, smelling like crisp leaves and home. Like everything Niles ever wanted. The Omega inside him wants to cry and cling, but he can't trust this feeling. His lower belly aches suddenly, a slight cramp twinging him as slick wells up inside, arousal getting the better of him. It seems he can't control his biology either.

"Once they got me on suppressants, I mellowed out," Tristan says, releasing Niles and having the courtesy to give him some space. "I'm still a bit of a rough guy but not *that* rough."

Niles chuckles through a slight smile, trying not to be charmed and failing.

Saving him from the moment, their dinner arrives. A blasé food runner with that omnipresent burgundy color laced through his black vest brings over a tray of dish after dish, and a perfect filet mignon au poivre appears before Niles in all its sinful perfection. His mouth waters. More than that, it tingles. Aches somehow. Longs to be filled by something so much thicker than a steak dinner.

Shit, why am I so hot right now?

He moves to loosen his collar and pulls his braids back into a thick loop, wrapping it in the hair tie he keeps around his wrist for when he needs to sweep it out of the way. Like an idiot, he only now realizes doing so exposes his glands, announcing his scent to anyone with the proper designation. With his emotions the way they are, Niles's desire may as well be screaming through a bullhorn, alerting everyone to the slick gathering inside him.

Swallowing a dry nothing, Niles tries to ignore Tristan's sudden heavy-lidded gaze as he heaps rosemary pomme frites on his plate, letting them suck up the juices from his steak.

His lower belly twinges again as he puts the first, succulent bite of steak into his mouth, just the perfect amount of saltiness to mix with the mild pepper flavor. The softness of its center offsets the crispness of its encrusted surface perfectly, making it worth every penny, no matter the how expensive it is.

Looking at Tristan, he admits, "God, this is good," with a lick of his lips and an honest little moan.

At the sound, Tristan's jaw tightens, and his focus narrows to a single pinprick, taking in Niles's expression with his nostrils flaring.

His heated gaze makes Niles even wetter down below before he realizes the error of his ways.

This is getting out of hand.

Pretending to focus back on his plate, he wonders if it's time for his heat. But no, it's too early, and he's been on his steady regimen of suppressants for years with no issues. Is his Alpha pulling him off-cycle? No, that can't be it either. Niles is trying his best not to breathe him in. It makes no sense. But it doesn't matter; it's happening anyway.

Unbidden, his next sound is a seductive sigh as he puts another bite in his mouth, rolling it around and feeling its heat on his tongue, wishing he had *other* things in his mouth instead. Things that are hot, veined, and silky smooth to the touch.

He closes his eyes, leans his head back, and swallows his food whole.

"Niles," Tristan says in a soft tone.

To which Niles trembles, his eyes snapping open and staring the Alpha down. He runs a thumb over his lower lip to catch any stray sauce, but moves all too slowly. The gesture holds his Alpha's gaze, and Niles's slick begins to trickle out in a warm rivulet that soaks into his briefs.

"Fuck," Tristan whispers, likely smelling Niles in that hypersensitive Alpha way, knowing exactly when his Omega is turned on. Tristan's pupils dilate into black galaxies, reflecting the pin lights all around them. "Niles, are you…?"

I am, Niles thinks as he whimpers softly. He slides his hand down to rest over his belly where it's starting to clench, its aching a blatant threat of what's to come. All the signs are there. He's hard in his pants, straining the fabric, stiff and leaking, and he's dying to be touched.

Tristan slides close, running his fingertips over Niles cheeks and down his throat, marking him with his scent. "Oh, please, God. Tell me you're not…"

Niles shakes his head weakly. "I'm sorry, I can't help it. I didn't mean to."

"Shh, Omega. Don't worry. I'll take good care of you."

Niles jerks away. "I don't want to be in a relationship." He presses his flat, pale palms against Tristan's shoulders, keeping him at bay. "But I can smell it on you. That's what you want, isn't it, Alpha?"

At the word "Alpha" a growl rumbles in Tristan's throat as he wraps a hand around the back of Niles's neck, caressing his mating gland and making him cry out. The sound is swallowed quickly in a kiss that tastes like whiskey, sin, and hope. Niles wants to give in—he does for a moment, his tongue gently touching the heat of Tristan's as it begs for entry—but he pulls back.

"We can't."

His Alpha strokes his gland, working him up higher. "No one will see."

"The waiters…"

"Fuck the waiters," Tristen forces out, his hand tracing around to the column of Niles's throat again and down the slight, muscular curve of his chest.

"No," Niles says more firmly this time, and Tristan drops his eyes, leaning back and taking the deepest of breaths.

"You still smell like honey." Tristan runs a hand through his loose, wavy black hair, clenching it while his tawny eyes remain glued to the table. "Do you still taste like it, too?"

"I need to go," Niles says. "I'm sorry. I just…I just can't do this."

Wonder of wonders, Tristan—his Alpha, always his Alpha—lets him go. He doesn't try to force him. He doesn't press his authority. He doesn't beg or guilt. He doesn't bully. All he says is, "Did you drive here?"

"Yes," Niles says, gathering his winter coat and draping his scarf over his neck, the itchiness of it immediately scouring his glands and making him grit his teeth.

"Good. Be safe, Omega."

His coat on, Niles prepares to escape, but Tristan stops him with one final thought.

"Niles?" He looks desperate, sitting there and smelling like pure lust. "Will you think of me?"

Niles wants to fall to his knees and beg for his Alpha, moaning that he'll think of him and only him, that he'll make his Alpha a perfect nest and be so good for him, but he won't. He can't. If he does, he'll fall back in love with the devil, he knows it. Instead, he turns on his heels without another word and bursts out into the cold winter night.

Niles is going to die. Or gush. Or die and gush. Or gush and die.

He clicks around his computer screen on a site he's not ashamed to admit he frequents. RnH.com—a place where hard-up Alphas heading into rut can hook up with Omegas suffering a lonely heat. It's a wham, wham, knot, bam sort of experience with no romance allowed. You send in monthly paperwork, so they know you're clean, and you're free to pair off with whomever you'd like. The site boasts "No Betas Allowed," and for that, Niles is glad. He refuses to entertain even a smidge of thought about Jason. That man is not what his body needs.

On fire as he is, Niles is infuriated to find no one is making his Omega beg for them. There are lots of dick pics but no faces. Nice knots, though. Still, their profiles describe them as soft lovers or kind lovers, and that's not what Niles wants. He wants to be railed. Railed and scratched and teased out of his mind.

Clicking in on the perfect picture with a strong hand wrapped around the smoothest, tan, most silky-looking member, the Alpha's profile says:

I just want to fuck. Fuck and suck and get you off. I'm wild in bed and get a little intense, but it's nothing you won't beg for. In fact, it's better if you beg. I want to fucking own you for a few days.
In an unrequited love right now, so no strings, but if I don't make someone mine tonight, I'm going to fucking explode.

Niles is hard again, imagining that silky skin sliding up inside where he's the wettest. Hitting him in that special spot. Flooding his Omega womb with his Alpha seed and making this horrible ache go away.

The cramps are insane, and Niles rests his sweating forehead on the desk for a minute to breathe through it. As soon as he lifts his eyes, though, he clicks to match with this self-proclaimed "intense Alpha" and crosses his fingers. Niles's profile picture has no face, either, only his back from the shoulder blades down as he presents his ass to the lens. He'd tried for hours to get that perfect shot the last time he was hard up, and the wetness that shows on his inner thighs has always been pure Alpha bait.

It's only moments before a black pop-up box notifies him with the word "Match," and a chat pane opens.

Your place, my place, or a hotel?

The Alpha is both asserting himself and being deferential to the Omega he's about to cater to. That's a good sign.

I can go in for a hotel, 50/50.

No need. I've got you, Omega. Do you prefer down and dirty, or do you want me to playhouse first?

I just want to lose my mind with you. Down and dirty, bottom or switch, just fuck me. Please, Alpha.

Niles likes spitting filth when he's like this. He likes to convince his more mild-mannered self to let the inner animal out. To not care about being nice or friendly. He just wants to be a turn-on who gets what he asks for.

Good boy. Meet me at Haverhill House. I'll get us a room. It's known for being a clean place to hole up, but why don't we go ahead and make it dirty, hmm?

Will you bring food?

He did mostly skip dinner after all.

Do you like grapes?

Why is it always fucking grapes?

If you suck me off, I'll put anything you want in my mouth.

And it's the goddamned truth.

Perfect.

I'm leaving now. Ask for Bad Boy at the desk. They'll give you the room number. What should I call you?

Why don't you call me your unrequited love's name?

There is a pause, then:

That's so fucking hot. I like that. Be my fantasy.

Leave now, Omega. I'll take good care of you.

And Niles doesn't need to be told twice.

***

Niles is alone in the elevator, making this the perfect time to put it on. He's been wearing these since Ari's mishap, just to make sure no one too enthusiastic takes advantage of him. Niles wraps the collar around his neck and does up the key latch, burying the little metal piece of sanity in the bottom of his overnight bag. The collar covers his mating glands completely. It's soft, silky, and sexy beneath the leather exterior, making the necessary precaution a turn-on more than anything else. The upcoming Alpha can still slip his fingers underneath, so he can tease Niles within an inch of his life, but he won't be able to bite him. To *mate* him. There will be no mistakes.

Niles is bad off. His legs are watery, so close to giving out from underneath him. He has no idea why his heat came on so strong, or came on at all, but all he can do is give in to it, the phrase *Alpha will take care of me* on repeat. He's shaking. He's sweating. His scent must have clouded the whole elevator by now, and he's glad the hotel staff let him take it alone. The woman behind the counter took one look at him after he gave his Alpha's faux name, nodded in understanding, and escorted him to ensure his protection. After all, Alphas come to this hotel when they're close to their ruts, and sometimes they don't care who the Omega is, as long as he or she is ready.

Niles leans against the smooth, bland, beige paint as he works his way down the hallway, muttering, "Room twenty-oh-two, twenty-oh-two."

He lets his eyes scan around. Much to his annoyance, the necessary door seems to be at the ass end of the corridor, unfortunately far away, although that does mean they might have nice, corner suite views of the city skyline.

"Please, Alpha," he begs in the deafening silence, nearly doubling over from another cramp as his slick wicks away into his special briefs, though those won't hold up much longer. Truth be told, they're not holding up now. The crotch of Niles's pants is wet down to his inner thighs, something sure to drive the upcoming Alpha wild. That's good. Niles requires some immediate attention.

At the door, he slips in his key card without knocking, but upon the sound, the already naked Alpha whips open the door and grabs Niles too fast for him to truly see, hefting him over his shoulder. Niles's tummy presses into a hard, round deltoid as he's walked deeper into the room, feeling it flex with every step. He has only a moment to realize the walls in this place have been padded and sound proofed, and everything is made of soft, waterproof material, meaning they can be as loud and dirty and wet as they want to be.

They pass a luxurious bathroom with a round tub that Niles currently refuses to bathe in. He wants to be coated in this Alpha's seed as fast and for as long as possible.

Until his scent catches Niles off guard.

It can't be.

The male carrying him seems to realize at the exact same moment he does, freezing in place and tensing his grip. After a moment and a deep breath, the Alpha nuzzles into Niles's side. "It's you, isn't it?"

"Tris?" Niles chokes out.

"Fuck," Tristan says softly, sweetly. "How can it be you?"

"The-the wonders of the internet." Niles lets out a pained gasp as another cramp hits him, slick trickling down all the way to the backs of his knees. Yes, those briefs put up a good fight, but they lost in the end.

"Sweet Omega. God, you smell perfect."

Niles wants to scramble away, but he can't. Instead, he's brought to the large bed that lies on the floor with excess cloth, towels, and everything needed for a nest folded neatly around the space.

"How can you be going into rut?"

"I was traveling last week," Tristan says, setting him down and running his nose over Niles's protective collar before whispering in his ear. "I forgot my suppressants at the hotel. I've been off them for a few days."

"So, this is my fault? My heat triggered your—" Niles can't complete his thought, letting out a gasp instead as Tristan takes his earlobe into his hot mouth and nibbles.

"Can we do this? Please, Niles, can we still do this?"

But he has to ask, "Am I the unrequited love?"

Face buried in Niles's neck, Tristan runs his cheek over everything to leave behind his scent, using his knees to spread Niles's legs wide. Mission accomplished, the Alpha presses his hips forward, letting his naked erection press against Niles's clothed one in a way that makes him shiver.

"No strings," Tristan repeats, like it said in his profile.

"Alpha, I don't want you to call me by a different name anymore."

"Don't worry. If it's you, it's you." Tristan offers another rock of his hips as he bites the edge of the collar and pulls, tugging it against Niles's glands and making his eyes roll back and flutter closed.

"Then we can do this. Just until our bodies are done, we can do this."

With one hand, Tristan drags Niles face to the side until they're finally staring into each other's eyes, tawny yellow to deep, earthy brown. "Good boy."

"HOW MUCH DO you like this T-shirt?" Tristan wraps Niles's fabric of the day around his fist in a whorl.

"What?"

"Scale of one to ten," Tristan continues. "It's pretty nice. I'd hate to tear it if it was a favorite."

"I don't give a fuck if you shred it in half," Niles groans. "Just get your skin on mine."

"That's it, Omega. Boss me around. I like it." Tristan's other fist bunches next to the first, and he pulls with a grunt. The cords of his neck stand out slightly as he bites his lower lip, those white teeth showing the sharp edges of his canines. There is a ripping sound, and a gaping hole blesses Niles's chest with cool air, kissing the sweat-stained skin there. Without hesitation, Tristan leans down and licks a stripe up his breastbone, lapping up the salt with the flat of his tongue until he reaches the collar again, sinking his teeth into the leather and tugging it upwards.

"I like this," Tristan says.

"Why?"

"It will keep me in check," Tristan says through a smile as he slides wet kisses over Niles's shoulders, helping him wriggle his way out of what's left of his shirt. "Add this to our nest."

"Yes, Alpha."

Tristan leans back, sitting up on his knees and showing off what God gave him. He, indeed, has that cut line leading to his groin, that perfectly deep V shape, and his erection stands proud—thick, long, flushed, and waiting for its chance to perform. He caresses Niles's jeaned legs, slicked-up and pinned open to either side of him.

"And these, too. They smell perfect." He plucks at Niles's button and zipper, popping open the one and dragging down the other, spreading his light, mocha brown fingers wide and pressing the heel of his hand onto the lower part of Niles's belly where he aches the most. "You want me in here, don't you? Deep inside you."

Niles nods, tears coming to his eyes. "Alpha, please. It hurts."

Tristan lifts Niles's hips, slipping down his pants and boxer briefs all in one go. "Will you still be my fantasy, like you said you would?"

Nodding again, Niles gasps as Tristan purses his lips, blowing cool air over Niles's hard length. He nuzzles his way down, giving a lick to Niles's base, sucking the skin of his sac ever so slightly before going lower and lapping at his inner thigh. There, he tastes Niles's slick again for the first time in nearly a decade, and curses with satisfaction. Licking again, around Niles's rim this time, Niles can only whimper and squirm.

"You want me to touch you like this?" Tristan pulls away just enough to press his fingers against Niles's pucker, swirling them gently.

"Uh-huh."

Those fingers dip in the tiniest bit before pulling out again. "Then you have to role play with me."

Niles gives a breathy chuckle. "What do you want me to be, Alpha?"

Pressing his fingers past the first knuckle this time, Tristan pulls forward and suckles Niles's erection, hollowing his cheeks and pulling back slowly. "I want you to be in love with me."

Niles twitches sharply, his adrenaline spiking.

"Just for now," Tristan soothes. "Just when we're like this." His fingers pulse in and out as he speaks against Niles's skin. Every pause in speech is punctuated by a lick or nip, sending electric sparks through Niles's groin. "Can you pretend with me?"

Another pain spikes Niles's belly as he avoids the question. "Alpha, I need you."

Inching forward, Tristan loops his arms under Niles's legs, angling him just right before positioning himself on his hands and knees, rocking the head of his cock against Niles's sopping entrance. "Then say something for me." He goes in the tiniest bit, making Niles's breath stutter. "Tell me you missed me."

Niles hesitates, focusing on those tantalizing nudges as they set fire to his insides, melting him and keeping him open wide.

"Pretend with me," Tristan whispers, reminding again, "No strings. Just us, right here, right now."

He goes deeper and Niles complies, saying a breathy, "I missed you."

Even deeper.

"I missed you," Niles repeats.

One more thrust, slow and shallow.

"I love you, Tris."

And Tristan snaps his hips with a growl, impaling Niles and hitting him at his deepest. "Say it again."

"I..." Niles starts, Tristan pulling out, "I'm in love with you."

He slams in again. "That's right. You can lie to me. We can pretend. Just don't stop fucking saying it."

So, Niles begins his chant as Tristan moves, keeping his legs hiked high, pounding until skin slapping skin, grunts, and gasps are all that can be heard besides Niles's sultry words. "I love you. I've always loved you. No one else. Be with me, Alpha. Stay. Never go."

It sounds real. It sounds like he means every word when he says it like this. Niles cries out as Tristan hits that perfect spot, panting above him.

"I need you so much, baby. You're the one that got away. Every Omega I fuck, I wish they were you."

"Don't talk about them," Niles snarls, instinct driving him to want his Alpha all to himself.

"I'd imagine you how you are now. I'd picture being inside you, just like this. Christ, Niles, I've always wanted it to be you."

Lost in the moment, Niles's heart squeezes, and he pulls Tristan down to his mouth in a kiss that's messy and full of clacking teeth and diving tongues. Tristan's knot starts to blow, but Niles won't let go even when all they do is moan with their lips touching, sharing breath and sharing the moment.

"Come for me, Alpha."

And he does. With a deep, guttural sound, Tristan fills Niles full, his knot stopping anything from leaking out and his seed immediately easing the ache in Niles's lower belly.

"We're not done yet, Omega."

Propped on one arm, Tristan slides his hand down Niles's chest and lower, taking a hold of his erection and pumping slowly, making Niles clench his backside and squeeze on the knot that fills him to the brim.

"How do you want to come? Like this?" He pumps fast, Niles's own slick and Tristan's split making it glide while Tristan's fist stays nice and tight.

Niles throbs as he gets up on his elbows, seeing his lover's hand work while he's stuffed full from behind.

"Or like this?" Tristan asks.

The motion slows down and Tristan's hand twists at the top, tugging Niles's foreskin in the most delicious pattern.

"Or do you want more of this?" Tristan tries to pull out, but his knot holds him tight. The tug of his Alpha against his insides sends a sizzle of pleasure through Niles's body, making him fall back against the bed.

"Or how about all of it?" Tristan starts a pattern of trying to pull out, making Niles tense, sucking him deeper and letting him hit his special place deep inside, then tugging Niles's length, two fast pumps, one slow. Then, he does it all over again.

"You're gorgeous. Sexy. Unforgettable."

Niles's ego soars at the praise as his body begins to tremble, on the precipice. "Don't stop."

Thrust.

"I just want to keep fucking you," Tristan groans.

Tug.

"Want to keep my Omega filled and wanting me."

Tristan's strokes take up their fastest rhythm, jerking him off so hard his hand is almost a blur.

Niles's balls tense beneath him. "Tris, please...I...I'm gonna..."

"Fucking right you are."

And a splash of white paints Niles's dark skin like an abstract painting, his mouth open wide in a silent cry. His body pulses as more spills out, coating Tristan's hand in his essence, a scented claim to keep those other imaginary Omegas far away.

Tristan collapses on top of Niles, taking his mouth in a frenzy of kiss after kiss, a sensation Niles both revels in and floats above, out of his mind. What is he doing? And does he even care?

Rocking them to the side, they flip until Niles rests on Tristan, his face tucked into the crook of his neck, hair splayed everywhere and coming loose. Trepidation starts to sink in, but Tristan hushes his thoughts.

"Don't. Shh. No strings, I promise. Just be with me now." His clean hand runs soothing strokes over Niles's back, lulling him into a sated sense of peace. But still...

"Am I the unrequited love?" Niles asks again, though he already knows the answer.

Tristan's arms wrap around him, holding him tight. "Since the day you left."

***

Niles's face is buried deep in the slightly damp edge of his nest, a silky fabric that smells like Tristan. Like him. Like sex and lust and need. His ass is presented in the air as Tristan tongues him, praising his slick as a delicacy and smoothing over every insecurity Niles has ever had.

Well, all but one. The one where everyone leaves him.

Even now, in the haze of his heat-induced stupor, Niles knows this isn't real. This is a game. A fantasy. A wet dream. Something you wake up in the middle of the night with, sweaty clothes stuck to your body and a leaking cock to remind you of your dirty thoughts.

There is one part of this that's real though, and that's the raw sensation. Tristan spreads him wide again and rams himself inside. Niles is about to lose his mind.

"Beg for it," Tristan says.

"Scratch me," Niles replies immediately. Eagerly. "Please, Alpha. Mark me up."

Buried deep inside him, Tristan swipes the tangled mess of Niles's hair aside, hooking his collar and dragging his head back until his spine is bowed and he faces the high ceiling. The pressure is barely on the good side of dangerous, keeping Niles's breath shallow and his head light. Tristan wasn't kidding when he said he would be intense… and that Niles would beg for it.

"White or pink? How hard?"

"Test me," Niles says, his voice raw. "See how much I can take."

Tristan releases the collar and wraps his hands around Niles's hips, focusing on fucking him, rocking him forward on his hands and knees until Niles feels he might collapse again. No matter how much he shoves himself back onto his Alpha's cock, hitting that spot, that *fucking spot,* it will never be enough.

"You're such a good boy, Niles."

Thwack!

Niles hisses in a breath through his nose as Tristan's hand collides with his backside, a stinging heat echoing off his skin.

"Again, please, Alpha."

And he is obliged, harder this time and in the same exact spot, making his nerves sing louder. Tristan smooths a hand over the sensitive flesh and squeezes Niles's rear tenderly, rocking Niles against him in slow thrusts. "You ready?"

"Please," he pants.

Eight of Tristan's fingertips alight onto his shoulder blades. Crooked into claws, their blunt nails rest against Niles's arching back. There is a gentle drag, almost a tickle, down the length of his spine.

"Harder," Niles says, gazing over his shoulder to dare the God of his heat, the man who owns him. The man whom he owns in return.

"You know I like it when you tell me what to do," Tristan purrs.

This time, there is more pressure as those nails drag, collar to sacrum, and Niles wishes he could be bitten. He's wished it no less than a million times.

"Please, Alpha."

"Always so hungry for me. Even when you were a teenager."

Those nails get rough, a scrape versus a drag this time, and the fine nerves under Niles's skin burn. Once more, the hardest yet, and Niles knows his ribs will show raised marks in the shape of Tristan's fingers.

"It's because I love you," Niles says.

On day two of their dalliance, saying it is as easy as closing his eyes, which may be exactly what he's doing. Hiding from the truth that this will be over soon. This heat will be short, Niles can tell, but Tristan's rut hasn't yet hit full swing.

Tristan loops his arms under Niles, and pulls him until he's kneeling upright, his back flush to Tristan's chest. Niles clenches his rear and Tristan's breath stutters, nipping his earlobe.

"Touch yourself for me, Omega. I want to feel you come when I'm inside you."

Strong hands wrap under Niles's sides and up over his shoulders as Tristen knocks Niles's knees wider, spreading him to the point of being imbalanced. He has no choice but to trust his Alpha not to let him fall. One handed, Tristan slides his grasp down Niles's forearm and curls it around, resting Niles's palm along himself.

"Fuck your hand, Omega. If you like to top, you can pretend it's me."

"Now that would be fun. If we ever fuck outside my heat, I'd like to try that." Rather than mentally castrate himself for that sentence as he rightfully should, he wraps his fingers around his base and eases them up, pulling the skin taut.

"If it's outside your heat, I refuse to fuck you," Tristan says. "I'd make love to you, instead."

Niles smiles to himself as he gets to work. Tristen's hand slides back up, plucking a nipple along the way as his teeth start to scrape just where the collar ends. It's so close. So close to his mating gland that Niles's slick runs in thick drips, and Tristan nips harder.

"Do you dream about mating?" Tristan asks, his arms bracing Niles as he begins to tug himself in earnest.

"S-sometimes."

"Is it with a strong Alpha?"

Unfortunately, "Always."

"Like me?"

Instead of answering, Niles uses his other hand to cup his balls, cradling them and squeezing ever so slightly. "Need you, Alpha."

And Tristan's hips begin to move back and forth gently. A barely-there movement that drives Niles crazy. He wants to scream for more, but takes it out on his own body instead, his abs tensing as his breath comes too fast.

"I'd want an Omega who can put me in my place." Tristan's lips drag over his flesh near the collar. "One who's smart and bold. One who smells like honey."

"Tris…" Niles sighs, almost there.

"I'd mate you, Niles. If not for this fucking strip of leather, I'd make you mine." With a rough growl, Tristan's hand launches up and pulls at the collar, riding it hard over Niles's mating gland until he lets out a steady whine.

Tristan rocks the inner fabric over his glands, letting the soft silk stroke him like a tongue would while Niles's hand feels every pulse in his veins as his pace picks up.

"Pretend I'm sucking on you," Tristan says into his ear, twisting the collar to the left and tugging it tighter. "Pretend I found that stupid fucking key, ripped this off, sank my teeth in, and tasted your blood."

Niles trembles in his arms, barely able to hold on.

"Now, Omega, imagine you tasted mine."

And Niles is lost. He comes with a shout and Tristan's hand takes over, still tugging at him and pivoting his hips.

"It's too much!" Niles cries.

"It's never enough," Tristan says through gritted teeth, pushing Niles to his hands and knees again and fucking him in earnest.

Niles's moans are screams of pleasure at this point, filthy words falling like the devil's prayers as Tristan pummels him from behind.

His slick squelches, the piston of his lover embedding himself in his body time and again.

"Say it, Omega."

"I love you, Alpha."

"Niles, please…"

"I love you, Tristan."

"That's it. That's right." His hips stutter against Niles's rump and he clenches as tight as he can, loving every inch of the man inside him. "Baby, I can't…I can't…"

"Come for me then, Alpha. Make me yours."

Colors ebb in cloudy pastels, swirling around in his floating mind, but a cool sensation pulls Niles slowly from dreamland. Peering out, he sees Tristan in front of him with a soft smile, lying on his side and close enough to kiss him. Niles wouldn't mind if he kissed him, would prefer it, really, but something else is pressing against his lips. He goes slightly cross-eyed before pulling back and finding a ripe, red strawberry.

"What's this?" he murmurs.

"Me taking care of you," Tristan says, flicking his eyes downward toward a small bowl full of the seed-speckled fruit.

"Your stupid online post said grapes."

"But then I realized it was you, and my Omega likes strawberries."

A ridiculously dopey grin spreads on Niles's face, and he gives no resistance. "You remembered."

"You'd be surprised what I remember about you."

Which is a sentence that makes Niles want to have sex again. Immediately. He leans in to kiss his Alpha but is met again by fruit.

"Ah-ah," Tristan *tsks*. "Mind shattering orgasms later. Food now."

Being a good Omega, Niles takes a bite. It's sweet and tart all at once, and his mouth waters. "Oh, yeah, I can definitely eat a bowl of these."

"Two bowls?"

"Maybe."

"Three?" Tristan asks with his eyebrows up.

"Why?"

He shrugs and frowns playfully, nodding his head to the side. "I may have ordered too many in my enthusiasm."

Chewing, Niles peeks over Tristan's shoulder. There is a room service tray laden with delicacies, selections of veggies, cheeses, prosciutto, cherries, edamame, and an insane amount of strawberries.

"I can't eat all that!"

Tristan only feeds him one more.

"Oh, but I think you can. Because you're a good Omega who wants to please his Alpha, and I'm going to satisfy you in every way possible."

Niles hums as he eats yet another. The indents on the skin of the fruit caress his tongue in sensual glides, his body still hypersensitive. Tristan's fingers trail from his shoulder down his ribs, over his hip, and back again, leaving a pattern of care behind.

"What else can I do for you?" he asks as he sits Niles up in their nest, pressing a glass of water to his mouth and letting him drink his fill.

"Just keep touching me."

Tristan runs the back of his knuckles over Niles's cheek. Then, his eyes go to half-mast as he splays his fingers on his throat, dragging them over his collar and down the center of his chest. His fingers slide lower, over Niles's abdomen, through his pubic hair, and to the tip of his length, causing a small sigh to fall from Niles's lips.

"Like that. Please, like that."

Tristan's smile is audible as he huffs through his nose. "So greedy. But I'll let you burn for me a little longer."

As he says it, he closes his fist around Niles and holds tight, not moving, only making him throb. Half turning, Tristan takes more food in his fingers, a slice of brie, Niles thinks, and caresses Niles with it, lips to chin. Obeying the silent ask, Niles takes a bite and is rewarded with a slow pump of Tristan's hand. He suddenly wants nothing more than to fall onto his back and beg.

"I'm going to feed you ten more things, Omega. And when we're done, I want you to feed me. First some food, then your cock."

Niles is enticed by another decadent stroke that makes him leak.

"And then I'll knot you, okay?"

Niles nods, his jaw moving in slow rhythm before he swallows, taking pride in doing what he's told.

"Good boy."

A fat cherry comes next, on the stem but seedless. It's round and fills Niles's mouth the way he wishes his Alpha would fill the rest of him. A bead of juice gathers in the corner of Niles's mouth, but Tristan is quick to dive in and lick it away, not kissing him, just tasting. His tongue is like silk and hot compared to the chill of the food. Niles tries to capture his Alpha, wanting to brush their lips together, but the man escapes, only pumping Niles's erection once more.

Breathing is a hiss, Niles lets his head dip back as he fake-whines, "You're such a tease."

Tristan sports a devilish look, reaching behind himself to gather something chocolate-covered this time. Niles takes it in and savors the crunch. Almonds.

"You should thank God I don't have a nut allergy." But another one is popped in, silencing him to his chewing. He chuckles, then gasps as Tristan gives him two hard pumps in a row, twisting his hand at the top to tug Niles's foreskin just right. "I think you're going to kill me."

"What a sweet way to die," Tristan says. "Seven more things. You choose."

With a smirk, Niles asks for the edamame, and as he expected, Tristan pops out the four light green orbs on his own, feeding them to Niles one at a time.

"Now only three things left," Niles says.

With adorable surprise, Tristan looks at the remaining bean pod in confusion, and once he gets it, he rolls his eyes. "That's cheating."

"Too bad. That's also what I want next."

Tristan leans in and bites just outside of Niles's collar, leaving a tantalizing mark. "So, boss me around. Make me obey."

Niles spreads his fingers through the black hair at the back of Tristan's head and clenches, tugging him backwards so he can admire those gorgeous eyes. "Hurry this up, Alpha. I need you now, and I don't want to wait anymore."

Slow and sensual, a grin blooms on Tristan's face. "As my Omega commands."

It's peaceful. The only sound is the hum of the air conditioner and Tristan's breathing. The man is dead asleep, head resting on his arm and his mouth skewed adorably to one side. Niles is staring and has been for a while. He was right about it being a short heat. He lasted three days, but here they are on the fifth. Niles has been helped through long heats before, where the Alpha was kind enough to stay even after their rut ended. He'd like to tell himself he's paying it forward, but it would be a lie. He just can't bring himself to abandon Tristan in his time of need. But his heat talk has ended. He no longer says "I love you" nor does Tristan ask for it. They had to order down for lube because Niles's never-ending well of slick has dried, but Tristan doesn't complain. Neither does he complain that Niles needs more sleep now, wants to bathe and get their liquids off him, and needs longer breaks in between. If there was such a thing as being a gentleman and in rut at the same time, this is it.

But it needs to stop.

The longer Niles is here, the less he can imagine going back to a lonely apartment. The less he can imagine going a day without gazing into those heavy-lidded, near-yellow eyes.

He's doing it, isn't he? Falling back in love with the devil.

He shouldn't. He can't.

Tristan stretches, his mouth opening into a wide yawn as he blinks his way awake. A slow, wide smile pulls onto his face when he sees Niles staring. "Hello to you, too."

Niles's lips curve up at the corners. "You seem coherent. How are you feeling?"

Tristan turns over, running a hand over his face and wiping the sleep away. He scratches idly down his naked chest and stares at himself. Niles also noticed.

"Not 'up and about,' so to speak?" Niles says, glancing at Tristan's non-erection.

He grimaces. "Part of me feels like I should be ashamed for not waking up with morning wood."

"And the other part?"

Tristan inspects his body. "Is probably in need of a shower."

Niles's smile is more real this time. "I highly recommend if you catch my drift. I'm certainly catching yours."

A bubble of laughter finds its way out of Tristan. "This was wild."

"Indeed."

"Was it bad?"

Niles whacks his chest. "Did any part of my body being absolutely amazing seem 'bad' to you?"

"Not that." Tristan frowns. "I mean…the rest."

But Niles doesn't want to talk about it. "The proper phrase is, 'The rest is said and done.'" He sits up, tries to smooth down his ruined hair, and scratches at his stubbled cheeks. "I'm going to hit the shower and then head out. You can take a bit to come back down to Earth and become a person again instead of an almighty Alpha."

A sad expression flits across Tristan's face, but he rallies quickly. "So, you think I'm almighty, do you?"

"Only in the sack." Niles ticks his eyebrows up and makes his way to the bathroom.

He tweaks the dial to scalding, mulling over work. He'd texted Katelyn and his boss as soon as he'd gotten home from the fated five-star restaurant but can't help but feel guilty. It's not his fault, but it wasn't his scheduled heat, and this is the kind of thing that puts off his Beta colleagues. It makes him seem unreliable.

He'd texted Ari, too. And Ben, but only because Ben would have been annoyed to be left out. He'd given them the address of the hotel and his to-be-Alpha's pseudonym, just in case. He'll text them again when he leaves. It's time to let the world know he's ready to rejoin it.

But what happens now?

He steps into the shower, ooh-ing and aah-ing a little at the skin-melting temperature before ratcheting it down a peg and starting to lather himself up. This stuff smells good. Like lavender and citrus. Nothing remotely like fall leaves.

He dashes the tears from his eyes.

There's a soft knock, and the door creaks open. Tristan's messy bed head pokes through. "Mind if I join you?"

"In a rush?" Niles asks, shy all of a sudden.

"I just…"—he shrugs—"thought it might be a nice way to say goodbye."

That word punches Niles right in the gut, and in a way it hasn't for many, many years. His father said goodbye, then never came home again. His mother said goodbye and went to die alone. His brother said goodbye and disappeared into the ether. Why does everyone leave?

"Hey," Tristan says, his eyebrows cinched and mouth pulled down. "Hey, are you okay?"

Niles turns his face into the water stream, pretending to wash it. "I'm having Omega hormones. You know how it goes. It's over, wah, wah, boo-hoo. I'll get over it."

The glass door slides to the side, a large body crowding in behind him. Tristan's arms wrap about Niles, and the man rests his forehead on the back of Niles's mess of hair.

"Sometimes Alphas feel that way too, you know."

Niles's lips tremble, a staggering hurt pulling at his heart.

"Can we be friends?" Tristan asks in a voice so soft Niles barely heard it. After a long pause, Tristan continues with, "I still need to hire you for all my ad campaigns."

Like a clock switching from tick to tock, Niles bursts into laughter. "What? What happened to Mr. 'No Strings?'"

The heavy weight of the Alpha drags on Niles's ribs comically as Tristan whines his name like a child.

"Fine, fine!" Niles faux gripes, enjoying this way too much. "We can be friends."

"Oh good," Tristan says, loosening up with the rush of a sigh. "Because apparently I suck at marketing."

CHAPTER 5
IT'S COMPLICATED

Debate is still considered a fine art, even when the one you're debating is yourself. Niles has ridden the elevator up and down twice now, caught in indecision. He hasn't seen Jason in a week, and with everything that went on, Niles never texted (doesn't even have the man's number), never asked Katelyn to tell him what was going on (though she would have loved a chance to get face-to-face with the Blond Beta), and, truth be told, he never once thought of that sweet, dimpled, comic book hero face. That means Jason had either sat waiting alone every day at their café lunch table like the puppy dog he is, or he got tired of being stood up and left, never to be seen again. Why wouldn't he? After all, last Jason knew, Niles was supposed to go on a date with his ex. And, oh boy, did he. Who knows what Jason's been thinking all this time.

The question is: Does Niles stop going to that coffee shop? Avoid it like the steaming pile of poop a wandering Karen leaves behind when she doesn't feel like picking up after her pet? Pretend it doesn't exist like the fart you know you squeaked out in the office, but if you just deny its existence, maybe everyone else will, too?

Or does he go downstairs, look that gentle giant in the eyes, and come clean?

What if that gentle giant isn't even there? What if he thought he scared Niles off with his ex-related anecdotes? He didn't. All he did was remind Niles that exes are exes for reasons. And then Niles took that sentiment and crammed it, quite literally, up his ass. Now he has to sit here in the muck and mire of confusion. It wasn't passing a heat with a stranger. It was more. And Niles doesn't know if he loves that fact, or if he hates it.

He fiddles with the new beads on his retwined braids—one of the very first items on the to-do list after rolling his head around on the floor for days—and peeks through the slit in the elevator door as it slides open to the lobby for the third time with its innocuously annoying little *ding*.

Announce me to the world, why don't you! Niles cries silently as he forces himself to walk out into the building's grand foyer, eyeing the café entrance tucked to the side.

His tiptoes are little, snipping steps, his bento box bouncing in his right hand as his left waggles outward, ready to grab hold of the doorframe so he can pivot behind it on contact. Sneaking a peek, Jason is definitely at their spot, hunched over an empty table and staring at his hands. Niles's heart gives a tug and a pitter-pat. The idea that someone is waiting for him, perhaps hurting due to him but holding on anyway, hits him in all of his soft spots.

Rallying, he smacks his own cheeks in little *whap, whap*s while he peps himself up. "Just go in and say hello. Just *go in* and *say hello*. This is not rocket science."

He only then realizes he's speaking aloud.

Shoving his hand over his face and preemptively very, very sorry, Niles opens the door and walks inside. Jason's head jerks up at the sound, and that sunshine smile appears without blame or accusation. Just happy to see him. If this man had a tail, it would wag.

Sliding into his spot across the table, Niles takes a page from the other man's book and blurts, "IHadAnOffCycleHeat."

Out of all the reactions Niles may have expected—surprise, confusion, embarrassment, worry—what he didn't expect was the smug expression that crosses Jason's face, his dimples showing beautifully as he props his chin on his upturned fist.

"I kinda figured it was something like that," he says.

Niles twines his fingers together. *In for a penny, in it for a pound.*

"And I didn't do it alone," Niles adds, wanting to blob up into a puddle of slime and slip down to the floor.

That doesn't seem to take Jason by surprise either, though his expression sinks. "Oh."

And now it's time to outright scalp himself. "I did it with my ex."

Now *that*, however, makes Jason's eyes go wide and round. A fine line draws its way up his forehead as his gaze flicks from one of Niles's eyes to the other. "But…"

"I didn't mean for it to happen!" Niles rushes forward and presses his palms to the table, not sure why he's so goddamn sorry, other than the fact that he is. "I went into heat, and it drove him into rut and—"

"He *rutted* you?" Jason's voice goes cold, his eyebrows dropping low.

This is when Niles should remind himself that he and Jason are not together. He has given no promises. He doesn't remind himself, though. Instead, his gaze drops, and his full lips press closed.

Niles isn't as good at smelling emotions as Ari is, but he can smell this. Jason's scent is like laser lights in the dark. That sharp note is overwhelming, and his hurt and anger vie for dominance in the air. It all swirls around in a miasma, clogging up Niles's every pore, but when he finally has the courage to look up at his Blond Beta, the scent breaks apart into sorrow and rejection.

"I wish…" Jason says quietly. "I wish you would have told me. I could have helped you."

Betas can't help Omegas the way they need, is Niles's first thought. A bitter, mean thought. A thought that's not necessarily true. He didn't even let Jason try.

"I'm sorry," Niles repeats. "I understand if you don't want to be friends anymore."

He goes to stand, but Jason catches his wrist at the last second. His eyes are a darkening blue, and his mouth is a grim line, but when he says, "Stay?" Niles lands on his chair again without a second thought.

Jason is holding his wrist, a soft circle of warm flesh against the gland at Niles's pulse point. The man won't meet his eyes, staring at where they connect and speaking only to that focal point. "I think I saw Bee-bee in the park."

"What?" Niles asks.

"Little white diamond shape on her back, right? I saw a dog like that bouncing around in the bushes. By the time I got there, she was gone, but I've been leaving food out for her every day at around seven o'clock. The squirrels are starting to meet me there on time, so I'm waiting for her clue in to the fact that there's a standard feeding hour. If she figures it out, maybe she'll come when I call. If she does, maybe I can grab her. Does her collar have her name on it?"

"The little blue one?"

"I'm sorry," Jason shakes his head. "I didn't see its color. I only heard the jingle."

Niles's lip trembles. "You found my dog?"

Jason's grip gets somehow kinder, dragging Niles near as he wraps another white hand around Niles's brown one. "I'm trying to. I'm good at this kind of thing. Hunting. Tracking."

Snorting crassly despite his misting eyes, Niles says, "I'm sure that does you a lot of good in the city."

Giving one of his patented shrugs, Jason says, "I'm not originally from the city."

It dawns on Niles that, for as many lunch hours as they've spent talking, he doesn't really know much about Jason. All he knows is the way he acts, not what made him who he is. But he's curious. For the first time, he's truly curious.

"Where are you from, then? Are you a Martian? Maybe Bee-bee likes Martians."

Finally, another smile lights Jason's face. "Think of me as the kind of guy who would have been a lumberjack in a past life."

"Living in the woods?" Niles asks.

"Definitely."

"Hunting for your meals and not for sport?"

"With bows and arrows." The smile becomes a grin, though Jason's still staring at the place where their hands meet.

"Well, what's stopping you from running wild and being free?"

That warm grip squeezes the tiniest bit. "I'd rather be here with you."

Niles stares at their hands together, feeling comforted, safe, and forgiven. Despite hurting this man, he is choosing to stay.

"Can I have your number?" Niles asks, knowing Jason has every possible reason to reject him, yet those fingers slide over Niles's wrist in gentle, soothing sweeps, leaving Jason's familiar, masculine scent on his skin.

"I'd love that."

"Well, this is a clusterfuck," Ben says in a flat, matter-of-fact tone, to which Niles can only thump his head on the table. Their terrific trio sits together in the mated pair's tiny half of a duplex at the end of a long day.

"Is it, though?" Ari asks. "Tristan said 'no strings.'"

"Yeah, after a weekend of making me say 'I love you' so many times my mouth went numb." Niles thumps his head a little harder. "I think the incessant repetition made the feeling stick. One day and I already miss him."

"But you're also goo-goo eyed for the Beta," Ben adds, refusing to let him off the hook. "And he's just as much of an idiot. Who doesn't freak out if the person they're into spends a heat with someone else?"

"You're an Alpha," Niles reminds. "You're growly and grumpy and always looking for a reason to start a fight. If it wasn't for Ari, you wouldn't have that marshmallowy inside."

Ari refills Niles's wine glass. "He's been a softie his whole life, he's just very selective about who he goes belly up for."

The wine is too tart compared to the wine Tristan had plied him with at that fancy restaurant. Or rather, Niles plied himself with. Suddenly realizing something, Niles asks a suspicious, "Why aren't you drinking, Ari?"

To which the soulmated pair both *bink* with grins. Sparkly ones. Ben's is self-congratulatory while Ari's is shy and giddy. Leaning over,

Ben tugs Ari's hair until she comes closer. He murmurs. "Should we tell him?"

"Isn't it too early?"

Niles's mouth drops. "You're pregnant."

Those grins shift to blaring supernovas, Ari turning all shades of pink and Ben puffing up and beating his chest like a damn gorilla, lifting his arms and jutting both thumbs in the air. "Goddamn right, we're pregnant."

Ari puts her hands over her face in absolute adorableness. "The doctor says it's triplets."

Those thumbs up become fist pumps on both sides, stretching Ben's chest to the ceiling.

"Damn, Benjamin. That's some potent seed you've got there."

"Don't let anyone ever tell you a decade in a coma will lower your sperm count." Ben ticks his eyebrows up.

"It doesn't tend to come up in conversation," Niles says, though his head is floating somewhere in the clouds. Three kids. That's, like, three kids too many. "No wonder you've been so weepy lately."

Ari gets up and starts fiddling with things, picking up the teakettle with no intention of making tea and rinsing it in the sink only to dry it off, find a tiny spot, and wash it again while rambling. "And why my feet have been swollen, and why I've been exhausted, and why I have to pee all the time. I even started hating Chinese food."

"You're obsessed with Chinese food…even when it gives you the runs," Niles says.

Ben blats a laugh and Ari shoots Niles a glare of pure loathing. "We. Don't. Talk. About. That. In. This. House."

"You don't have to say anything. Your bathroom does it for you."

Flinging her arms in the air, Ari grunt-growls and begins a huffy walk away, stomping her apparently swollen feet. "I'm going to do the laundry."

When she turns the corner, Ben mouths, "Moodiness is part of it, too."

"Screw you, Benjamin Allein!" Ari calls from halfway down the hall toward their basement steps. Both men cringe as she slams the door behind her.

"So is a heightened sense of hearing," Niles notes, and Ben nods so fast, his black hair falls into his bourbon brown eyes.

Niles cocks his head, knowing Ari and Ben emotion-share—part of being soulmated versus regular mated—and has to ask, "How are you doing with all of this?"

Ben slides his eyes in another direction, his smile becoming wry. He tips one shoulder up before lacing his fingers together over his belly. "I'm happy. I'm fucking ecstatically happy."

"But?"

Ben reaches over and shoves his walker a bit, the steel glinting in the kitchen lights. "I have concerns."

"About?"

"How am I supposed to help with diapers and carrying babies when I can barely walk? If it was one, that would be something she could maybe handle most of, but *three?* What happens if they're all crying at once, and I need to go grab one, but I can't? What if one is going to, I dunno, stick a fork in a socket, and I can't get to it fast enough? And we're going to feel it all together, you know? I'll actually *feel* her frustration and disappointment when I can't help the way I should. And she'll feel my depression about it. And then she'll pity me. You know how much pity I already get from people? The last person I want it from is my mate." He shoves his walker harder, getting it slightly out of reach with a rubber squeak across the tile flooring.

"Can you get a nanny?"

"You think we can afford a fucking nanny on pro-bono lawyer salaries? Never mind daycare. One of us might have to quit our jobs. It's not like the kids are gonna have grandparents to come help. Or even a fucking uncle."

"Ben?" Ari calls from downstairs, likely sensing his change in mood.

After a rough sigh and a deep breath, he calls back, "It's alright Ri-ri. Do your thing."

With a quiet "Okay" she shuts the basement door again and they listen to the sound of her walking down the wooden, creaky stairs.

"I can't even help with the laundry." Ben crosses his arms again, pursing his lips and seeming far away.

"I can come help."

"What? And give up your life to babysit or watch your best friend start to hate her husband?"

"Ari could never hate you. It's, like, biologically impossible."

He snorts, saying nothing. Niles gets quiet too. His brain can't fathom what life will be like now. For Ari. For Ben. And, selfishly, for himself. No more nightly texting because Ari's going to be overwhelmed with children. No more wine weekends. No more terrific trio outings. Where the hell does he fit in now?

That loneliness fills him up with a constricting hurt, shoving his lungs against his ribcage. He'll have no one to distract himself with at night anymore. No one to numb the pain of being detached from the rest of the world. He doesn't date. He doesn't anything. But maybe he better start, or else he'll truly be on his own.

"But I am happy," Ben murmurs. "It's not one feeling or the other. It's all mixed together. I've lived my life in a constant state of anger and self-loathing, to be honest, clinging onto one person to save and be saved by. I'm used to that. But this? I've never felt so much at once before. So hopeful, proud, excited, afraid. So furious at myself for not making different choices in my life. Everything could have been different if I'd never gotten into that car crash. I ruined so many lives. Yet here I am, about to be blessed with three little angels I already love with my whole heart, even though I haven't even met them yet.

"I just want to be a good father," Ben continues. "If I can do that, maybe it won't all be for nothing. Maybe I'll have lived for a reason."

Niles scoots his chair over and lays a hand on Ben's arm. The Omega in him lets off every calming pheromone he can, trying to soothe his favorite Alpha. "You're going to find a way. And they're going to love you so much, you're going to burst from it, I know. Never mind Ari loving you, she kind of can't help that, but I'm a walls-up, sarcastic prick, so if I can love you, anyone can."

"Thanks." Ben pats a hand over his and squeezes it. "It...well, it means a lot. I've never had a friend before."

"Don't let it go to your head."

They both have a chuckle, and Niles takes a sip of his wine.

"Do you think you'll ever want kids?" Ben asks.

"God, no. You know how hard that is on a male Omega's body? No thank you. I'll leave the parenting to those who are ready and willing."

"No one's ever ready."

Niles rocks his head side to side, pulling his lips down at the corners in agreement. "But you've got one thing wrong about all of this."

"And what's that?"

"Your kids will definitely have an uncle." Ben stares at him blankly, so Niles clarifies. "Me."

It's small and more than a little sad, but Ben manages a smile. "Yeah. You're right."

The light streams in, snow falling gently outside. It's always so pretty until it hits the ground. At that point, cars run over it and people smash through it, turning it all into gray slush. Niles had to wear his boots today, and they wrap around his feet like heavy burdens. He asked Jason out for coffee on a Saturday afternoon, needing to decompress with someone he seems to be able to be vulnerable with. Jason is in rapt attention, never looking away, his chin resting on his fists as they clasp together, elbows on the table.

"I worry I'll be left behind." Niles words come out with a gust of air, and he rubs his temple, a headache threatening. "I feel like that happens a lot."

"Why?" Jason asks.

"Because I got shipped off to foster care. Because as soon as my brother was old enough, he basically ran away. Because my dog did, too. Because my best friend, someone I love more than anything, left me alone in this city to go be with her Alpha. Because now she's going to live a life that's going to be too full to fit me. I'm going to have to force my way in, or else I'll be forgotten."

"That must feel lonely."

Niles falls silent. He stares at the coffee in his hand, unable to bring himself to drink it. His stomach is sick again. His phone buzzes, screen-down on the table. Out of habit, he flips it over and sees a text from Tristan. It simply says, "I hope you're feeling okay. Thanks for taking care of me."

Lips quirked up at the corner, Niles realizes he's proud. The old Tristan would have texted him the night they left each other. Hell, the *moment* they left each other. Now his Alpha—for some reason, always his—gave him space and waited a whole seventy-two hours to ping him. Maybe he *has* grown. Changed. Maybe Niles could…

Realizing his impoliteness, he flips the phone back over again. "Sorry. Anyway, I'm being depressing again. I feel like I've dragged down our last few chats."

"I know." Jason smirks. "Where did my funny Omega go?"

Niles scoffs. How would a Beta feel about being called by his designation? It's a normal thing for Alphas and Omegas to do, but not Betas. A true sign this man is trying to live in their lifestyle. An Omega fetish. Maybe it's kind of sexy to be fetishized, though. After all, who is he to yuck somebody's yum? Especially if he's the yum.

A knock at the window startles him, and they both look up. Waving behind the glass…is Tristan. If Niles could go pale, he would. His Omega lets out a soft cry of pleasure that Niles tries to tamp down like an Irish step dancer, but it doesn't work. Tristan points at the door to the café and holds his finger up, mouthing "One sec" before walking a few steps and ducking inside, snow leaving little melting spots on his long winter jacket. It fits him perfectly, and his heavy-lidded, tawny eyes fall on Niles, squinting with the breadth of his smile.

He pops over to the table, seemingly without a care in the world, and ruffles the melted droplets from his messy, wavy black hair. "Imagine seeing you here."

Niles wants to run away. Instead, he puts on his big boy pants and smiles back. "Wow. I didn't know you hung out in this part of town. This is my friend Jason. Jason, this is Tristan, a friend from high school."

Tristan ticks his eyebrows up at that but puts his hand out to shake with the other man, neither of them seeming to understand how intensely weird and awkward this is...or maybe they do. Tristan sniffs the air slightly and turns to Niles, Jason following his gaze.

Niles does his best to leave his smile frozen, despite his panic. "So how are you?"

"Happy to see you" is Tristan's easy reply, making Jason frown a bit. Tristan doesn't seem to notice. "I was scoping out your firm. I have a meeting on Monday to see if it makes sense to hire them. Well, hire you specifically. You said you'd help me, after all."

Oh, yes, he did say that. Something he should have thought through a little better.

"I'm horrible with this damn city. The streets make no sense. It's easier when I walk, so I figured I'd check out the parking situation and work my way over. I want to make sure I get to the meeting on time."

"Not from around here?" Jason asks.

"Nah. Niles and I went to school in Springfield." When Jason knits his eyebrows, Tristan shrugs. "Just think 'Very Poor' and 'High Crime' and you'll probably get a good enough idea."

"It's about two hours west," Niles explains. "But at least they have a theme park."

"One we could never afford to go to," Tristan adds.

Seeing his opening, Niles says, "Speaking of affording things, I need to go back to the office. I've got some stuff to finish up this weekend, and I need the power of large-scale printers to do it."

A total lie.

"Oh!" Tristan says. "Wanna show me up?"

God no.

"Sorry, you need a badge to get in, and if I let you piggyback, security will have a field day with me on Monday."

Tristan smiles at him all too softly. "Alright. I'll leave you to it." Moving to leave, he gives the Beta a wide berth. "Nice to meet you."

"Likewise," Jason says, though that's another lie if there ever was one.

Before Jason can ask even one question, before Tristan is even out the door, Niles makes his excuses and tries his best not to outright run away.

To Niles's credit, he does scrounge up some work to do. He'd left his laptop at the office and pokes around for a bit, checking his emails. He's still catching up from his unexpected heat leave and pretending to be a stellar employee by emailing his boss on the weekend. To which his boss promptly replies, "Get offline, it's the weekend." What a good boss.

Time ticks by slowly with nothing to do. Niles finds himself playing games on his phone to blow away an hour until it's finally safe to leave his empty office and make his way home. The gloomy shine of the winter sun is long gone but the snow still fluffs its way down, starting to gather in the nooks and crannies of the city streets. The chill makes Niles shiver, even with his coat buttoned all the way up and his hands shoved deep into the pockets. Cement walls greet him as he turns into the narrow parking garage he pays a monthly fee for—one that should be immediately discounted because the elevator hasn't been working for days and the stairwell is sketchy and smells like pee. Niles is forced to get his steps in by walking the long and winding way from one parking lot floor to next, aiming for lucky number seven. It's where Niles usually ends up every day. He's come to think of it as his personal space.

Twisting around the strut that braces level four, Niles walks past a smattering of cars without noticing them, too busy obsessing over babies, Ben, and Ari being as big as a mountain. How the hell triplets are going to fit into that tiny body is anybody's guess. She's going to blow up like a bounce house, kicking kids and all. A shudder runs through Niles as he imagines six little hands stroking the inside of her belly, fingertips showing through her skin like little alien parasites.

Yeah, no. He should never have kids.

There is the telltale crunch of someone else walking behind him, their shoes scuffing along the salted asphalt. Niles scans over his shoulder and catches the shadow of a shape back on floor three, working its way up as well. Poor bastard. Someone else caught out in the freezing cold.

Floor five and the cars have thinned out. Only a handful in sight. Those footsteps still climb behind Niles, which shouldn't bother him except those scuffing steps don't sound like a normal stride. They get silent, almost to the point where Niles assumes the shoes must have found their vehicle, but then they shuffle forward again. They're not nearly as loud as Niles's own steps. Softer, almost like the person is trying to mask their footfalls.

A chill works its way up Niles's back that has nothing to do with the cold. Glancing over his shoulder again, he sees no one, which makes him feel worse instead of better. He picks up his pace, skirting around to floor six.

Once he rounds the corner, those stalking steps shamble forward again, and Niles's skin turns to gooseflesh. He may be tall, but he's not thick and definitely not a fighter. He digs his hand deeper into his pocket and grabs his keys, working the rigid metal through his pointer and middle fingers until it sticks out of his fist like a claw. If he's only got one punch in him, he'll make sure it will carry a nice surprise.

Casting another look behind him, Niles sees someone duck behind a car—a red sedan covered in splashes of winter street guck—but there is no sound of a door opening. No one gets in. No lights turn on.

Fuck this.

Niles breaks into a run. There are no more footsteps behind him, not that he can hear over the slaps of his own feet, anyway, but that doesn't stop him from picking up his jog to a gallop, ramming the key fob's unlock button until he hears the familiar *cheep cheep*. Throwing himself inside, he slams the door and locks it down. The key is turned with a sweaty hand, and he flicks on his headlights, backing out without looking. If he hits the sonofabitch, so be it.

He has to go slowly down the tight spiral of the garage, or he'll never make the turns, but it helps him scan for danger. When he gets to the red sedan, he sees it. A figure slips behind the car and out of sight. Niles's gaze snaps to his rear-view mirror, rocketing back and forth between every reflective surface his car has to offer, waiting for another car to speed up behind him, or for the garage boogeyman to jump out, grab hold of his wiper blades, and bash his forehead through the glass, grabbing Niles by the throat and dragging him through what's left of the windshield.

It's an overactive imagination, Niles tells himself. *You've always had one. That's what artsy-fartsy people are like. It's night-time, you're stressed out, and you're seeing things. Or maybe you just avoided being mugged.*

That seems like a fair enough explanation. Niles nods to himself, clenching his steering wheel tighter with one hand as he scans his monthly pass with the other. The barred gate of the garage opens in a slow, metallic creak, and Niles gets the hell out of there.

THE PAST

Ten-year-old Niles's guts tore from his throat as he wailed. This was worse than anything that ever happened to him before. All the pent up hope for the future he dreamed about, day after day, night after night, was gone. He was abandoned yet again.

Thirteen-year-old Trey held Niles's small hand in his, watching him with those denim blue eyes. They shimmered, but no mourning tears fell down his smooth, brown cheeks, even though they were ripping holes down Niles's. His were acid tears.

"It's going to be okay," Trey said.

But he was wrong. He was wrong because Mama was dead, and now they were never going to get out of the foster home. They were going to stay there forever in a small room with other broken, angry kids who were more than happy to take out their frustrations on the little boy too weak to stand up for himself.

He and Trey were wearing borrowed black jackets. They came with long, matching black ties that clipped to their collars neatly, making them look fancier than they ever had before. All around them was rain. It beaded up in Niles's buzz-cut hair, trailing down the back of his neck in drips and drops. His white shirt was going see-through, but he didn't think he'd get in trouble for it. They were out in the rain to say goodbye, after all, and even God was crying.

"I want my mama!" Niles wept, not bothering to scrub his arm under his running nose. "I want her right now!"

His brother said nothing but got to his knees, putting himself at eye-level with Niles. He ran his thumbs over Niles's cheeks and then squeezed him from shoulders to wrists.

"Don't you dare tell me it will be okay ever again!" Niles yelled. "I hate it! It's a lie!"

"You're right," Trey said. He lifted Niles's chin and gazed at him, steady and sure. "We're going to miss her for the rest of our lives. We're going to think about her and remember everything we've done together. We—"

"No one's ever coming to get us now!" Niles screeched louder than he should but didn't allow himself to care. Everything in him was boiling in thick, poison bubbles. "No one will love us! No one will tell us stories or hold us and kiss us goodnight! We're *stuck!* Just some stupid orphans!"

"Not stupid," Trey said, squeezing him again. "And I'll love you. I'll tell you stories and hug you and everything okay? Don't cry. You'll make me cry, too. Mama told me I've gotta be strong now. I'm the big brother, right? I've gotta take care of you."

Niles flung himself into Trey's arms, planting his face in the crook of his neck and gasping through hiccups and sobs. "She said she'd come back!"

The arms that encircled Niles were just firm enough, keeping him upright when all he wanted to do was throw himself on the ground and scream.

"It wasn't her fault, kiddo. She was sick."

"Yeah, well, she *shouldn't* have been sick!"

Trey had no reply. He only held Niles tighter. Moments passed as the rain continued to soak into him, seeping deeper than his clothes. He was frozen to the bone even as warm weather spring flowers bloomed all around him, promising the lie of life and rebirth.

Looking over Trey's shoulder, so many people in dark church clothes were staring at him. He recognized some as his mom's friends, but there was also a blur of faces he didn't know.

Mama would have told him not to make a fuss if she were here. She'd have said to keep his head high and remember that he was loved from beginning to end. That he was not alone. His brother was there, a rock to cling to in a storm, and he always would be. That thought became a safety line in his heart, snicking closed with a thick, metallic lock.

"Promise you won't leave me," Niles murmured against his brother's wet, softening collar.

His grip tightened further. "I promise."

Niles nodded his head against Trey, pulling back and snuffling before scrubbing at his eyes. An umbrella unfolded over their heads, and he peeked up to see his social worker, her mouth a flat line.

"It'll be okay boys," she said.

Those horrible words.

Trey stood, gripping Niles's fingers in his own, and led them out of the umbrella's haven. Niles was glad. This rain was meant for him. Though he was cold, he could at least feel it. If science class was right, the chill, the damp, and the water running over his skin were all lighting up his nerve endings and sending signals to his brain. It was precious. Holy.

It was something his mother couldn't do anymore.

"Sneaky footsteps," fourteen-year-old Trey whispered, setting his pointer finger to his lips.

"You're too old to talk like that," eleven-year-old Niles griped, though not without smiling.

"You're never too old for anything," Trey said. "Now, do you want it or don't you?"

Niles lifted his hands in surrender and followed. The night kept most of the stairwell in shadow, but Niles knew exactly how many steps it took to get downstairs and into the kitchen. He knew where to pivot to sneak around the corner table, avoid the lamp, and pass over the creaky board without sound. Years of doing it with his eyes closed as a sort of challenge for himself had paid off. Now, with the moonlight barely shining through the windows, he was glad to have gained that skill.

Trey let him take the lead once they got into the kitchen, where it got considerably darker. The pantry was four steps in on the left wall, and Niles skated his hand over the wallpaper at hip level until he found the doorknob. It filled his whole palm and then some, but he grinned at his co-conspirator—who couldn't see him anyway—and eased it open.

It was Trey's turn to step forward again. He was taller but still had to stand on the tips of his toes. Up high was the candy shelf, replenished after the shopping for the week had been done. It was a ritual. Every time cookies were bought, one of the kids would sneak down and grab a few. Trey always helped, since he was the only one who could reach them without jumping. In payment, he got one cookie on every mission instead of just one turn every month or so, but he never took anything from Niles. Niles's score was his and his alone. Trey was good like that.

The proffered delicacy this time around was mint chocolate chip. Not Niles's favorite, but he wasn't about to turn down sugar, no matter what form it came in. Every crisp crinkle of the wrinkling bag under Trey's grip was like a grenade, putting Niles in a constant state of cringe, his body taut and thrumming with nerves. He'd only been caught once, but getting grounded in this place meant a week's worth of nothing to do except homework and reading the encyclopedia. From the beginning. Every time. As much as Niles liked the idea of an aardvark, he had no desire to read about one ever again.

Pulling the plastic inner container from the bag was slow death. Even Trey, as little as Niles could see him in the blue light, had his lips pulled back, showing his teeth in a never-ending wince. The cookies themselves were like black circles. Harmless but not delicious-looking in the slightest. Niles knew better. He pulled three from the front where their foster mother had already cleared out half the row. These shouldn't be missed. He hoped. If one of the kids got too greedy, they'd all be screwed.

As was custom, Niles offered the first one to his brother who shook his head daintily, bowed, and lifted a hand in deference. Niles held back a snort at the butler-esque submission and tucked the cookies into the pocket in the front of his hoodie. He would crunch and munch them tomorrow morning on the way to school. If he did it now, it would be another noise violation he couldn't risk. Their foster mother's bedroom was beside the kitchen, and he had no desire to awaken the kraken. The hassle would very much outweigh the treasure.

With agonizing, painstaking slowness, Trey pushed the row of cookies back into the bag and sealed it up. Treats replaced and pantry door shut, they snuck their way back upstairs to their room, sneaky smiles lighting up their shadowed faces.

"What's happening to you?" twelve-year-old Niles asked, his voice pitchy.

Fifteen-year-old Trey was leaning over, clutching his belly and panting. Sweat made little droplets on his forehead and soaked stains into his shirt, both down the line of his back and in the crooks of his armpits. "It hurts."

"Want me to get Mrs. Strauss?" Niles asked.

"Don't you dare. I don't want to go into quarantine."

That's what she did. To avoid getting all the kids sick, their foster mother would lock the infected one away. No school. No TV. No nothing except suffering. She'd leave your meal tray and a few bottles of water outside the door with whatever medication the doctor inflicted upon you, but that was it.

"This sucks," Trey groaned. "Why does this suck so bad?"

Niles got down on his hands and knees beside his brother, his palms up and unsure of what to do with themselves. "What's it feel like?"

"Like a fever, but I'm too hot instead of too cold. I want...something...but I don't know how to explain it. My skin is so sensitive, it's like it burns or aches or...I don't even know. I just wanna cry, and my belly hurts."

"Do you have the stomach flu? Are you gonna crap yourself or something?"

The strained huff of a laugh Trey let out was concerning. "When did you get to be so vulgar?"

"Crap isn't a swear."

"Do your teachers let you say it?"

Niles tipped his head to the side sheepishly. "No."

"Then call it something else."

"Shit?" Niles grinned while Trey only narrowed his eyes at him. "Defecation? Diarrhea? The poops? Do you have the poops, Trey?"

"Oh my God, shut up. If I don't die from whatever the hell is happening to me, your mouth is gonna kill me."

Niles took that for a win.

With a gasp, Trey curled over again, resting his forehead on his knees. "I...I think I know what this is."

"I told you. The poo—"

Trey lashed a hand up and covered Niles's mouth. "Whatever you were going to say, don't."

Niles shrugged his brother off but not without good humor.

Trey's fingers were like claws as they scoured backwards over his scalp. He let out a pained little mewl, and it was at that inopportune moment Erik popped in, eating from a bag of orange barbecue chips and wiping the crumbs on his shirt. He was going to get in trouble for that.

"What's going on here?" Erik said with a slimy tone of glee, always happy to take part in someone else's suffering. His face was a mottled land map where one couldn't tell the difference between acne and freckles, but he never took shame in it. Puberty was a trial by fire, he said. Zits or not, he was winning.

"I dunno," Trey said. "Nothing like this has ever happened before."

Erik popped another chip into his mouth with an audible crunch. "You're a fucking moron, you know that?"

Both brothers flung their eyes in the boy's direction.

"You're presenting," Erik said, mouth full and chomping.

"How would you know?" Trey muttered.

"I take freakin' health class. Don't you? The question is: do you want to rail somebody, or do you want to be railed?"

The question was lost on Niles. Trey only cringed with a whimper. Erik took another tack.

"Jesus. Do you want to, like, hug someone or be hugged?"

"Be hugged," Trey said pitifully.

"Then you're an Omega." Erik's eyes dropped down to the chip bag as he plucked another from the silver foil and shoved it in his face. "Want me to get Strauss?"

"Can she actually do anything about it?" Niles asked, truly curious.

"Nah." Erik shrugged, as if it didn't matter. "It is what it is."

"D-does this mean I have to do that…what do they call it?"

"Dry heat?" Erik offered.

"Yeah," Trey said with a wince.

"Yeah," Erik echoed. "Strauss isn't gonna rent you out by the hour to some Alpha at your age."

"They do that?" Niles gaped with horror, but the bully only laughed at him.

"Probably. Sucks to be you." Erik stared at Trey, who started to shiver at that point. "Wasn't your mom an Omega?"

Trey nodded.

"Males are rare, you know. Maybe they have a registration for freaks like you."

This time, Trey flinched. Niles knew he hated that word. He was a freak for being black in a white neighborhood, a freak for having blue eyes, and now a freak for being an Omega male.

Niles wanted to stand up for his brother, but then Erik would wail on him, he was sure of it. He wanted to yell "Go away!" but he was too much of a coward to open his mouth.

"Fine," Trey said through gritted teeth. "Go get Mrs. Strauss. If I have to get locked up, then whatever. Just tell Josie to look after Niles."

Erik snorted. "Josie's gonna be eighteen in about three days, and then she's outta here. You gonna finish…whatever…in three days?"

Why does this have to be so hard? Niles thought. *All you have to do is promise not to beat the crap out of me!*

"I'll figure it out," Trey said, all too seriously. "Niles, go to Josie right now."

"But I…" *I don't want to leave you. Not when you're like this.*

"No buts, kiddo. C'mon."

"Yeah, move your ass, or I'll move it for you," Erik chimed in helpfully.

Niles had half a mind to deck him and eat the rest of his chips just to be a prick about it.

At a quick clip, Niles was down the hall knocking on Josie's bedroom door, angsty-bellowing music playing behind the thin wooden surface. When she opened it, her black-makeup eyes were narrowed, and her penciled-on eyebrows were up. Niles pointed backwards toward his brother, still on his knees and bent nearly in half while Erik called downstairs for their foster mother.

Josie's arm wrapped around Niles's shoulders with a sigh. "Alright. Get in here, kid. I got you. You're gonna stay with me for the next few days, ok?"

Niles couldn't stop staring at his brother, who at this point had begun to cry. A knot worked its way into Niles's stomach as he heard their foster mother tromp her way up the stairs calling out, "Oh, hell!"

Without further ado, Josie tugged him in and slammed the door behind them. Grimacing, she leaned down to her stereo and switched to pop music instead, the kind Niles liked. She gave him her goth side-eye. "You will tell absolutely no one I've listened to this music. Ever. Get me?"

Eyes locked on the door, Niles nodded. What else could he do?

Trey grabbed the awkward fourteen-year-old Niles and dragged him outside. "We know what it's like," he scolded.

"Yeah, well maybe I don't want to deal with other people's baggage. I've got enough of my own."

"Everyone's got baggage. If you're ever going to have friends, you're gonna have to get over yours."

Niles scowled. "I don't need friends, I've got you."

"Yeah, and I turn eighteen next year. Where will you be then?"

"You're gonna get a house next door, and I'll see you every day," Niles said, digging in his heels. He hated this conversation every time his brother tried to have it.

"Again, I don't have the money to live anywhere."

"She said you can have a job next year."

Even though Niles knew it cut into her weekly paycheck from the state. She was greedy, but at least she had enough kindness not to toss them out into nothing.

"What, you think I'm gonna flip burgers and somehow afford to live around here?"

"Dude, this neighborhood is *not* special."

"I think you need to sincerely reevaluate your understanding of how finances work, Niles Matthew."

"Ugh, don't call me that, Trevon James."

His brother rolled his eyes, but was otherwise unmoved as he yanked hard, nearly knocking Niles off his feet into the dirt. Petulantly silent, Niles allowed himself to be led to the creek behind the house, a dirty trickle of a stream that only served to pass the time somewhere that wouldn't get you tapped to buy drugs or pressured into joining a gang. A white girl with brown hair sat on a low hanging tree branch, a skinny leg swinging down as she picked at the bark. She was so lost in thought, she didn't seem to hear the two of them stomping up, one with more enthusiasm than the other.

"Hey, new girl," Trey called up, startling her to the point where she almost fell out of the tree. "You and my brother are the same age. You'll be going to school with him starting tomorrow, so I wanted to introduce you to each other. He can look out for you."

Niles snorted. He couldn't look out for anything.

The girl's face was misery personified. Her eyes were swollen from crying, and she seemed to have a permanent frown. Her broken arm was in a cast, and she held it tight to her chest like it hurt. Pity came easily when Niles truly took her in.

"Our parents died, too," Niles said, cutting to the quick like a damned idiot. She stared at him as if he'd gutted her, and guilt took a hold of his heart with an uncomfortable squeeze.

"Oh yeah?" she said softly. "And did someone kill your parents like they did mine?"

An uncomfortable silence followed, one Trey broke by saying, "Our father got shot when Niles was little. Our mom died of because she was sick, though."

Her face crumpled in what looked like sympathy. Niles loved her that very moment. Not in a boyfriend/girlfriend way but in a kindred spirit kind of way. A "will you be my friend" way.

"It gets easier," Niles tried again.

"I don't want it to get easier," she sobbed. "I love them, and they're gone, and I have nothing! I don't know these people. I don't know how to live like this. My friends are far away, and I'm all alone!"

Trey tugged Niles a few steps closer, and he went willingly this time. "You're not alone. The other kids here were abandoned when they were little, so they won't get it, but Niles and I...we do."

She cradled her head in her arms, curling up on the tree branch with her pink sneakered heels digging in. "I don't want you to have to get it! I don't want anyone to know what this feels like!"

She teetered, and Niles rushed in, catching her, and reseating her back on the branch, his hands around her waist. It was a moment that sped by, his body acting without him asking it to, and it was officially the first time he protected anyone.

His brother beamed at him.

Niles's face got warm. "What's your name?"

"Ari," she said, rubbing her reddened eyes.

Niles took her unhurt hand in both of his, petting it with his thumbs. "I'm Niles, and this is my brother, Trey. We've been here for about seven years. It's...not horrible."

"Pfft, high praise," Trey scoffed.

"Kat, your roommate, she's quiet, but she's alright. Stay away from Erik. Brandon is creepy, I swear he eats bugs, but he's getting adopted soon. He's young, and he's smart, so those ones tend to go. Kids our age stay."

"Good. I don't want another family." She shook her head, turning her face up toward the sky and tearing up again.

"How about some friends, instead?" Trey asked. "It doesn't hurt to have allies."

Niles's thumbs continued to stroke back of the girl's hand as she quieted.

Trey said, "And know it's okay not to be okay. You're going to miss them forever. But we're here to listen to you talk about them if you want. Maybe we'll talk about our parents too."

"And what? Be miserable together?" Ari asked.

"They say misery loves company," Niles replied. "And we're about as miserable as it gets."

The girl finally huffed a pained laugh. "We can be The Ruined Kids Club."

"Oh yeah," Trey said. "We're gonna like you."

Niles sat on his bed. Trey was across the room at his own and stripping off everything—the blankets, the sheets, and the pillowcases. What was left was a stained, flattened, overused mattress, likely decades older than Trey was at the ripe old age of eighteen. The age kids got kicked out of there.

"It's gonna be okay," Trey said.

No matter how many years had gone by, Niles still hated those words.

"Boston's not too far away."

"It is when you don't have a car," Niles said.

Trey tossed his laundry in a heap on the floor and plopped down beside Niles, making the springs creak. "One of my roommates has a car. Maybe she'll let me borrow it."

"And how are you going to find time with your three jobs?"

Trey puffed out a sigh.

"And you don't have a cell phone."

"You say that like you do."

"No, but I have a house phone," Niles insisted. "Are you gonna have a house phone?"

Niles wanted to clobber something, but Trey leaned back as if he didn't have a care in the world. He rested a wrist over his forehead, staring up at the dingey ceiling as if it held all the answers of the universe.

"You know, Ari will be with you. She'll keep you on the straight and narrow until I get myself sorted out. And I'll get a phone soon. Hell, I'm pretty sure my jobs will make me. I used Mrs. Strauss's number on all my applications. I assume that's not gonna fly forever."

The *harrumph* that pulled from Niles's throat was childish, and he knew it. He crossed his arms and turned away from his brother, more than happy to review the familiar crack in the wall. He listened to the rustling sound of his brother turning over and poking his back.

"I've opened up a bank account for you. I'm gonna put money in it every paycheck so you can go to college."

"Pfft. You're not going."

"And thus, I need three jobs and two roommates to make ends meet."

"What would I even go for?"

Trey seemed to consider. "You love to draw. Maybe something with that. Or maybe making movies. I can picture it now, the award-winning blockbuster *Tales of Niles the Know-it-all!*"

"You're an idiot," Niles gripes. "Besides, don't artists make, like, no money?"

"Maybe if they work for big businesses, they do." His brother continued to poke him as if he'd taken up shiatsu. "What about me? What should I go to college for?"

Now, there was a question with many answers. The gears clicked and turned in his mind before Niles offered, "Maybe you could be a social worker. Help people find new places when they lose their homes."

"Now that's a thought. Or maybe I can be a therapist and help people overcome what's holding them back in life. Maybe I can help them stop being so afraid. That would, I dunno, make it like my life matters. I want to do something that sticks."

Some inexplicable ice in Niles's heart melted. "You already have."

Trey shoved him hard, knocking him off the bed with a punishable curse. "You're making me blush, kiddo."

Gathering Trey's blankets, Niles got up to take them down to the laundry. "You don't get to call me that anymore."

"Oh yeah? And what will I call you instead?"

After a beat, Niles had his answer. "Niles, Commercial Artist Extraordinaire."

THE PRESENT

CHAPTER 7
FOLLOWING IN HIS FOOTSTEPS

MONDAY AFTERNOON, almost at the magical hour called "quittin' time," Niles stares at his computer screen, squinting at an abstract commercial outline and hoping to make it worth putting on film. He's on a deadline, which usually makes him more creative. As much as he hates calendar squares marked with little red circles, he also loves them. They add the excitement of pressure to his otherwise humdrum life.

He sets pencil to paper, starting a rough storyboard. Some people draw on the computer, but Niles kicks it old school, loving the sensation of graphite dragging on twenty-four-pound pressed white sheets. His strokes are choppy and hatched, his faces circles with Xs on the backs when they're turned away and little emoji faces when they are directed toward the camera. He likes it when the actors follow his emotional beats, if feelings are even a part of it. Sometimes it's only sultry voice-overs and cars. Lots and lots of cars.

His phone buzzes. It's Tristan.

I got the contract.

It doesn't explicitly state that you are in control of all my campaigns, but your expertise was promised to me, either way.

I think your boss was surprised I asked for you.

> For as popular as I am, I've never quite made it up the corporate ladder.

Well, let's change that.

> You forget. Black. Gay. Omega. Every box to check is checked in the wrong way.

Well, I happen to be a Latino. Gay. Alpha. And I seem to get what I want.

> Alpha being the key word. People are intimidated by you. They think I was born to be walked on.

To drop your eyes and submit like a good Omega?

That sounded sexy somehow. Niles shifts on the seat in his cubicle.

> I know you better than that. Though, I have to admit, when it does happen, it's a thing of beauty.

And now they are in very dangerous territory. Before Niles has a chance to scold him, Tristan is already apologizing.

> Sorry. That was inappropriate. I really intend to be professional, honest. If I slip up, put me in my place, okay? I don't care in what capacity you're in my life, I'm just happy to have you in it again.

> Thank you for giving me a chance.

> You and I are going to make Geriatric Gamers a multi-million-dollar company!

Niles snorts.

High hopes, my young friend.

We're the same age.

High hopes, my aging friend.

Tristan sends him a GIF of an old man walking with his back bowed and shaking a thick black cane at children who scatter. It's captioned with: "Get off the lawn!" Niles has to run a hand down his face to quell the grin that lifts his cheeks.

Made you laugh, didn't I?

Hush. I'm at work.

Tristan sends a winky face with its tongue out and then says no more. Niles wishes he would, even though he shouldn't.

When he'd left Tristan in high school, it was because he'd become violent. He'd tell Niles he loved him, and the very next moment, slam him against a wall to try to fuck him. He'd be rough and mean, biting Niles's inner thighs to keep him in heat. At first it had been exciting, but eventually, it got scary. Especially when Tristan became obsessed. Stalking him. Leaving emotionally bloodletting notes in his locker. Alienating him from his friends. Trying to manipulate him into giving up everything he cared for.

The man today doesn't sound like that. He's more like he was when they thought he was a Beta. Calm. Charming. Considerate. Even during their sexual escapades, he did nothing Niles didn't ask for. Beg for. If there was a lesson to learn, it seems like Tristan learned it.

Is it possible for people to change, or is this a trick? If not, is it wrong to still blame him for the past when he seems so sorry, wanting to make it right?

They'd loved each other for more than a year, which in teenage-hood is like forever, yet it took less than a month for Niles to give up on him. He'd never watched an Alpha present before, but if Tristan was telling the truth, then his was an extreme case. He was three or more years late to the party, after all. Normal boys presented at fourteen or fifteen. Not two months away from their eighteenth birthday.

Perhaps Niles should have been there for him. Helped him. Instead, he ran away. For someone afraid to be abandoned, he was quick to do the leaving himself.

Another text comes over. With a twinge, he checks to see if it's Tristan again, but it's not. It's Ben of all people.

> What the fuck am I supposed to put on a baby registry?

> And you're asking me because...?

> Shit. Who the hell is even going to buy things from a baby registry?

> Me? Ari's friends at work? I could take up a collection plate.

> Do you think she'll need a chair that rocks or leans back? Or both?

> Again, why me?

> Because you're my only friend!

Ah. Well, that's kind of nice.

> Ari is crying at work because she doesn't know what to get for the babies, and we have no one else to ask!

> Aren't you at work, too?

> Yeah.

> Do you have anyone in your office who looks like a grandmother?

Yeah.

Go prey upon her wisdom.

Oh. Yeah. Okay.

Eloquent, that one.

And don't forget, half the crap they say you need, you probably don't. Cave people managed to keep babies alive without high-end onesies.

What's a onesie?

Internet searches will be your friend.

To which, Niles receives a humble thumbs up and then no more.

Niles was smart today and wore a nice button up under his tailored peacoat. It was one of his splurges for himself. The thing cost an arm, a leg, and two testicles, yet here it is, keeping him dapper and snug as he waltzes through the department store. They're always less likely to follow him around when he dresses like a rich person, and after the incident in the parking lot over the weekend, Niles is in no mood to have strangers trailing behind him.

He pokes around in the baby aisle, checking out presents and price tags. The bitch of it is, no matter what he decides on, he'll have to get three of them. Ari's house is about to be stuffed full of crap. Literally and figuratively.

There goes my favorite guest bedroom, Niles thinks with pursed lips and a furrowed brow. It was just big enough for one dresser and a queen bed, but now Ari and Ben are going to have to shove multiple cribs in there.

A crib…that's the *perfect* gift. Yet, on second thought, the sheer cost keeps the item firmly placed in the *im*perfect gift column.

He peruses them anyway.

There are kinds that only fit newborns—a complete waste of money —and kinds that convert from crib to toddler bed to regular kid bed. They cost about the same, but the newborn bassinets come with frills, ruffles, and little mobiles already hooked to their delicate hoods. It's trickery, pure and simple. As a marketer, he sees right through that ploy, and before his best friend gets starry-eyed when she sees all the little giraffes printed on the fabric, Niles vows to ensure more rational decisions prevail. With an internal gripe, he considers his upcoming bonus and kisses its mental image goodbye. Three convertible cribs are about to be procured for his poor—meaning both financially and emotionally—friends.

"Dreaming of the future or is there a secret you'd like to tell me?"

Niles's heart thumps, and he drops the hand twirling the stuffed animal mobile, whipping around to see Jason standing with his hands in his pockets. He's wearing a nicely fitted black polo shirt and…a name tag.

"I'm looking for stuff for Ari," Niles says, fixated on that little red badge. Somehow, he'd always pictured Jason blundering bluntly in one of the tall office buildings nearby his own, not in a depot-sized warehouse of aisles and randomized prizes to tempt you at the checkout counter. "You work *here?*"

Jason turns pink. "I'm a manager if that makes it any better. Not, like, a shift manager, but a district manager." His head drops to watch his shuffling feet. "This store's been a bit of a problem lately, so I've been coming here more often. It's not a glamorous job but, well, you know." Jason shrugs, seeming embarrassed and a little hurt.

Niles realizes at that moment he's being a snobby dick. "Do you like it here?"

Jason peeks up at him, blond hair hanging in his eyes. "It's a great place to people watch." When Niles only cocks an eyebrow at him,

Jason waves his hand in a circle, beckoning Niles forward. "Come here."

Standing next to him, Niles starts to scan the shoppers, but Jason *tsks*. "Don't be so obvious," he murmurs, a mischievous look on his face. "Pretend you're asking me about baby stuff."

Niles picks up the first thing he can get his hands on, a turtle that lights up and plays obnoxious music when you press its buttons.

Jason snorts. "Remind me to never bring you on a covert mission."

Niles puts it down a bit too hard, turns around, and picks up a complicated looking car seat from halfway down the aisle, lugging it to his…friend.

"That's better," Jason praises, and the Omega in Niles heats his cheeks.

"Now take a gander at the woman down the aisle in front of you. The old one."

Niles glances up. A gray-haired woman with a frown on her face is in front of the greeting cards, picking up one and putting it back in the wrong spot, then picking up another, huffing, and doing the same.

"Do you know my people are going to have to spend at least a half hour fixing her mess?" he says in a gruff undertone that gives Niles a familiar thrill of excitement. "Anyway. You'd think she's looking for the perfect card, right? The perfect little quip or sentimental blah blah blah."

Niles nods.

"Nope." Jason's eyes squint with his dimpled smile. "She's looking at the price tags. Knowing someone like her, she's probably looking for the ninety-nine cent cards. She's going to see if there's something she can scratch out on the inside, changing 'Happy Birthday' to 'Happy Graduation' or something. But check out her clothes. They're expensive, yeah?"

Niles peeks and nods again.

"That means she comes from money but is either a cheapskate, a bitch," Niles gapes at his Good Boy cursing, "or she's found herself on the wrong side of a fixed income. What do you think?"

Niles blinks at her, unsure.

"Now put that car seat back and get a different one. When you do, take a gander at the man to your left."

Like a good boy himself, Niles dutifully lugs the one away and drags forward another. Seriously, how are you supposed to carry kids in these?

The aforementioned man is in the lingerie area, which is placed directly in front of the baby things. The people who designed this floor plan must have automatically assumed only women would be scouring these toy-riddled shelves. They're ninety-nine-point-nine percent right.

The man is poking through lacey white things with an amused expression, touching this or that as he scans through the lines of hanging silk and cotton.

"So what?" Niles asks. "He's getting something for his girlfriend."

Jason hums. "Could be. But look at the size of those panties he's picking at. They're on the big side, right? And look at how happy he is. Either his girlfriend is sexy plush, or he's going to wear them himself."

Niles sputters. "Oh, come on, how could you know that?"

Jason bites his lip with glee. "I don't. But the best part about this job is that these people's lives become *Choose Your Own Adventure* books. Turn to page three if Bobby over there is going to have a night with his lady. Turn to page forty-four if he's starring in a drag show tonight. Bonus points if it's his first show and he's about to live out a lifelong dream." Jason's voice drops low. "Or maybe he's a pervert and likes the way they feel in his fingers. Maybe he'll jerk off to them later, dreaming of dear old grandma's granny panties."

And Niles dies. His burst of laughter is so loud, everyone stops to stare at him. It doesn't quell his reaction, though. His eyes tear up and his shoulders shake with unstifled guffaws. "Oh my God, the mouth on you!"

Jason leans close, whispering, "Not such a good boy now, am I?"

"Not at all. You're a very, very bad boy." Tears are beading up in his eyes as he throws his head back and laughs again. Jason chuckles alongside him.

"There's my funny Omega."

"You're the one that made the joke."

"Yet you're the one that made me laugh. I told you I like laughing."

Niles tries to get himself in order, pressing the heels of his palms against his eyes in quick swipes as the last of his hee-haws work their way out.

"Buying cribs for Ari then?"

Niles nods, having managed to dial it back down to snickers.

"Three?"

He nods again.

"You saint. Tell you what, I'll go in for one of them."

"What?" Niles says, sobering. "Why would you do that? You've never even met her."

"No." Jason shrugs, hands in his pockets again and cheeks pink. "But I met the babies' soon-to-be-uncle. That's good enough for me."

Niles glances at the price placard before his eyes sweep over to Jason's department store name tag again. He opens his mouth and shuts it quickly. Opens and shuts. Jason leans down to catch his eyes.

"Don't worry about me. I'm a trust fund baby. I've got more than I could ever need."

Niles jerks back in confusion. "Then why have a job at all? Why not be a lumberjack, like you said?"

"Well, I didn't want to brag, but my family owns this chain. We're kind of rolling in it. I'm just helping to keep up the family business. I'm not the CEO type, though. I'm the people watcher type." He peers over Niles's shoulder. "And that's how I know that kid is about to steal something."

Niles pulls back as Jason skirts around him. The kid is maybe ten or so, looking at a display of little cars, two to a pack. He checks down one aisle with his hand on one of the packages, lifting it slowly from the rack…before shoving it under his coat.

"Nah, nah," Jason's meaty hand falls on the boy's head with a *plop*, and he squawks. "You sure you want to do that?"

A mother, a genuine dress-up doll—one that looks venomous— stomps up the aisle with a "Hey!" Jason doesn't flinch, just keeps his hold on the kid who seems like he wants to crawl into a hole. "Hey! Get your hands off my son!"

"Happy to. As long as he takes the store's merchandise out of his jacket and puts it back on the shelf."

"How dare you! My Decker would *never*—"

Jason lifts his hands up in surrender with a placating smile. "Would you check him, ma'am?"

"There are real shoplifters out there, you know! Why would you think my son of all people would—"

And that's when the cars fall out of Decker's coat with a *plunk*. There is a silence in which three things happen. The little pissant gapes at the cars like he's never seen them before, Jason crosses his arms in utter triumph, and the Diva Doll stares at her son with something akin to hate. Without a word, she grabs her little angel's arm, drops her full shopping basket on the floor, and drags him toward the exit. Decker half tries to keep up and half lets himself drag, first one, then the other. Niles is very glad he doesn't have to be in that car ride home.

"Um," is all he can say.

Jason unhooks a little walkie-talkie Niles hadn't noticed from his belt. "Sam, you there? We've got a customer who abandoned their shopping experience in the middle of aisle twelve. We need to reshelve some stuff."

Niles doesn't hear the sigh, but he knows it happens before the person on the other line replies back with a clipped, "Roger."

"I'm going out for a bit. I need someone to step up. You got this, Pepi?"

This time, a new voice jumps on. One that's a bit...well...peppier. "You got it, boss!"

Tucking his radio into his back pocket once more, Jason says, "She's going for manager. She likes it when I let her run the show."

"Is she any good?"

Jason shakes his head. "Not at all. You want to head to Quincy Market for some delicious desserts or would you rather have a full five course meal at the Pru?" He takes off his little badge and untucks his polo shirt, letting it roam free over his belted khakis. It gives him a perfectly reasonable, respectable, relaxed look. Niles approves. Even so, he's not ready for another official date.

"How about dessert? I'm in the mood for something lava cake-y. My treat, since apparently, you're buying my best friend a crib."

Jason gestures at himself. "Trust fund baby."

"Model citizen." Niles splays his finger on his own chest, earning one of those Good Boy smiles.

"Then come on, model citizen. I can't wait to share something spewing molten chocolate with you."

"Who said I was sharing?"

Jason dips down and takes Niles's hand, squeezing for a few seconds before letting go. Niles half wants to catch it and bring it back. Lace their fingers together. Lean on the big bear's shoulder.

Why is he so haunted by his past that he can't take control of his present? Why can't he let go of the person who hurt him so terribly in favor of a man who does nothing but try to please him?

For better or for worse, he wants both of them. He wants to cram them together into one person. Someone who makes his blood scream for sex but who is also the most genuine person Niles has ever met. Honest to the point of discomfort. Deferential to the point of stupidity. Funnier than Niles would have given him credit for.

Sweeter than he deserves.

He follows behind Jason, matching his stride, one that is undoubtedly shortened for Niles's benefit, and debates taking his hand for real.

"Come on, dog, where the hell are you?" Niles mutters, searching through the frost-speckled evergreen bushes.

He's been at this for at least a half hour, but, alas, his beloved Bee-bee is still nowhere to be found. LOST DOG posters remain strewn about the park's hard surfaces. Benches. Railings. Poles. Both he and Bee-bee's grins gleam in photocopied black and white with his phone number printed neatly across the bottom. Those stupid signs are all he can do. That and wait.

His shoe makes a halo in the snow as he pivots, heading back toward the train station. He has food shopping to do and an extraordinarily mundane meal to make. The subway train is filled with college kids. Sockless males trying to be cool and a smattering of high-skirted females trying to be hot even in the freezing cold. Niles must be getting old to look down on them like this. He was once a sockless idiot himself after all, his shoes reeking to high heaven but his ankles on prominent display. Why that mattered, he can't remember.

Bodies hover, holding onto the metal bars to steady themselves while glancing at their phones and each other in that perfunctory way that says, "I have nothing better to do, and you happen to be in my line of sight."

Niles takes in people as well, flitting his gaze over an old man so crinkled he looks like a scrunched paper bag, a mother with a child who looks like he hates her with an unbridled passion, and shadows of passengers behind the tinted glass of the next train car. One shape seems to be watching Niles, but he can't make out a face. Just a masculine shape. Unfazed, Niles continues his review of the lives around him. Thinking of Jason, he imagines everyone as the hero of their own story. It's strange. Humbling in a way. Channeling his friend, he tries to come up with reasons for them to be who, what, and where they are.

That guy over there is texting his side-piece girlfriend but is about to realize he's actually sending his messages to his real girlfriend instead. Niles smiles at the sudden rush of schadenfreude. *And that girl tapping her foot has to pee so bad she's going to get off at a stop that's not hers, find an alley, and make yellow magic happen.* Futzing with his braids, he looks toward the next train car and the face in the tinted window. *And that guy over there thinks I'm hot.*

He snorts.

His apartment is far from the train stop, but since he has a car, he's never really complained about it. More people mill about, some chatting on Bluetooth headphones, some jogging miserably, and some like Niles have their hands in their pockets, just trying to get home. A few flow in his direction, ambling behind him at a reasonable saunter, not too close but not too far.

Until he feels it.

There is a prickle that runs up Niles's back and a sudden stutter in his heart. Something brushes his elbow, and he turns around only to see people simply walking both toward and away.

Someone bumped him, maybe? But no one was close enough.

Shoulders hunched to his ears, he keeps walking. Minutes pass, and this time he feels a shiver at the back of his neck, as if someone were running their fingers through his braids. He whips around again, still seeing no one of consequence, though a woman behind him glances up as if wondering what his problem is. Niles wouldn't be able to answer even if she asked out loud.

Clutching his coat closed, he reviews the people walking away from him. It's a sea of tans, beiges, and blacks, everything nondescript. People sidestep him as he looks backwards, his feet stuck to the ground as he breathes in, tasting the air and checking for scents he doesn't recognize. All he can smell is the residue of Katelyn, Jason, and marijuana wafting from a man sidling by.

It's the stalker. A paranoid twirl worms its way into Niles's mind, a sickly slime leaving a trail in his thoughts. Maybe it's the man from the train—the one who never took his eyes off him.

About-facing, he quickens his pace, immediately feeling it again. That sense that someone is all too close. That fear that someone is reaching out to touch him. That certainty that he's being hunted.

A rocketing terror clenches a fist around Niles's insides as he runs, readying himself to scream.

Niles shoves his apartment door open and slams it behind him, immediately leaning against its pressboard wood surface. His chest heaves and his heart hammers. He was being followed again. Some doubt dances in his mind, but he knows there was someone.

Was it another mugger?

No. The streets were peppered with people. The person—no, the *man*—would have been an idiot to attack him in a place like that. So why else would he follow him?

Tristan used to do it to make sure Niles was telling the truth. That he was going where he said he'd go, seeing who he said he would, and staying for only as long as he promised. There's no one in his life that would care that much about him now, although "care" is the wrong word to use.

Niles spins around, twirling his locks. Doorknob, deadbolt, and latch chain. He stares at his door as if preparing for an ax to splinter the flimsy wood. To hack and slash until he sees the wild eyes of his tormentor staring at him through a thorned chink.

He shudders, taking a thumping seat on the puffy chair that faces the only thing standing between him and the dangers of the hallway. He takes in the tobacco smell from Keller next door and catches the scant traces of Janet, the bitch from upstairs who always seems angry at the floor.

He listens. The stairs in his building tend to creak and snap, begging those who tread on them to please stop, but Niles doesn't hear anything. No footfalls. No doors opening and closing. Nothing but a distant TV playing some sport Niles doesn't care about.

Whipping out his phone, he goes to text Ari...but hesitates. He might upset her. She'd been stalked too. Her first mate, Caleb, had haunted her every step. Just like Tristan, Caleb kept a close watch on her, but she sets him on such a pedestal now, it's as if he never did the things they knew he did. Ben doesn't help. Ben's love for his twin brother runs deeper than Niles can fathom, but maybe that means he understands the minds of people like this.

Choosing his words with care, Niles types.

> Don't tell Ari.

> I don't want her to worry, but I think I'm being followed.

Niles stares at his phone, praying for little bubbles to distract him from the silence. They take so long to come that Niles finds himself trembling.

> Call me.

No. Ari will hear.

I just want to—I don't know—complain for a minute?

There is a long pause.

Do you carry a weapon?

Pfft. My keys maybe.

That's good. That'll work.

You're not a gym rat, right?

God no.

Put me on a treadmill and I will sit down and slide.

Another pause.

Do you need me to come over?

Niles bitterly wants to say "And do what? Roll him over with your wheelchair?" but that would be the cruelest thing he could ever say.

I only wanted to vent.

I didn't know if you had any tips or tricks or anything.

I have no idea why someone would do this.

Look, you're not MY Omega, but you're my Omega anyway, get me?

If someone is bothering you, I'll beat them to fucking death with my walker.

Of that, I have no doubt.

I'm serious.

Want us to spend some time with you?

Ari and I can stay on the pull-out couch.

Yeah, if those two come, it's technically six people hanging out. Not that Ari is showing yet, but it still freaks Niles out a little.

Maybe get second-chance romance asshole to watch out for you.

Or Beta Bumfuck.

They have names.

I like my names better.

Niles manages a smile. His heart rate has come down, but he has the sudden need to be held. To be comforted. It's the Omega in him, he knows. The need to be protected.

I miss Bee-bee. She would have been a great guard dog.

She would have yapped her brains out.

Exactly. Perfect alarm system.

Get a new dog.

That's like asking you to get a new...I dunno...me.

You're a dog in this analogy?

I just mean she's not replaceable.

So, what are you gonna do? Was this a one-time thing?

Twice.

In a parking lot a few days ago and then coming home tonight.

I can only guess the person is trying to figure out where I live.

There are bubbles then not bubbles. Bubbles then not bubbles. Ben is all huge thumbs and no skill.

I'm serious about coming to protect you. You feel unsafe, you call us. Or call the other guys. They're closer and if they're trying to impress you, the best thing they can do is save your ass.

It's a good ass.

...

Trust me. If you ever saw it, you would know it's a good ass.

If you're making jokes, you must be feeling better.

He is.

Thanks, second place bestie.

Oh. And by the way, be nice to Beta Bumfuck. He and I are pooling together to buy you three cribs. One for each baby Benjamin.

There is a long pause.

I told Ari.

Shit. You made her cry.

Like, good cry.

Fantastic. Someone's gotta be the happy one.

He sends a winky face, a hug emoji, and some XOs.

Letting his screen go dark, Niles stares at his hands in contemplation. Jason is big, maybe he could help. But Tristan…he'd really understand what was going on. This is something he has instigated before, after all. And he'd definitely have that Alpha instinct to do whatever he can to save his Omega.

Niles's heart twinges.

His Omega.

Eyes filling with tears, Niles clutches his phone, doubling over and wrapping his arms around his middle. He wants to belong to someone. To be hugged by and loved by someone. To have a future with someone. But who?

He must be crazy. Stupid. Foolish. That doesn't stop Niles from unlocking his phone once more, scrubbing the tears from his eyes, and sending a message to Tristan. A horrible, idiotic message.

Can we talk?

The minute he hits send, he already wants to flay himself. What is he trying to accomplish here? Does he think diving into the psyche of a psycho is going to change anything? Is he mental?

He needs a tissue.

Sure, what's up?

So nonchalant, as if Niles wasn't climbing out of his goddamned skin.

Never mind, actually. It's stupid.

Of all the attention-seeking…Ugh! Niles throws himself back in his puffy chair and moans. When the phone rings, he considers flinging it across the room, watching it shatter in his mind's eye. Instead, he takes a deep breath, runs his sleeve under his nose with an impolite snuffle, and answers.

"I'm not needy, I swear to God. Get off the phone with me before I put my foot in my mouth and keep it there."

Tristan's chuckle is warm. "Sending someone a text doesn't qualify as needy."

"It's not about work," Niles says, facepalming.

"I assumed it wasn't."

"It's about…shit. I don't… I just…"

"Is this where I promise not to be offended, hang up on you, or ghost you forever?"

"Yes?"

"Then I promise all those things," Tristan says, sounding sure of himself.

"What…" Niles swallows hard. "What makes someone want to stalk somebody else?"

He's met with silence. An indelible, painful silence that goes on for decades as Niles ages into a wrinkly prune in his own mind, his hair going white from the years he's held his breath, waiting for the next sentence.

"Oh," Tristan says.

Yeah. Oh.

He asks, "Are you talking about me?"

Can Niles slam his head against the wall? Can he knock himself unconscious? He's quite sure he's physically able, but he might be too much of a self-preservationist to try.

"Someone's been, like, following me places."

"What?" Tristan asks, an edge to his voice.

"I don't know who it is, but they followed me to my car and to my apartment. It's like I see them, but I don't. Like they're right in the corner of my eye, but when I turn around, they're gone. I thought if maybe I could understand why someone would do something like that, then I could figure out how to make it stop."

Tristan grunts. Niles can imagine him standing up and pacing.

"Do you have a roommate?" he asks.

"I used to have a dog but—"

"What kind of locks do you have on your door?"

"One of those twirly ones on the knob, a deadbolt, and a chain."

"And all of them are set?"

"Yeah," Niles says, getting freakishly paranoid the more agitated Tristan sounds.

"Do you have a spare key floating around? On your doorframe or under a welcome mat or something."

"No. Ari has one, but she lives far away."

"Good," Tristan says, but then Niles can hear him hiss a curse. "Shit, not 'good' like *good*. Good like no one can steal your keys from her."

Niles blanks for a moment before remembering how Tristan used to try to separate them. He had said they were like conjoined twins, two brains and one heart.

"I knew what you meant," Niles says quietly. "So why would someone do this?"

"Isn't it obvious? Because they want you."

"Want me? Who the hell would go so far for something like that?"

Tristan huffs on the other end of the line. Niles wishes they were on video chat for a moment before he remembers his weepy face and reconsiders.

"No offense, Niles, but you don't look like a millionaire."

"Hey," he gripes.

"So, they're not gonna go through all that trouble just to rob you. I know you already went through your heat,"—Niles's spine tingles, hearing that word—"but that doesn't mean another Alpha can't smell you and want you for his own. You know how rare you are."

Much to his chagrin. He wants to feel complimented, but he's too busy being petrified. "Why did you used to do it?"

Niles bites his lips during another one of those heavy silences. There is a soft, puffing sort of sound, like Tristan landed on a heap of pillows. If Tristan's anything like he used to be, he'd be rubbing the furrow of his brow to stave off a headache.

"Because I thought you belonged to me."

In a whisper, Niles says, "I did."

There is a short, pained laugh.

After another beat, Tristan says, "When I went crazy, everything was a threat to me, and I mean with a capital T. My inner Alpha looked around and only saw people who could steal you away. That woke up another capital letter. P. *Protect.* Anyone who touched you made my skin crawl. I didn't know what they were going to do to you. Even if they didn't try to take you from me, they might hurt you. Your body. Your feelings. In my fucked-up head, I thought I was preparing to be your hero. I wanted to swoop in the moment anything went wrong. But then that wasn't enough. I just liked watching you. I needed to know you weren't a liar, that you weren't tricking me, so I tried to track every word you said and put a pin in it. Part of me wanted you to run, so I could catch you. So I could prove how strong I was."

Niles is silent on the other end.

"I know you're not an Alpha," Tristan says, "so this won't make any sense to you, but when I was bad off, everyone and everything became an object to break. But the only thing I never wanted to hurt was you. That's why I didn't come after you when you left. I deserved it."

The air leaves the room.

"I'm sorry," Tristan says. "I can never take it back, and I can't even say I didn't mean it at the time, but I'm not like that now. I smoothed out my pointy edges, you know? I've succeeded, failed, had hope and lost it again. I've run through everything there is to feel and kept myself in check. Both with jobs and relationships. I learned how to keep my monster at bay."

"Can you teach the guy who's about to come rape me to death?" Niles meant it to be a joke, but a sick dread sinks into his stomach. Always that word. *Dread.*

"I can come stay with you if you want. No strings."

"You keep saying that as if you really mean it."

A smile in his voice, Tristan says, "You called me, if I remember."

"No, I *messaged* you. You had to go all voice-to-voice about it."

There's another chuckle. "Well, if I know you, you were about to lock yourself in the bathroom and never message me again."

Niles's lips become a flat line. "Then you know me too well."

It feels like Tristan should say something. Hit on him. Say "I'd like to know you more" in a sexy way that would make Niles gooey inside, but he doesn't say anything.

Suddenly, Niles hates the space in between them.

"You could come over if you want, but I require food. I was going to go shopping, but I find myself in an unfortunate predicament at the moment."

That warmth comes back into Tristan's voice. "Barbecue chicken pizza?"

Niles outright salivates. "Oh, yes, please."

"Text me your address. I'll come right over."

"No strings?" Niles asks meekly, fiddling with the edge of his shirt.

"Not unless you want there to be."

CHAPTER 8
LOVE TRIANGLE

THE FRENCH FRY bounces off Niles's chest without sound but with much offense. "Hey!" he grumps.

Tristan only smirks, putting another innocuous piece of stringed potato in his mouth and raising his eyebrows. "You started it."

Another French fry soars and whacks Tristan off the forehead with a silent *ping*. He eats that one, too.

The pizza box lies dead between them, having given up all its cheesy, flavorful treasures. The roof of Niles's mouth is blistered because he never waits long enough for the cheese to cool. He's just like Ari when it comes to stuff like that.

"So," Tristan says, mouth half full. "Strategy."

"Run," Niles says simply.

"And?"

"Get to where there's lots of people."

"And?"

"If I can't get away, scream and kick."

"That's right." Tristan offers the last fry and shoves it in his face when Niles declines. "You're stronger than you think."

"You don't get it. I'm an Omega. With shows of force, something in me wants to go belly up."

"Why?"

Niles shrugs. "It's because it feels right to give in."

Tristan hums a low note, wiping a paper napkin over his fingers. "Well, you definitely can't say anything like that in front of your new stalker friend."

"Not a friend. And why?"

"Because if he was ravenous before, he'd be frothing after hearing something so submissive."

Niles tosses his hands in the air and claps them down again. "It's biology!"

"And we have to be better than that. Besides, you're selling yourself short. Where's the Omega who stood up for himself and walked away from something he didn't want? The Omega who held his own in a foster home? The Omega who life dealt a shitty hand, yet look at him now, excelling at life."

"I wouldn't call it excelling," Niles mutters.

"What would you call it?"

"Getting by."

A long-suffering sigh puffs out, and Tristan gets a faraway glaze to his eyes. "I can understand that. Even though my successes make me feel good, it's not what I'd call happy. It's proud and excited, but once the dopamine hit wears off, I feel...empty."

That resonates with unfortunate intimacy. "Me too. Why do you think that is? I mean, nothing's specifically wrong, things might even be good, but that doesn't mean I'm happy."

Tristan considers. He sucks the insides of his cheeks and fiddles with his napkin again, tearing off triangular shreds and letting them fall into a white Styrofoam container lined with crumbs and French fry grease.

"For me, it's because I'm lonely." He looks away, and Niles can't read his expression. "Do you ever feel like that?"

Only every second of every day.

"I don't think I have the right to," Niles says. "I have a best friend, and despite my continuous efforts, I really like her mate. I've got a colleague at work I talk to. I've got a...lunch buddy."

"But do you have someone to love?"

The sounds of the street outside make their way into the pause of conversation. They reverberate over the hum of the old heater, swaying the air in waves and whooshes as cars sweep by, no thought for what's happening in this room at this moment, living their own lives oblivious to the world around them.

"I've only ever loved one person," Niles admits quietly.

"Me too."

The unspoken words have a thickness. The tension between them is a real thing, seeming to keep them one phrase away from melting into each other.

"Tell me more about you," Niles says. "You're all grown up now, so what's different? What are you into? Do you have a group of friends? How long have you been in Boston? When did you start your company? Did you do it with friends, or did you work up the cash yourself? What do you do in your spare time? Do you have any pets? Like a goldfish or a chinchilla? Maybe an iguana. You seem like the iguana kind of guy…"

"You want me to answer any of these questions, or do you just want to ask them?" Tristan's half-lidded eyes squint as he smiles. "I've got some for you, too. But I'll start with one. Will you call me the next time it happens? The next time you feel like someone is following you?"

"Why?"

"Because the need to protect my Omega never went away."

He doesn't lean over to steal a kiss, though Niles would give in wholeheartedly. He doesn't reach out to hold his hand, which would make Niles's heart throb. His Omega cries, *Yes, yours. Always yours. Forever yours. Please be good to me, Alpha,* and Tristan seems to smell it on him. His full bottom lip pulls between his teeth as he scans down the length of Niles's body.

"If we keep being friends, I'm not sure I can keep my hands off you," Tristan murmurs.

"That's not being friends."

Tristan reaches over and rests his fingers on Niles's knee. The touch is electric, and Niles's slick gathers inside him, getting him wet and ready. Tristan knows, somehow he always knows, and his nostrils flare.

"I should go."

Niles whimpers. It's a short, quiet thing, but it happens. Tristan lets out a low purr in return.

"Call me, okay? It doesn't have to be about this. I'd love a chance to answer all those questions." He stands, never taking his eyes off Niles…until he does, and it's a loss that hits Niles right in the chest.

Stay, Alpha. Make any excuse. Even one thing, and I'll let you stay. An hour. The night. My whole life.

And the strength of that feeling scares him.

"Okay," Niles agrees, trying not to let his emotions get the better of him.

"Lock the door behind me, yeah?"

Niles nods, keeping his eyes down.

Swooping in and hooking his fingers under Niles's chin, Tristan lifts his face and whispers, "I don't want to go. Let me make that *very* clear. I don't want to go, but you need me to go."

His eyes moist, Niles asks, "How do you know what I need?"

"Because I'm your Alpha. And you're not ready for me." He lets the pads of his fingers skate over the soft flesh on the underside of Niles's jaw. "But when you are, I'll be waiting. We won't have to be lonely anymore. I promise."

Niles does cry then, a single tear tracing down the curve of his cheek. Tristan leans down and brushes a feather-light kiss over his skin, tasting the salt of it.

"When you're ready, I'm ready."

Niles nods. What else can he do? He wants to throw his arms around his Alpha's neck, but he knows Tristan is right. He's weak right now. Not in his right mind. If he did something tonight, he'd regret it in the morning.

"Lock the door?" Tristan asks again.

"I promise."

"Good boy." It's as if Tristan will say something else. His lips part, and sweet breath sighs out, but he changes his mind, shaking his head and forcing a smile. "Goodnight."

Niles holds in the rest of his tears as he watches Tristan walk backwards, not turning away until the very last moment. He fiddles with the three locks, and with each one that comes undone, Niles's heartache worsens. Finally, Tristan slips out, and when the door shuts behind him, Niles gets up with heavy limbs, walks his way over, methodically works his fingers, and locks out the man who obviously still loves him. Who's always loved him. A man he might love right back, all rational thought be damned.

Her legs crossed as she sits on the floor, Ari levels a look at Ben, pointing a screwdriver in his direction. "What was it like when you presented?"

Niles puts down a pamphlet of instructions that attempt to explain how to put together a crib with only a jumble of pictograms and iconography. He stares at the frowning Ben who perches with slabs of wood laying across his lap as he tweaks tiny screws, melding two pieces of fake mahogany together.

"When I what?" he says.

"Presented. Did you go all—" Ari waves her hands wildly with wide and bulging eyes, making an ooga-booga sound that very obviously offends her mate.

"Are we really talking about this?" Ben gripes, but upon receiving only doe eyes from the Omegas in the room, he gives in with a huff. There is a long pause while he clenches his jaw, petting the wood's stained finish as he gathers his thoughts. "Caleb and I presented when we were twelve. Too young, I know, but it didn't happen all at once. Over time we just kept getting angrier, losing our tempers at the drop of a hat, and wanting any reason to start a fight. We were vicious little fuckers. We went to an all-boys school, and everyone was always butting heads to see who was top of the pack. Caleb and I fought liter-ally tooth and nail to claw our way up, but it never seemed to stick.

"Our uncle ran the place, and he thought we needed to learn how to control our inner Alphas on our own, so we didn't get suppressants until we were sixteen. Hell, they barely got us new clothes when ours were splitting at the seams. We were bulking up, getting thicker and broader everywhere. It only made the other Alphas want to fight us more.

"We knew something had to change. Lashing out was only getting us in trouble, so we chose to start fighting back with words. Those hurt more. A bloody lip heals, but having your insecurities picked apart keeps you festering. That's what made us want to be lawyers, actually. We wanted to beat people with words. We wanted to use our brains instead of our fists. Only when we got suppressants was that even possible, though. I could barely think straight otherwise. I wanted to mark my territory and kill anyone who trespassed. What was mine, was mine. There was no room for anything else."

"And what did you define as 'your territory?'" Niles asks.

The answer is a firm "Caleb," and it makes perfect sense. "I don't know if that's what you wanted to hear, but that's all I can say on the subject. It sucked. And having the family we did only made it worse."

"That's depressing," Niles says.

Ben has no reply.

Niles turns away, taking a tool from Ari, jamming it into the head of a screw, and twisting clockwise, cinching two pieces of wood together at a right angle. Ari picks up the instructions this time and scrunches her face.

"I wonder if all Alphas struggle like that," she says.

"What's it like for an Omega?"

Niles shrugs. "We don't know if ours was typical, either. We lived with a bunch of strangers, right? As soon as they got a whiff of us changing, we were on suppressants and blockers immediately. They said it was to keep us safe. I didn't get to have my first heat until I was seventeen, and Ari didn't have hers until she was twenty-five."

"I don't want to talk about that," she says, her voice clipped.

"Health class said it was supposed to be like a Beta girl's period cramps, and we wouldn't be able to control our emotions or slick, but they skipped over the rest of it. God knows I wish they'd explained more. What did they tell you, Sir Benjamin?"

"Pfft. To pray."

Niles takes his perpendicular piece and aligns it with Ben's, holding it together while the Alpha starts hammering in little dowels.

"Are you sure these things are actually going to hold your kids?" Niles asks.

"With our craftsmanship?" Ari asks. "It's debatable."

"Oh, ye of little faith," Ben mutters, getting the crib rail in place. "Remember we have to make three of these. We'll have it down to a science when we get to the last one."

"That means you get to pick a least favorite baby," Niles says. "Put it in this nightmare test-construction and prepare for ultimate collapse. You can afford to lose one."

Ben and Ari's eyes snap together, look at the pieces all around them, and then at the vague directions.

"Do you want to unbuild it and start again?" Ari asks, her voice high pitched.

"Y-yeah." And Ben starts unscrewing.

Niles has no one to blame but himself. He takes another swig of wine and begins to undo all his hard work. "Should I give Tristan a pass for everything that happened?"

"Do you want to give him a pass?" Ari asks.

"That...is a very good question."

"Beta Bumfuck out of the equation now?" Ben asks.

"Don't bite the hand that feeds you, Benjamin. One of these cribs will be anointed in his honor. Do you know how expensive these are?"

"Don't tell me!" Ari covers her ears. "All it will do is make me feel guilty."

"Just be glad I have trust fund baby friends."

Ben drops his tool with a dramatic clatter. "Trust fund? Beta Bumfuck is rich?"

"*Jason*," Niles emphasizes with a huff, "did allude to having more than he needed. But it's not like he's some useless froofy guy drinking and partying and throwing his money around on private yachts and stuff."

"That you know of," Ari adds.

"Is this where I tell you to just go for the rich guy?" Ben asks.

"Tristan's got prospects, too. He has a whole company."

"You know who else has whole companies?" Ben asks. "Self-published authors, and do you see them making any money?"

"Fair point." Niles clucks his tongue in disappointment. Katelyn had tried to do that for herself, but ironically enough, she was bad at marketing. She could design her own covers like a badass but create a social media strategy? She'd rather hang herself.

"Jason is so nice." Niles wraps his arms around his legs and bunches up. "There's absolutely nothing wrong with him. He's cute. Sweet and funny. Incredibly honest. Sometimes he even gives me stupid butterflies."

"And second chance asshole?" Ben asks.

Niles props his chin on his knees. "Isn't so much of an asshole anymore."

"Well, who do you want to fuck?" Ari asks, then squeaks.

The men's eyes go round as they gape at her, and she goes as far as to cover her mouth. Vulgarity is new for her; her soulmate must be teaching her well.

"The audacity, missy," Niles says with a grin.

She untethers all the wooden pieces and lays them out according to the directions again, her face flushed with embarrassment. "All I'm saying is that your Omega should be telling you something."

He snorts. "Not like it's very trustworthy."

There is a buzz in his pocket, and he takes out his phone. It's a text from Tristan. He doesn't read it yet, just tucks it away again, but the look on his best friend's face is telling.

"Pick that one," Ari says. "Whichever one just made you make that dopey, swoony face is the one."

"Shut up and build your crib." Niles picks up his wine and downs the rest of it before snatching up the screwdriver and getting back to work. Tonight's going to be a long night.

"Yes!" Tristan shouts, his arms flinging wide as if to embrace Niles, even though he's a solid twenty feet away. "You came!"

"It's kind of my job," Niles says with his hands in his coat pockets.

Tristan waves off the dismissal, instead taking Niles's elbow and making a broad sweeping gesture with his free hand. "How do you like it?"

The brightly lit space is nothing like a standard reception area. The *Geriatric Gamers* team must have put a lot of thought into concept and design...and production. This thing must have cost a fortune. The check-in desk is a swooping curve that matches the elegant arc of the double-wide computer screen behind it, which is currently showing off the high-resolution photo-realism of a flight simulator demo. The receptionist seat is a gamer's chair in blacks and flashy reds, sleek and stylish. Along the sides of the desk are life-sized statues of game characters. An unrealistically wide-eyed RPG shaman-priestess-something with flowing ribbons around her body dominates the right-hand side. The left sports a burly, square-jawed man in combat fatigues, a dangerous look on his face and a rifle the size of a mule lying against his shoulder. Along the desktop are cutesy figurines from much more benign adventures, as well as several recognizable game board pieces.

"You do board games here?"

"Hell, yeah," another man says, poking his head up from beneath the desk. He's holding a white cord of some kind and pursing his lips at the metal tines coming out of the bulky plug. "Gaming is gaming. We've got a chess league, too. Old timers don't only play with their youngins here, they play against each other. Sometimes, we even narrate to give it some spice and make those wrinkly geezers smile."

"We should strike the phrase 'wrinkly geezer' from your vocabulary," Niles says to the all too thin, stereotypically nerdy guy. He even has thick, square framed glasses, but in camo colors instead of dorkish-black.

"This is Gunner," Tristan says.

Niles's eyebrows go to the sky. "Seriously? Or is that a nickname?"

Gunner stands up and brushes off his witty t-shirt. "It's a calling."

"He's an expert at first person shooters. And he's also my business partner, and therefore one of your clients."

Niles slaps on a grin. "Well, then, nice to meet you." He puts out his hand to shake, but Gunner snaps away with a grimace.

"I don't touch people."

"Well, that makes one of us," Tristan cuts in, slinging an arm around Niles's shoulders. "Come on, take off your jacket, and I'll show you around."

Around is the absolute right word. The wide expanse is a circle of glass with beveled doors leading to a series of rooms. Everything is tinted, but one can still see the glow of TV screens and the flicker of seizure-inducing, arcade-like blips. Intricate, die-cut borders drape the top and bottom with explanatory room names like: Battle Central, Questing, Roll the Die, Builder's Paradise, and more.

"This is insanely impressive," Niles says, shrugging his shoulders to get his jacket off.

"Can't convince people you're the coolest place to be without being, you know, cool."

Tristan takes Niles's coat and throws it atop Gunner. The man catches it with a grumble but doesn't complain, disappearing to a spot behind the desk, which seems to contain unisex restrooms and medium-sized lockers.

"My brain is bubbling with ideas right now," Niles says. "I can picture a panning shot that pivots on an angle—an extreme twirl for the young crowd, gentler for the older one. We can cut to people enjoying the games together. Young and old. Or old and old, apparently."

"And I've got actors lined up for you, too," Tristan says.

"Oh, no. Bad idea. You might think you know who can act, but you're wrong."

"Why act?" Tristan says, shrugging. "I've got a couple kids hyped up to be on TV, and their parents are equally starry-eyed. All we have to do is plant some cameras, light it well, and let them play their two-hour session. Snag the footage we like and cut the rest."

"Two hours?" Niles asks, blinking. "That seems long."

"You, my friend, are obviously not a gamer. Two hours is nothing. Do you know how little you can get done?" He leans in close and drops his voice low. "We give you just enough time to really get into it, which makes you desperately want to come back to finish what you started. Do you know how many people walk back to the front desk asking, 'same time tomorrow?'"

Niles ticks his head to the side. "Ingenious."

"Yeah," Gunner says, appearing out of nowhere and making Niles nearly jump out of his skin. "Three hours, and they usually get bored or come to a good stopping point, which is exactly what we don't want. We need to end them on a cliffhanger."

"No wonder you guys are doing so well."

Both Tristan and Gunner grin at him, smarmy, smug, and all sorts of proud.

"You'll meet Azure, too," Tristan says. "She and Mikey take over the night shift, but they overlap with us from noon to three. Helps us get in lunch breaks and business meetings. Azure is our third partner."

"And the genius behind all our fabrication," Gunner says. "Woman is an insane sculptor."

Niles's jaw drops. "Did she make those?" He points to the two guardians of registration.

"And I hired the legal team that got them licensed for use," Gunner says with a snort. "Told her not to use real characters, but she told me to go eff myself."

Niles scoffs and Tristan's tawny eyes fall on him with such obvious affection it makes him lower his head and smile shyly.

Gunner seems to pick up on the vibe and says, "Tristan, take off. Get this man something to eat."

"It's barely eleven," Niles says.

Tristan only ticks his brows upward, a seductive, half-lidded look to his eyes. "Business over brunch. I like it."

"Don't you have guests to deal with?" Niles asks.

Gunner scans the numerous sets of rooms. "Everyone just got in session. We're solid."

Niles tries to come up with eight million excuses but arrives empty handed. He sighs heavily. "Alright, but I require pancakes."

"And mimosas?" Tristan teases. When Niles tosses him a frown, he amends, "Sorry, how dare I? I mean Bellinis."

"Peach over orange every day," Gunner agrees with a few somber nods.

Relenting, Niles takes his handy-dandy tiny notebook from the ass of his jeans, trying to keep his eyes on the day's mission and not on the beautiful man before him. "Lead the way, mon capitaine."

Instead of walking in front of him like a normal person, Tristan rests his hand on the small of Niles's back, immediately sending a thrill up his spine. The Alpha looks at him askance with a knowing smile, and Niles can smell the upward spike in his interest level.

"What are you doing?" he asks quietly, but Tristan only sweeps him forward, opening the main doors to the elevator.

"There's a nice restaurant downstairs. Can I get you tipsy during the workday?"

Niles's cheeks heat, but he rolls his eyes. "That's a career limiting move."

"Only if I tattle." Tristan's smile is playful, but more sexy than cute. His plush lips curve up at the corners, and Niles finds himself staring, which the Alpha notices and seems to enjoy much more than he should. Tristan presses the elevator's down button. "Consider it business relations. If there's anything I've learned about making deals, it's that they happen best over drinks."

"The deal's already done. I'm contracted to you."

"Oh, that's not the deal I'm talking about." Tristan's hand sweeps up Niles's back and toys with his braids. "I really do like these."

The tingle that goes through Niles is unexpected but not entirely unwelcome. His mind flashes back to the other night when Tristan came to him, soothing all his fears away. Work flies from his mind, and instead he's back there again, his Alpha hovering over him and saying, "I'm waiting."

"You're not holding back when it comes to me, are you?" Niles says in a breathy whisper, embarrassingly excited.

Tristan must smell it because he only advances instead of backing down. "I am, though. Believe me, I'm being such a good boy for you, you don't even know."

Niles's heart throbs so hard it hurts, beating against the inside of his ribs in heavy thumps.

"And your scent tells me everything," Tristan purrs. "You like this."

He's not wrong.

The elevator dings, and by the grace of God, there are other people inside. They smell benign, so Niles walks in with his head held high, Tristan behind him with a cocky grin, hands in his pockets and chin tipped up.

This might be the longest, most tempting, sexiest brunch of his life. And he is not sad about it.

***

Pastries are one of life's great joys. Cream puffs, specifically. They're the perfect balance between flakey, croissant-like shells and creamy, frosting-ish insides. When you squish them, they erupt like rounded volcanoes—ones that look much less suggestive than their cousins, the bursted eclairs.

That's what Niles is thinking as he squeezes a puff the size of his palm in his hand. It oozes pale yellow goo from the top, making his salivary glands praise the Lords of Sugar as Niles suckles the deliciousness that tries to drip over the back of his hand.

Tristan pings over a text—his own special, identifying ringtone now living in Niles's settings—but Niles ignores it for now; his winter-chilled fingers are too powdery with sugar as he laps at his prize, sauntering down the empty streets. He likes walking the city, otherwise, he would have moved away long ago. It's quiet, almost quaint in places. Little historical buildings are peppered amongst skyscrapers, and one-way, nonsensical streets remain at the ready to disorient you if you don't know what you're doing.

He heads toward Rowes Wharf and his favorite gazebo, a place where middle-class people spend an ungodly amount of money to get married against the backdrop of a sunsetted ocean, all bright oranges, pinks, and purples. The pictures must be great shots for the photographers' websites, making them come off as artistic when it's really mother nature and makeup artists who do ninety percent of the work.

Niles's pocket pings again from the unanswered text, and he licks his fingers clean enough that he can dig for his phone. He and Tristan have been messaging a lot over the past few days, and Niles is tripping steadily forward on the balance beam of love. With every letter on his screen, his fear seeps away. They don't talk about romantic things on purpose, but they tend to pop up on their own. Niles says things that leave the door open just wide enough for a comment filled with longing to peek through.

God, I really am attention-seeking, aren't I?

Not that it would stop him at this point. The idea of a man who's loved him despite years and distance is too heart-achey to pass up.

> You got something sugary, didn't you?

> Just because I said I wanted something sugary doesn't mean I went out and got it.

Tristan sends an eyeroll emoji.

> Alright, I went to the North End for cream puffs.

> More than one?

> Perhaps…

There is a pause, then:

> Wanna share?

Niles is giddy. He hasn't felt this way in so long, he can barely remember what it was like. The freshness and newness make the baggage Niles carries seem to disappear in these now-moments that have him looking forward to the next point of contact. A text. A voice call. A chance to see Tristan again in real life. He's a teenager all over again.

> I dunno. I'm busy being melodramatic. I'm gazing out at the ocean and seeing a hazy sky that should be stars but isn't.

> Are you asking me to come find you? Because
> I'd gladly hunt you down.

Well, now. That was not only romantic, it contained a sexual oomph. If pinging for pining was a sport, Niles would be on the winning end of it.

> Do you know your way around enough to be
> able to spot me? Shall I let you chase me
> around the waterfront? I hear Alphas like that.

> Don't tease. You know what Alphas do when
> they catch you. Or is this an invitation?

Niles gets a shiver that has nothing to do with the weather. One handed, he takes another bite of his delicacy and decides how he's going to respond. What should he say? How should he say it? Does he flirt? Does he pull back? Does he spread his legs and take a nice picture? Now that would be something.

> I'm at Rowes Wharf near the archway. Can you
> look it up?

> Already am. Am I meeting or chasing?

Niles grins to himself.

> Let's see how the night goes.

Biting his lips with a rush of excitement, Niles does a little dance. Not a big dance. Not enough to be considered a weirdo by the absolutely no one around him, but enough of a wiggle to matter.

There is a nearby chuckle. Niles turns his head in the direction of the sound, his cream puff half in, half out of his mouth, but sees nobody...

Except a shadow. One that doesn't belong to the shape of the building, a lump unsuitable for the straight lines of concrete around the corner of the nearby hotel, far enough away to make Niles question himself, but near enough for his sixth sense to prickle.

He swallows, his treat turning bitter in his mouth. It's been two weeks since he was followed, enough time that he'd written it off as unwarranted paranoia—like he was a hypochondriac but for stalkers instead of sickness. He figured he was safe now, but an increasing, compounding thought creeps into his mind. What if he hadn't been safe as much as he just hadn't caught sight of the man who tiptoed in his footsteps? What if the man was being more careful? Cautious? Cunning?

What if that man was behind him now?

Niles picks up his phone again.

> You know how I thought the Big Bad Wolf had decided to stop his prowl?

> Well, I think I was wrong.

Shit, what?

Niles tries to keep the shadow in his periphery, but it's hard without being too obvious.

> There's something that might be a person, but it's not moving. Someone laughed, but no one is around.

Safety plan, Niles. Find a crowd.

Get back to where the cake shop was.

Not a cake shop, but now's not the time to correct him.

> That's a fifteen-minute walk.

Make it a seven-minute run.

> But what if he's an Alpha? What if he likes it?

Then you better not stop.

North End?

Yeah.

Go. I'll find you.

Yes, Alpha, his heart calls.

Tucking his phone back into his pocket, Niles chucks what's left of his dessert into the ocean, feeding the jellyfish and sunfish or whatever the hell else lives in this crescent bay. He doesn't want to seem too panicky. He doesn't want to cause a scene in front of his possible audience of one. He just wants to work his way under the lit arch and start a jog, then a trot, then a dash.

The shadow's distant voice is a low growl, something the wind carries in little wisps to Niles's ears. "Stay right where you are, Omega."

That word. Something about it falling through the air in such a threatening undertone forces everything in Niles to yell to *submit*, but like Tristan says, he needs to be better than his biology. His Omega can go fuck itself.

He jolts into a run, his long legs taking wide lunges as he hears someone coming after him. He doesn't have time to look. He doesn't have time to cry out. He only has time to pound his soles against concrete and pray.

His breath sucks in the icy weather, making it hurt to fill his lungs. There is already a stitch threatening in his ribs, but his adrenaline is overpowering it. Green street signs streak past under overhead lamps while those matching, unwanted footfalls thump in a staccato pattern behind him.

Is he getting closer, or is it Niles's imagination? Is he falling behind? One thing is for sure, he's not stopping.

Niles takes a sharp right onto Hannover Street, where people are milling about. Some are bar-drunk, and others filter from a nightly comedy show that has a reputation for being mediocre. Italian restaurants blur by even as Niles is forced to slow, slamming shoulders with strangers and scrambling to work deeper into them, putting a buffer between his body and the horror movie villain.

Finally, Niles spins around, dizzying himself as his beaded braids smack his collar with the speed of his motion. He looks for someone out of breath, panting like he is. Someone out of place, dressed in dark garb with a tell-tale ski mask. Someone looking at him with hungry eyes and a steel-bladed knife in his hands. But there is no one other than Betas who glance at the Omega with a heaving chest, clutching his jacket around him with a nearly forgotten plastic bag of sweetness dangling on his arm.

The pastry shop.

Tristan wanted Niles to get back there. There's more than one in the area, but if he can get to the one nearest the road, maybe Tristan will find him.

Live wire nerves and trembling hands find the brick wall outside a shop housing café-style tables filled with tourists who don't know Niles thinks he's about to die. They sip their cappuccinos and espressos and pretend to be posh, not seeing Niles as he slams his back against the hard exterior, leaving his eyes free to roam.

"Niles?" a voice asks, but it's not who it should be. Somehow, out of everyone in the world, it's Jason.

Niles barely glances at him before throwing himself into the man's arms. Jason cinches around him, resting a hand on the back of his head while the other winds its way around his waist.

"Hey…hey, what happened? Are you okay? What are you doing on this side of town?"

The in-and-out rhythm of Jason's breath rocks Niles as he finds himself speechless. He can only clutch and tremble, so Jason holds him tighter.

"Let's get you out of the traffic, yeah?"

Niles nods against him, and Jason weaves them around a corner, not away from the shop but away from the flow of sightseers.

"S-someone's been following me lately. Watching me…" Niles manages, trying to calm his panic. He should be better than this, a strong male ready to take on the world, but it's impossible. He just wants to be protected.

"What?" Jason asks with concern. "Lately? As in 'for a while now?' Why didn't you tell me?"

Why *didn't* he tell Jason? He'd had a reason, but it escapes him. Oh…it was because he was trying to stay funny. Jason likes him best when he's funny.

"I didn't want to worry you," Niles says.

Those arms close tighter. "I don't care about that. I'm here for you no matter what."

There's something soothing about Jason's scent, the familiarity of it, but there's an undertone of something. Hope? Fear? He can't read people the way that Ari can. He wishes his nose was sharper.

"I don't know who the person is, but now they know what car I drive, where I live, and if they followed me here, where else have they gone? My work? Ari's house? Why me?"

"It's because you're special."

"Why does everyone keep saying that?"

Niles hates it. If being Alpha bait causes issues like this, then he wishes he was a Beta, like Jason. Then none of this would have to happen.

"Who the fuck are you?" someone hisses.

Niles is yanked out of Jason's arms and wrapped in another set, one that smells like fall leaves.

Peeking up, Jason has his hands outstretched as if reaching for Niles once more, but Niles's Omega is too busy swooning in his Alpha's arms. Tristan smells like he was fresh from the shower before he decided to haul ass, but also like safety and home and everything Niles has ever wanted.

A car is parked on the street where it's absolutely not supposed to be, and it makes Niles smile in spite of himself.

Alpha came.

Jason's voice drops. "I remember you."

Tristan ticks his jaw up. "Yeah? Well, that makes one of us."

His arms cradle Niles like he's precious. The adrenaline seeps out, and he wants to sleep in his Alpha's embrace. To recover somewhere soft that smells like them.

"You're the ex-boyfriend," Jason says.

"For now," is Tristan's lofty return, and suddenly, Niles is uncomfortable. Yes, he is undoubtedly in the middle of a love triangle, one of his own making.

He is ashamed.

Pulling out of Tristan's grasp, he slips his hands over his jacketed biceps to hold himself, trying his best to self-soothe. "Tristan, you met Jason in the coffee shop, remember?"

His chest puffs up. "I don't bother with people who aren't worth remembering."

Niles bristles on Jason's behalf. This is what Tristan used to do. The old Tristan. The bad Tristan.

His wide palm splays on Niles's back.

"This guy smells wrong," Tristan says. "I don't trust him. Who the fuck is he?"

Now, how to answer that question? Niles sounds more pathetic than he intends to when he says, "Tris, I don't like the way you're acting."

Tristan ignores the comment. "God, Niles, look at you! You're shaking! Did that fucker run you down? Is he here?" He glances left and right before letting his eyes fall on Jason once more. "Was it you?"

Jason's back straightens like a lightning strike. "Excuse me?"

"Tristan, stop," but it comes out meekly.

"You stink, dude. You smell like you're hiding something. You got something you wanna tell us?"

Jason's fists clench, and in his mind's eye, Niles can see it. He can see his poor Blond Beta being trounced by the slightly smaller but genetically stronger Alpha.

"I told you to stop!" Niles yells this time, jerking away.

The Alpha's eyes go wide with confusion, soften with hurt, and then close in understanding as he lets out a heavy, tortured sigh. "I'm sorry. It's not what you're thinking. I don't care who you hang out with, this isn't like that. I'm just freaking out a little over here."

"Like I'm not?"

"I came out here to help you."

Jason's face is triumphant. "Sorry buddy, seems I've got that covered."

A pissing contest. This has become a fucking pissing contest.

Tristan walks closer and shoves Jason. "Why do you smell like that?"

Because he's a Beta.

"Why the fuck are you here?"

Because other people have a right to live in this world.

"What the hell do you want?"

"Enough!" Niles snaps, grabbing Jason by the hand and pulling him away from Tristan. "Go home and take a cold shower or do whatever the fuck you need to do to stop behaving like that. This is my *friend.*"

Jason's hand grips his tighter.

"He smells like—"

"I KNOW what he smells like!"

Worry and anger and his normal, sharp smell.

Tristan is stunned. His lips part, and his shoulders round as he seems to deflate. "You want me to go?"

He sounds wounded. Niles's heart aches, but he needs to set a precedent. This is unacceptable.

"You said you wanted an Omega who would put you in your place. Consider this getting what you wanted."

Niles hears the opening in that statement. It wasn't something that said "I never want to see you again." Instead, it was something that said "You asked for me, and now you have me."

Tristan takes it that way, too; Niles can tell. His scent calms, and he drops his eyes. His gaze lingers for a moment on where Niles and Jason's hands are clasped together, but he nods. "Will you text me, so I know you got home safe?"

There's some defensive shield in Niles that drops, his anger flying from him. Tristan was terrified on his behalf, that's all. His blood was up. In a situation like this, the Tristan from before wouldn't have backed down. He wouldn't have left, no matter how much Niles yelled. If he'd have seen Niles holding hands with another male, then that male wouldn't have walked away unscathed.

He is growing. This is proof.

"Yeah, I'll text you," Niles says. After a moment, Tristan starts to turn away, but Niles can't leave it at that. Pulling from Jason, he shoves his bag of pastries into Tristan's arms. "There! Now you can't say I didn't share." Niles has the acute sense that he's being an idiot. "And…thank you for coming to save me."

His Alpha looks at him with a crooked little half-smile, nods, and gets back into his car. People skirt around him as he winds his way through the crowded streets, likely unsure of where to go or how to turn around. This place is a maze of alleys and corners, and he was willing to brave them all for Niles's sake.

His Omega heart throbs.

"You okay?" Jason asks, sounding gruff and upset.

"I'm sorry. He's overprotective."

"So am I." Jason wraps an arm around Niles's back, leading him down the empty alley.

"He's always been aggressive. Possessive."

"All Alphas are like that." Jason says the words with utter contempt. "I'm like that, too."

Before Niles has a second to think, Jason pivots around, pinning him against the rough brick wall. Niles's wrists are held high over his head as Jason clenches them tight around his scent glands, swirling his thumbs and leaving a trace of himself behind. He leans in, his breath a whisper away and his lips so close, all Niles would need to do is pout to taste him.

"I'm insanely jealous right now," Jason murmurs.

This is it. This is when he should bid Jason goodnight. Maybe goodbye. But part of him wants attention like this. To be wanted. Needed. Required. He whimpers and Jason presses closer, resting his elbows on the brick and caging Niles in, intertwining their fingers.

"There are limits," Jason says. "Boundaries. But for you, I'm not afraid to push them. Maybe even break them."

He's acting like an Alpha. Niles's slick starts to gather within him, threatening embarrassment at his obvious arousal.

Jason brushes his nose against Niles's, and his knees go weak. Pressing their chests together, Jason keeps him steady. "Let's get you home."

The weight lifts as he releases Niles to stand on his own, his watery legs doing their best to stay beneath him.

"Y-yeah," he stammers, trying to dismiss the past minute from his mind like a swipe of sand off skin, wanting to hold on for just one more moment before he needs to tell this kind man that all his attention has been for nothing. "It's been a hell of a night."

Jason's smile isn't the same. It's darker, tinged with desire, and it makes Niles hot and cold all at once. "I'll bet."

CHAPTER 9

LET'S BE FRIENDS

Niles stands in the shower, his chest in the hot stream as he runs soap over his body in slippery strokes, leaving behind stripes of white bubbles that trace down to his navel and beyond. His mind flits over the evening's spike of emotions, the ups and downs like a heart monitor's green line in jagged peaks and valleys. Blip, blip, blip.

He was happy. He was afraid.

He was relieved. He was tense.

He was angry. He was cared for.

He was seduced.

Seduced by Jason and not Tristan. And not in a sweet way either, but something more primal. Something dominating. Something that made Niles want more for the first time. Not some childish "holding hands in the park" vibe, but something with mouths and teeth, those denim eyes locked on him.

He's getting hard. Again, there is that guilt, but he reminds himself he's made no promises. "No strings" as Tristan would say, a lie every time he said it. What he'd meant was, "No strings for you." But Niles wants strings. He wants them wrapped around his heart and his body.

The glands at his wrists still smell like Jason because he has yet to wash them. It's exciting in a way it's never been. There is a fantasy here. One where Jason is on his knees in this very shower, his thick fingers spreading over the jut of Niles's hips as he sucks him into his mouth.

Niles bites his bottom lip and moves his hand over his length. If he's going to fantasize, let him commit to it.

He would hit the back of Jason's throat and feel that wet clench as Jason swallows around him. Jason would make a tiny, high-pitched noise and pull back with a strong suck, the flat of his tongue laving over the veins on the underside of Niles's cock.

"I want you," Jason would say, nuzzling into Niles's public hair, his broad shoulders pressed against Niles's thighs. "Any way I can have you. Please. Please want me, too."

"Just like you want me," Tristan would say, standing behind Niles with his heavy erection slipping between Niles's cheeks. His arm would wrap up and around Niles's chest, fingers flicking over his nipples before they landed on Niles's throat with a tentative squeeze. Tristan would lick his mating gland then, slow and firm, and Niles would tilt his hips only for Jason to suck him in again.

"Not him," Jason would pant as his hand moved over Niles's length, a steady tug where each crest would end in his thumb running over Niles's head, gathering the precum beading there. "Pick me."

"No," Tristan's fist would clench tighter, his teeth nipping up to Niles's ear as he spoke in his honeyed voice, "You've always been mine. For a decade, you've been mine, and I want you for a decade more. This isn't a fling for me. I want you for life. I want to mate you and be owned by you. I want you to love me forever because that's exactly what I'll do for you."

And just like that, the fantasy Jason is gone, and Tristan's imaginary hand strokes him instead. In real life, Niles works himself to the same beat, pound for pound.

He would murmur Tristan's name if this was real life, so he does it now, turning to lean over and rest his head on the cool tile wall, letting the hot stream hit his ass and make him ache for attention. His inner thighs are wet with slick.

"We'll travel the world," Tristan would whisper, nosing Niles's mating gland and running his face over it, marking him. "I would never leave you because I've wanted you since I first laid eyes on you.

I've always been looking for you, no matter who I was with, but no one could ever replace you. You and I are meant to be."

Niles's rhythm picks up now, hard *fap faps* slapping as his fist hits his groin. "I want you, Tris," Niles groans to no one. "Why do I need you so badly?"

"Because I'm your Alpha," Tristan would say. "Only yours. Be with me. Stay with me. Trust me. *Come for me, Omega.*"

And he does, his essence coating his hand in thick drips as he rides out his high, his strokes slowing to sensual glides as Tristan stays conjured in his mind, the Alpha holding him, loving him, needing him.

There is no longer a choice to be made. There is no love triangle.

Niles knows exactly what he wants.

"You did what in the shower? Ew! Ew! I will never get that out of my head." Ari icks out across the line and Niles can almost see her crunching up her body and rolling around.

"Like you've never imagined getting double teamed."

He wants to add "With Caleb and Ben" but, ah, that would be a landmine.

"Anyway," Niles continues, "you should be proud of me. I've come to a grand epiphany."

"Does this mean I need to pay Jason back for my crib?"

Niles winces at the thought. "Yeah, we probably should. I mean I should. I was going to buy all three, anyway."

She blows him smooches through the phone, wet and smacking. "But what changed your mind?"

Filling his chest as full as he can, Niles holds the air for a beat before he lets it out in a gust. "I realized Jason is the safe choice. He's warm and fuzzy, but I want to burn. I want risk and adventure. I want Tristan. His jokes. His eyes. His strength and smile. I want his protectiveness and desire. I want our history, patchy as it is. And I want our future, you know? This blank open space of whatever comes next."

"Sounds romantic," she says.

Niles takes in the room around him, its muted, sensible colors and generic mall-quality art, and regrets the blandness of it. The lack of personality. Anyone could live here. There are no photos of life's joys or forever-captured memories of places he'd been or silly snapshots with friends who he can trust will always love him. It's all so empty. Lonely. Tristan said he was lonely, too. He promised, together, they wouldn't have to feel that way anymore.

Niles's heart flutters. "I want to be head over heels, you know? Like when I was younger. My feelings...they never really died. I just hid them away for a while. Now it's like they're reclaiming their space in my brain, and I can't hold it in anymore."

"We're Omegas. We like strong males. He's definitely one of them."

"But he's so soft, too. He gets this look in his eyes, and I can tell he, I dunno, yearns for me in a way beyond sex."

He can hear the grin in Ari's voice as she whispers. "Ben gets a look like that, too. It's like he's saying 'I love you' without ever opening his mouth."

"Yeah." Niles twiddles his toes together on the bed, hooking the big ones together. "I want that. I want to be mated someday with someone who I can smell loves me. I want our scents to mix to remind me that I'm never alone. I already want Tristan to bite me."

"Isn't it a bit too soon?"

"Pfft. Don't you talk to me about that," Niles starts, but she grunts in annoyance, so he placates her. "How are the babies?"

"I want you to touch my belly."

"Like, rub it? Try to get a genie from the lamp? Now that would be a twist in the fairy tale no one would see coming."

"What should I name them?"

"Frick, Frack, and Frock."

She snorts.

"Thing one, thing two, and thing three?" Niles tries again.

"I wonder if they're boys or girls. Or a mix. Do you think they'll be identical?"

"If they are, I require facial tattoos so I can tell them apart."

She pauses. "Do you think they'll love me?"

Niles's heart gets a gentle squeeze. He can picture her in his mind's eye, fiddling with something around her, keeping her fingers busy and tearing up. He wants to hug her. "I'll tell you what I told your mate. If I can adore you, anyone can."

"Is that supposed to be praise?"

"Of the highest order."

Giggling, she changes the subject. "So, what are you going to do about Mr. Blond Beta?"

Rolling over, Niles shoves his face into his silky pillow. "Mmphhlll-blaaarg."

"I take it that's an 'I don't know?'"

"Oh, I do know, I just don't want to do it. I've never broken up with anyone like this before. All my heat flings were just that. Flings. This guy actually likes me. I'm gonna break his heart."

"Would you rather break Tristan's?"

And there it is in a nutshell. There is no choice to make. "I'll tell Jason this isn't going to work. He might hate me forever…or he might just get really sad…but this isn't about him. And that's the thing, it never has been."

"Go on, then. Get off the phone with me and text him 'Thanks, but no thanks.'"

Niles's eye twitches. "That's horrible! He deserves better than that!"

"You're so nice," Ari says dreamily. "I love you." Then, she's overcome by sniffles. "I hate being pregnant."

"Tell me again in six months."

"Oh, I will."

After more than a few minutes of chatting and a few grunting complaints from an irate Ben, Niles finally says his goodbyes with lots of "Yes, I'll visit tomorrows" and "Tell Benjamin I said to shag you gentlys."

Taking the phone from his ear, Niles eyes it like it's the enemy. Only two hours ago, Jason had him pinned to a wall, something completely out of character, so maybe that's the out Niles needs. It could be the moment their situation "became too much for him to handle" and "made him realize he can't do this."

There we go. That's the plan.

He texts Jason, asking if they can walk during lunch tomorrow instead of going to the coffee shop. His reply is an immediate yes.

Niles hides under his pillow again with another *mlurf* of anxiety over the conversation to come. This is going to be the opposite of a good time.

OhMiGawd OhMiGawd, Niles chants silently, walking beside Jason in what seems to be the most fluffy, romantic, Christmas-story snow he's ever seen. The Beta's cheeks are nipped with cold, rosy and dimpled as he smiles and saunters beside Niles without a care in the world.

He has such puppy dog eyes. Eyes that are about to look a whole lot different in a few minutes.

Niles wants to put himself in a weighted bag and drown in the depths of the ocean. He can imagine the *blub, blub,* which seems almost preferable to this situation.

"It's nice, just walking with you like this," Jason murmurs, his eyes crinkling.

"You're only saying that because your tree trunk legs get secretly cramped under those café tables, I know. Charley horse is your middle name, but you're trying to be a badass and keep it to yourself."

The man's laugh should be endearing. So should it be when he reaches over and dusts the snow from Niles's shoulder, smiling like he's the happiest man in the universe.

"Hey, I've got to talk to you," Niles says.

Jason's face falls in slow motion and his steps lag. Of course, they do. It's an opening line that only ever means bad things after all. Still, Niles can do this. He can shove words from his mouth. He can take his brain, strangle it, put it into a blender, and make sentences happen.

It comes out in a gust, breathless on the last word. "I know you've been looking for something from me, but I can't give it to you even if I wanted to. It has nothing to do with you as a person, you've been so honest and good and sweet, but I can't think of you that way, no matter how hard I try. And I did try, I swear!"

Jason's footfalls completely stop, and he stands on the sidewalk, stunned, as other people skirt around them. Niles had figured it would be easier if he didn't do this in close quarters where they would be overheard by the barista who serves them every day. Better in a place where it would be easier for one or the other to walk off into the sunset.

"Is it because of last night? I'm sorry, I went too far."

Niles lifts his hands, palms out. "I know why you did it. It was… well, an incredible turn on, to be honest…but I realized it wasn't you on my mind. I….well…"

Jason's jaw sets. "You were thinking about your ex."

Nodding, Niles grabs Jason's shoulder and turns, pulling him along into a walk again and keeping them from causing a scene.

"You said it didn't end well between you."

"I know." Niles sighs, dropping his hold on Jason and pulling up his collar, keeping out the flakes that melt on his skin. "But he's better now."

Jason scoffs. "Better than me, apparently." His scent petulant and angry, Jason kicks his feet against the concrete, leaving stripes in the snow. The tendons in his temples work as he grinds his teeth.

Niles says, "I like you as a friend."

And the bark of Jason's laugh splits the air with its morose and defeated sound. "That's worse. It's one thing to like him more than me, it's another thing to put me in the *friend* category." He growls the word *friend* like a curse. His wide hand streaks through his blond hair, tousling it.

"You don't want to see me anymore, do you?" Niles asks quietly, that fear of abandonment creeping into his heart, constricting it and making it hard to breathe.

With a huff, Jason snags his arm and pulls them to a stop again. "I didn't say that!"

There's a tenderness in those blue eyes that keeps hardening and softening, as if he's weighing his next words carefully. He jams both hands into the deep pockets of his jacket and ticks his jaw to the side. "We've been hanging out for a month or two now, right?"

"A month and fourteen days," Niles says, not knowing if that's anywhere near right.

A quirk comes to the side of Jason's lips. "Twenty-three, actually. All I'm saying is I enjoy spending time with you. I like how you make me smile. I like listening to your stories about the office and art and creativity. I like hearing about your friends and the upcoming doom of babies. I like it when you can tell me what's bothering you. I don't see why that has to stop. If that's what it means to be friends, if that's all we can have, then okay. I can deal with that."

Niles swipes a finger under his eye, catching the moisture there. "You don't have to be so nice to me. It would feel better if you were mean."

"Is that really what you want?"

"I..." Niles sniffs his nose. "I'm just so sorry."

Jason reaches out as if to caress his face but corrects his action, resting a heavy palm on his shoulder instead.

"Don't cry." He leans in with a playful arch to his brow. "They'll think we're breaking up."

Niles sputters into a laugh. Isn't that exactly what they're doing? They were never a real couple, but they were a couple, anyway. "We're not?"

"Nah." Jason shrugs, keeping it light. "Who could break up two clowns like us?"

Niles scrubs at his face once more with both hands. "I feel stupid. I mean, I *am* stupid, but standing in the middle of a winter storm and growing icicles on my tear-filled face is so anti-me I can't bear it."

With a rumbling chuckle, Jason nods at the ground, shuffling his feet as he shifts his weight back and forth. He still smells angry and hurt, but who could blame him?

"This is your way of telling me to get lost so you can go inside, isn't it?"

"You're being too blunt again." Niles forces a motherly frown on his face, shaking a finger in a scolding gesture.

Jason doesn't seem to mind. "Alright, fine. I'll take off."

"But I'll see you at the coffee shop?" Niles asks, a hopeful look on his face.

"Yeah," Jason replies. "I'd like that."

The pain in Niles's chest dissipates. Someone is choosing to stay, even though he's inconvenient. Even though he's not giving the person what they want.

He doesn't deserve this, but he is grateful.

The man nods more than once and takes his leave. Niles watches Jason's back as he walks away, congratulating himself. He did it. And it went so much better than he'd expected. He gets to have the dark prince and keep his teddy bear friend. What more could he ask for?

***

"Just shut up and help me," Ben groans.

"How you win over anyone in court is beyond my ken, Benjamin," Niles says, his arm woven under Ben's and across his back, his walker cast aside like so much metal junk.

"It's not like I have to be charming. I state the facts, catch people in lies, and intimidate the fuck out of everyone."

"I can see that." Niles grunts, trying to heft Ben's weight a bit higher. "Why are we doing this again?"

Ben takes another tentative step forward and lists to the side. Niles snags him tighter about the ribs and rights him.

"Because I can't afford to be in physical therapy twenty-four seven, so you get to hold my ass up when it's after hours."

"Let me reiterate my question."

Ben winces, hissing through his teeth as he tries to keep himself upright this time. "I'm practicing."

"You know you're strong enough for this, it's your inner ear that's screwed. No amount of wobbling around on me is gonna help with that."

"Say that a-fucking-gain, and I'll rip your dick off."

Now that would truly be a loss.

"If my core is strong enough, it should help," Ben says.

Awkward step after awkward step, Ben works his way from the kitchen to the living room again without touching the handrails sticking out in straight lines along the walls parallel to the floor. They reflect a dull silver, like something that's been handled a bit too much, and Niles feels bad for his friend.

"Figure if I can take a few steps on my own, I can grab one of the little guys before they get into too much trouble," Ben says.

"Or you could fall on them."

"Consider more closely a dickless life."

Truth be told, Ben's steps are improving. They do another circle around the little living room, trying their best not to plow Ben into the coffee table. He now only needs Niles to catch him every few steps or so. This is a vast improvement over the first lap when Niles was dragging Ben more than walking alongside him.

Ari enters the room with a huge yawn on her face, making her eyes disappear as she stretches her arms up high, showing a slice of belly skin that may or may not be showing a little pooch.

"Hey, sleeping beauty," Ben says with entirely too much love.

Not that Ari takes in the romance of it. "Hey," she says, scratching her pink pajamaed ass and ramming the heel of her hand in her eye to rub it. "How long was I out for?"

"'Bout an hour," Niles says. "Fell asleep just before I got here."

"Oh, crap. I'm sorry. I didn't mean to!"

Niles shrugs the best he can with man meat strewn over his arm. "S'ok. Benjamin and I are bonding."

Ari purses her lips, checking them up and down with her eyebrows to the ceiling. "Ben…"

"Quiet, you," Ben says. "I already told this one I'd cut off a piece of his body for harassing me, don't make me threaten you as well." He winks at her, throwing his equilibrium off and making him lose his balance, almost dragging Niles to the floor.

"Yeah, well, what part of me would you cut off?" Ari asks. "You like all of me too much."

"Got me there," the Alpha says, finally letting Niles lead him to the couch, which he lands on with an exhausted *plop*. They're both slightly sweaty but not the smelly armpit kind. Just wet beads dappling their foreheads and between their shoulder blades.

Niles flops beside him and casts his head onto Ben's lap, throwing an arm over his forehead and speaking in a falsetto southern accent. "God's truth, I do believe you're gonna be the death of me."

Ben boops his nose, of all things.

"So did you break up with him?" Ari asks through another yawn.

"Ooh, I didn't hear about this," Ben says, continuing to tap Niles's nose and making him go cross-eyed. "Who are we losing? Second Chance or Bumfuck?"

"Bumfuck," Ari says, and Niles shoots her a look.

"*Jason*, please and thank you. But he said we could still be friends." He slaps Ben's hand away but makes no move to take his head out of the man's lap, his braids splayed over those meaty thighs.

"And what did Second Chance say when you told him he's the chosen one?"

Ari comes over and lays on Niles's legs, putting them all in an *oofing*, wriggling pig pile. "Oh, yeah, did he lose his mind with glee? Do you have another date set up?"

Niles goes blank. He blinks up at Ben, then over to Ari as she snuggles in on his chest, and says, "I forgot to tell him."

Ben's eyebrows lift. "You did what now?"

Ari sits up, kneeing Niles in the groin more than slightly and making him cough up his testicle. "Niles, the last time he saw you, you sent him packing while you were holding hands with another man!"

Ben repeats, "You did *what* now?"

Niles rolls, getting Ari off him and landing with a *thump* on the floor. "Shit," is all he says.

"Ya think?" This time, Ari puts herself in her mate's lap and curls up.

"Should I call him?"

"No," Ben says, "You should show up at his apartment with nothing on under your coat."

Niles flips him off.

"Then a call will have to do," Ben says, running his fingers lazily over Ari's mating bites until she starts to smell like arousal.

"Don't do that in front of me."

Ben grins and does it softer and longer, making Ari gasp and thwack him.

"Phone call it is," Niles says, getting up and walking as far as possible from the soulmated pair.

In the kitchen, he plunks down onto a bargain bin chair, threadbare in places, and picks up his phone from the table. That giddy feeling bubbles up in him again, but he still shoots a concerned glance at his friends. Both give him thumbs up.

He unlocks his screen and finds their latest text message—stuff about the stalker he absolutely has no desire to think about—and presses the call button.

First ring and Niles's heart is in his throat.

Second ring and he gets fidgety, wiggling on the chair and bouncing his knees.

Third ring and he starts to frown.

Fourth ring and the voicemail picks up. He takes a moment to listen to Tristan's baritone before hitting the little red button with a huff.

"What?" Ben says. "You're not going to leave him a message that says, 'Dude, let's be boyfriends.'"

Niles grimaces. "Thank God you're soulmated, Benjamin, because you have literally no game."

The man spreads his arms wide with a grin.

"I'll try him again tomorrow," Niles says. "I don't break up over text and I don't ask someone to go out with me over voicemail. I have standards."

"He's going to be really happy," Ari says with a sleepy smile.

"I think so, too."

"After all this?" Ben says. "He better be."

Pressing the edge of his phone to his lips, Niles smiles sweetly, his brown eyes crinkling as his heart flutters. "I'm going to be happy, too."

The highway traffic is barely there at this time of night. The haze of the moon casts a glow over every outline and rectangular window as Niles drives over the cable bridge back into Boston. Its white, straight lines radiate from a central strut and attach along the length of the bridge in a geometrically satisfying pattern, fanning out like rays of the sun. He likes this bridge. It's like a citadel gate with no toll, only pretty, colorful lights shining up the cables' angles, leading the way toward home.

A call comes in, his Bluetooth overwriting his be-bop music and ringing through the console of his car. It's already eleven o'clock, so he's not sure why anyone would reach out so late, but it's Jason. His name lights up in white pixels, and Niles debates whether or not to answer. In the end, he presses the accept button.

"Hullllllllllllllo, *Dave's Roadkill Diner*. You kill 'em, we grill 'em."

"Heh," Jason laughs quietly. Then, without preamble, "I found Bee-bee."

Niles's eyes widen.

Bee-bee...

He had completely given up hope of finding his dog, assuming the worst but refusing to think about it. He'd stopped talking about her, worrying about her, or remembering her, all with a purposeful intent, but Jason hadn't forgotten.

There's nowhere to pull over properly, Niles having ducked down into the tunnel at this point, so he just lets happiness fill his body as he clenches the wheel. "You did?"

"Yeah." Jason seems out of breath somehow, but a familiar little yip in the background fills Niles's eyes with tears.

"Hey girl!" he coos, although Niles has no idea if his dog can hear him. "Hey sunshine! Where have you been?"

"Sorry, I found her earlier but didn't get...get a chance to call." Jason makes a slight grunting sound, and Niles's happiness sours somewhat. "I'll bring her to your house this weekend, okay?"

"No, I can come get her now! If it's not too late for you, I mean. I'm in town. I need your address, but I'm sure I can get there soon. Hell, you found my dog, I'll grow wings at this point! Or maybe you should grow wings, you angel."

There is a soft chuckle followed by a hiss.

Niles's brows knit. "Is something wrong?"

There is a long pause. Then longer.

"Jason?"

He sounds gruff and exhausted. "I don't know if I should tell you."

"Tell me what?"

"I, ah, I got...attacked. I was bringing my trash to the alley dumpster and...well...I'm a little beat up."

"Oh my God," Niles says. "Are you alright? Did you see his face? Did you call the police?"

There is a concerned whine from his dog, and the musical jingling of a collar, as if Jason was giving her a nice scruff scratch. That alone fills Niles with a deep well of affection atop his concern.

"No police, and yes, I saw his face."

"What did he look like?"

There's that pause again, then a heavy sigh.

"We'll hunt him down!" Niles says. "You and I, we'll go all whoop-ass and haul him into whatever the right police place is."

"Have you ever even been to a 'police place' before?" He can hear Jason's smile.

"Truth be told, I've spent the entirety of my life trying to avoid them."

Jason grunts painfully again.

Niles's concern ratchets up a notch. Two notches. Five. "Tell me what's going on. I want to help you. That's what friends do."

"Yeah...friends." Jason clucks his tongue on the other side of the line and draws out the moment. "Are you sure you want to know?"

"Okay, you're starting to scare me." Niles is at a place where he can finally pull to the side. He's double parked, but he throws on his flashing lights and will happily let the cars that pass every few minutes swerve to avoid him.

"I'm sorry," Jason says.

"You don't have to be sorry, you—"

"It was your ex."

Niles's blood runs cold. "What?"

The weak laugh is dark this time. "He came over to claim his territory, I guess."

Throat closing in on itself, Niles's mouth goes dry. "He wouldn't…"

"I tried to tell him you already made it…ah"—he hisses again—"clear that nothing was going to happen between us, but it didn't seem to matter. He just kept saying you were his."

No. Please no.

That's the old Tristan. The one Niles wants to be gone.

"Has he done anything like this before?" Jason asks. "Is this what you meant when you said you guys didn't end well?" Something shifts on his side of the line, and he grunts again. "You know, I wouldn't be surprised if he was your stalker."

Niles rests his head on his steering wheel, trying hard to make himself breathe. "Why would you say that?"

"Doesn't he show up at the most convenient of times? He texted you at the coffee shop when you were with me, and you didn't answer. That was him, right? And then he just appears. *Poof.*" There's anger in that spoken rush of air. A bitterness. "How did he even know where you were?"

Niles cinches his eyes shut, nauseated. "He was looking for my office. It was just a coincidence."

Though he'd fantasized it was fate. Just like meeting up for his heat. Just like meeting at the department store in the first place.

"And when you were with me last night, didn't he show up a little fast? I don't know where he lives, but for him to rev up like that, maybe he was already nearby. Maybe all he had to do was jump in his car after he was done chasing you down."

"He would have been out of breath," Niles tries.

"Not if he's an Alpha."

Niles is going to be sick. Is it possible? Could Tristan really have done that?

No. He won't believe it. Not for a minute. Because, if he did, it would make his every feeling for Tristan part of an elaborate lie.

But the fighting though…that he can see as clear as day.

This is all his fault. But is it for pitting the Alpha and Beta against each other or for getting involved with Tristan in the first place? Niles doesn't know. Minutes ago, he was so sure about everything, yet here he is. This was going to be his future. But his Alpha—even now, always his—hurt someone for no reason.

Niles asks, "Do you need help?"

There is another long pause. Another deep sigh. Another heavy wince. Jason's voice is weak when he whispers, "Yes."

Then that's exactly what he'll do. Getting Jason's address, he jabs it into his GPS and shoves down his cyclone of emotions. This territorial behavior is what Alphas do for their Omegas. This is what Ben would do for Ari if he sensed a threat. But Jason is his *friend*, not a stranger, and that makes all the difference.

As Niles turns back onto the road, another call comes through, a specialty ringtone Niles had programmed in himself. It's Tristan. With a sardonic smile and fury in his heart, he shoves his tongue into his cheek and scoffs. He can't hit that little red button fast enough.

He doesn't want the old Tristan. The old Tristan tries to take away his friends.

This was all a mistake.

THE PAST

NILES AND ARI said goodbye for the night, looking at each other for a beat too long, like they always did. Niles struggled in his shared room. Erik, now his unwanted bunk mate, hated him more with each passing day. No amount of snark or sarcasm could get you out of trouble if someone wanted to do you harm for no reason other than the fact that you existed. And exist Niles did.

He'd tried to get their foster mother to let him and Ari share a room instead. Niles insisted that, since they were both Omegas and he knew very much that he liked boys, there should be no problem. Their foster-whatever had been disinclined to let males sleep with females, though, because the state wouldn't care who Niles "wanted to bone," as she put it. All they'd see is a risky situation, and then one—or both—of the children would be taken away, cutting the woman's weekly paycheck by half because she housed only four orphans in her derelict, rickety house now.

"You'll be okay," Ari whispered. "He can't hurt you."

"Not with his fists," Niles replied, his meaning clear enough. There were things that hurt more.

Niles was morose as he clicked his locker shut, twirling the padlock with a snicking spin and dreading the next class. It was gym. He always got hungry looks from the Alphas during gym. All Omegas did. Their sweat did something to the males that couldn't be denied. Some Omegas preened over the attention, but Niles wanted none of it. He was intimidated by the Alphas' intense stares, even though they made his insides quiver. If he fell in love, he knew it would be hard and fast, and if he gave in to his baser desires, he'd be just another Omega to be revered, railed, and rebuffed, all in that order. Those who had gone through their first heat already—missing exams and coming back walking funny—were tight lipped about it. Possibly because none of the Alphas wanted to stay, no matter how much they vowed otherwise. Niles thought it broke most of the Omegas' hearts.

Well, no one was going to break his.

***

"Hey," a voice said, a kid Niles recognized standing across from him at the lunch table.

At sixteen, this seemed taboo. Ari and Niles had a clique of two and he didn't remember opening up for membership.

A skinny boy set his food down without care. The sharp clatter of the tray mixed with other sounds as they echoed across the cafeteria's expansive space, other teens also roosting and shoving fried delicacies in their faces.

"Hello to you, too?" Niles tried, his cheek half-stuffed with chicken nugget. "And you are?"

"Tristan." The guy plunked down without preamble and shoved a carrot in his mouth, talking right through the crunch. "You looked lonely, so…" He shrugged, as if that said it all.

"I'm waiting for my friend," Niles replied, suspicion trailing up his arms. Though, with one sniff, he could tell this boy was non-threatening. He asked a forward, asinine question. "Are you a Beta?"

With a chagrined smile, Tristan grabbed another carrot. "Seems like it. You got a problem with Betas?"

"No," Niles admitted. If he did, he'd never get on in life. Alphas and Omegas were on the rare side. If there was ever a hostile takeover, Betas would win due to sheer numbers alone.

"You're thinking something strange, aren't you?" the boy asked.

Niles admitted, "Dystopian, maybe."

He was met with a grin, a fleck of carrot stuck in the boy's—Tristan's—teeth. He had shaggy, wavy hair and a flannel shirt that made him look more like a twig than he would have otherwise. It was too big and swam over his straight lines until it hit his mid-thigh.

"I've kind of been ousted by my friends, so I'm in the market for some new ones," Tristan said.

"Did you do something wrong?"

He sucked the insides of his cheeks and ran a tongue over his teeth, clearing his mouth. For some reason, his movement drew Niles's direct attention, and his eyes lingered on those lips. "I didn't present. At this point, I probably won't. It's no fun to try to keep up with the pack when you don't have what it takes to try."

Niles considered, staring the boy down. "Do you know what I am?"

"An Omega, right?" Tristan picked up a handful of burger and took a bite so big it should, in a reasonable world, choke him. "Iy wike Omegahs," he managed through full cheeks. His sharp swallow sounded like a rock squeezed down his throat.

"Why is that?"

Burger hanging in front of his open mouth, Tristan blinked. "You guys just calm me down, I guess." He dove into his meal once more.

"Aren't there, like, a whole plethora of people you could pick to be your token friend?"

Tristan snorted a little through his nose. "I told you, you looked lonely."

"Night guys," Ari whispered, ducking back through the open window.

She, Niles, and Tristan had been sitting on the rooftop of the foster home, watching the moon rise. Everyone inside was asleep, even goddamned Erik, so they'd snuck out to sit under the stars.

"Night," Niles said back, just as furtive and nervous as she was. They had yet to be caught, but it was only a matter of time. After the window had safely sealed shut with a *snik*, he asked Tristan, "Shouldn't you be going, too? The night progresseth and all that. I'd hate it if your mom caught you dallying with two orphan miscreants."

"Don't call yourself that," Tristan said, pushing Niles slightly. He glanced down at his hands, a quirk surfacing on the corner of his mouth. "You're worth more than you think."

The thought was a cherry placed atop all the wonderful things Tristan had said to him today. All week. All semester. He always spoke of Niles like he was a piece of art hung in the most prestigious space in a fine gallery, showcasing how unique he was even in a collection of colorful brush strokes.

Tristan looked at Niles then, and Niles looked back. Tristan's eyes seemed to catch the moonlight, draining them of all color and leaving only a crescent twinkle reflected in each black pupil. Slowly, the boy lifted his hand and brushed the back of his knuckles over Niles's cheek, his skin leaving a trail of warmth.

They'd danced around this. They'd stared at each other far too long and left unsaid things hanging in the air, but this was the first time they'd touched like that.

"Do you like guys?" Tristan asked, drifting his gaze from Niles's eyes to his lips. Tristan bit his own, either in nervousness or interest, Niles couldn't tell.

"Yes," Niles said.

A slow smile spread on Tristan's face as he replied, "Me, too." After a pause, he scanned down Niles's chest and shoulders, his eyes skirting over the dark skin of Niles's biceps until his fingers followed, drawing invisible stripes down his flesh, and making the thin hairs of his forearm stand at attention. "What else do you like?"

Niles could barely comprehend anything beyond the sensation of Tristan's fingerprints as they trailed over the glands at his pulse point and across his palms. "I—I suppose I like loyalty. I want to trust the people I love would want to…" he trailed off.

"Keep you?" Tristan filled in the blank. "Is there an Alpha you want to keep you, Niles?"

Hearing his name sent a tingle from his heart to his groin. It was spoken with something beyond tenderness. It was spoken in a way that made Niles ache. His Omega, oftentimes silent, took notice, and Niles couldn't stop the low hum of want that crept from his throat.

"I'm not sure an Alpha is in the cards for me."

"Another Omega, then?" Tristan's fingers cascaded in a slow slide back up his arm again, leaving fire in its wake. "Not a Beta, I'm guessing." When Niles's eyebrows knit in confusion, Tristan ceased his stroking and put his hands back in his lap. "Omegas don't see Betas as potential mates. We can't claim someone. We don't have knots or ruts. Our…" he gestured downward and then outward, not saying the most embarrassing part. That a Beta's seed could never ease the distress of an Omega's heat in the same way an Alpha's would.

Maybe that was true.

And maybe Niles didn't care.

"It doesn't matter," Niles said, unable to take his eyes off the boy in front of him. His terra-cotta skin had turned blue in the darkness and the moonlight made his edges glow.

"Then what does?"

Niles angled toward him and lifted his own hands. Tristan's hair was made of silk as Niles slipped his fingers through it, and those tawny eyes slipped closed, a soft sigh filling the space between them. Niles let his fingers roam over Tristan's ears, down his throat, over where a mating gland could be but wasn't, though that didn't stop Tristan from trembling, anyway. Niles's palms slid down Tristan's chest, feeling his heart thrum under his skin, a beat that matched his own in a seductive rhythm. He leaned closer and pressed a kiss over Tristan's breastbone, and the boy's arms latched around him, not dragging him closer, but holding him where he was. Niles's blood rushed both up and down, his body unsure of what it wanted other than *more*.

"You." Niles let his lips catch on the thin fabric of Tristan's shirt, his chest inflating and deflating in short bursts. "I don't care about your designation. I don't need an Alpha. I just need you."

Tristan did drag him closer then, burying his nose against Niles's mating gland and exhaling little soft puffs of air over it, making Niles quiver. Tristan ran his cheek over the rough skin for a moment before doing the same with his rolling tongue.

Niles whimpered. "Tris, what are you doing?"

"Claiming you as best I can," he said, his voice breathy, sexy, and perfect. Niles was so hard, it hurt. "I can't bite you, Niles, but I want to."

"I wish you could." His mind was like spun sugar, his thoughts wading through nothing but sweetness. Young love was an eternal thing. Something wrought by destiny, bringing together two souls who belonged to each other since birth. Niles felt the incandescence of it, as if he could shine like a god.

Tristan's hand slid down, grazing the hard length in Niles's pants. When he gasped, the hand retracted, but Niles pulled it back again, pressing Tristan's palm harder while his jaw dropped.

"I've always wanted you," Tristan said, nuzzling. "I think I've loved you since the moment I saw you."

His hand did nothing but keep a firm weight on Niles's erection, but for now, that was enough. He was leaking and had no control over the wet spots that bloomed, both precum and slick, front and back. It was the first time anyone had made him feel this way.

"Kiss me," Niles begged, skating his cheek over Tristan's, marking him in the same way. "If we're going to do this, then I want everything."

Tristan's sound was guttural when Niles placed the heel of his hand against Tristan's zipper as well, his fingers splayed before cupping slightly, wrapping around nothing but heat.

"Good. Because I'm gonna suck you dry," Tristan said, dragging flat teeth over Niles's mating gland and sending another rush of slick into his britches.

For all his talk, Tristan's mouth was soft when it finally connected with Niles's. That erotic pressure disappeared as Tristan took Niles's face in both hands instead, keeping their lips brushing, testing, and dragging over one another.

"Will you fall in love with me?" Tristan asked, his tongue touching Niles's when the words "fall" and "love" tumbled out.

Niles's chest was thumping, his belly fluttering, and his glands pulsing. "I already have."

Sunday evening came too early, and Niles wasn't ready to leave the cocoon of the weekend. Tristan hiked his shirt up and groped his chest, his thumb swiping over Niles's nipple. He lapped heavy strokes against the roof of Niles's mouth, the curl of his tongue catching on Niles's teeth as he moaned. Niles's slick seeped out, and Tristan growled low in his throat.

"I can smell it, you know."

Before Niles could get self-conscious, Tristan ran his hand down over Niles's stomach and slipped his fingers under the hem of Niles's pants.

"I love it. I feel like it's driving me fucking crazy. Does that make any sense?"

"I've...I've been wet for you before," Niles panted out as Tristan's fingertips grazed the swollen head of his erection in sinful swirls.

"But it's never been like this. I want to taste you. Omega, let me taste you."

And something in Niles burned, a low cramp starting in his belly. Tristan had called him that many, many times—but never in moments like this. It was enough to make his mouth water and his backside soak through his pants.

"Tris, something's happening to me."

"I feel it, too." Tristan started grinding against Niles's groin. "I feel like I want to...tear something apart. But"—he gasped when Niles tugged at the hair on the nape of his neck—"but I also want to do anything you want me to. I'd do anything for you."

"My belly hurts," Niles confessed. "I'm too hot. I'm sweating everywhere."

"I know," Tristan said, yanking Niles's shirt off and diving into the crook of his neck. His tongue skated around Niles's skin before taking his mating gland into his mouth and sucking. Niles cried out just as Tristan made a high whine. "I want this. God, Niles, why do I want this so fucking bad? I hurt, too. I feel like I need to be inside you or something in me will break."

"We've never done that."

"But we're going to tonight."

The only words Niles knew were: "Yes, Alpha."

The noise Tristan made was obscene. "That's what's wrong with me. It's happening."

"What?"

"I'm presenting. Fuck, Niles, I think you're putting me into rut."

Instinctively, Niles wrapped his legs around Tristan and tugged him forward, riding against him. "I need you. I ache everywhere. I wanna cry."

"Shh, shh, no baby. Alpha's going to take care of you."

And that's exactly what he did.

Ari told Niles their foster-whatever took all the kids to a hotel with a pool. It was a vacation—their first one. With a sly grin, she leaned forward and bumped his arm, saying the whole house could hear them moaning, growling, and spitting more swears than Ari's virgin ears could stand. Their foster-whatever had muttered, "Goddamn heats," and that was all she said on the matter. She just got everyone out of the house as fast as possible, only stopping to hit the pharmacy for extra doses of suppressants, blockers, and morning-after pills.

That was when everything was euphoric. Blissful. Everything that was missing snapped together like puzzle pieces, just like Tristan had interlocked their bodies with his new and delicious knot, something

Tristan never thought he'd have, something he'd always secretly yearned for, and now he had it.

Alpha and Omega, more in love than their bodies could contain.

It was bliss.

Everything about Tristan was rigid, veins and corded muscle standing out on his arms as his jaw flexed, his teeth bearing down on nothing. "Stop hanging out with her."

His voice was a low, soft threat rumbling in his chest with a sound that had once made Niles's heart flutter. Now, it filled it with dread. The dread his mother taught him about. The dread that came with fear for tomorrow.

"She's my best friend, Tris. My only friend."

"I'm your only friend."

"No," Niles tried to placate, oozing every calming pheromone he could. "No, you're my boyfriend. My perfect, sweet boyfriend."

Niles attempted to run his fingers through Tristan's short hair, but the man snagged his wrist instead, fast and tight, his tawny eyes boring into Niles's.

"No. I'm your Alpha, and there's a difference!" His teeth were bared, his incisors sharp and dangerous. Still, something inside Niles, some ancient monster, begged to be bitten. Claimed. He trembled, and the sight gave Tristan pause. He ran his palm over Niles's cheek as his threat dipped into pleading. "Why are you always looking at other people? It makes me want to jump down their throats. Can't you see that? Why would you do that to me? Don't you want to make your Alpha happy? I can give you the world if you'd only prove how much you love me. Always me. Only me. Please."

A tear traced down Niles's skin as he shook his head. "I can't. I love Ari, too. And when my brother comes back—"

"Trey abandoned you!" Tristan roared suddenly, gripping harder to the point of pain, and making Niles cry out. This was no longer fear for tomorrow. This was fear for right now.

"That doesn't mean I don't love him. People make mistakes and then turn it around, right? Like now. Please, Tris. Please let me go."

Niles was flung to the floor, palms slapping on the hard wood as Tristan reared up and began pacing. Up. Down. Left. Right. His shoulders rolled back, flexing under his shirt as he pinned Niles down with his eyes like a predator. "Don't you run, Omega. I can smell it on you. If you run now, I will chase you down and fucking mate you right here."

Niles went completely still. "Okay, Alpha. I'll stay."

Tristan's feet made no sound as he padded along the floor. "Everyone leaves you. Your father. Your mother. Your brother. How long until it's that little bitch? Leave her first! You don't need anyone but me!"

A small whimper escaped Niles's throat. "Why would you say that? Why do you have to hurt me like this?"

At that, Tristan dove down and took Niles's face in his hands once more, his eyes wide and wild. "No. No, no, no, sweet Omega, Alpha would never hurt you. I love you. You're the only thing in this world to me. You're all I can see."

The raging bull of a man swooped in to try to kiss him, but Niles turned his face, offering only his cheek, something his Alpha didn't forsake, instead tasting Niles's tears as if they were aphrodisiacs.

"I want you, Omega," he whispered. "Please, let me have you."

"Not if you don't let me have my friend," Niles replied, everything in him bracing to flee.

"She'll leave you! But I never will!"

The words came out cold and detached, though Niles felt them with his whole heart. "Maybe I want you to."

"What?" Tristan asked, high pitched and breathy. His arm wound around Niles's lower back, dragging him somehow even closer.

"Maybe I want you to leave me." Niles cinched his eyes closed, more terrified of this man than he'd ever been of anything. "Maybe if this is who you are, I never want to see you again."

THE PRESENT

CHAPTER 11

SYMPATHY GONE ASTRAY

THE BUILDING IS HIGH-END. When Jason said he lived near Boston Common, Niles knew he had money, but he should have realized the man was outright rich by that statement alone. To his great surprise, the Brownstone is all Jason's, not shared with some bottom or top floor neighbor. Three stories for one person. Given Niles's one bedroom apartment, the luxury seems excessive.

A winding staircase of old wood, well stained and glossy, brings Niles from a spacious entry level to an expansive main floor. Though the stairs continue their spiral to the bedroom level above, Niles is frozen to the long lines of pale pine flooring. "Bowled over" is the phrase that comes to mind, first by the open floor plan and second by his dog who yips and yaps like she's going insane when she sees him.

Bee-bee is tiny, in no way large enough to knock him down, but when he squats to fling his arms out and hold her, she covers his face in kisses so wet, he falls back if only to pull his mouth away from her slobbering excitement. He hears Jason laugh at them, but his eyes are too squinched shut to see the man's face. Niles sputters, getting a hold of Bee-bee's furry chest and pushing her down far enough to hold her wriggling, writhing body in his arms.

"Who's a good girl? Yes! Yes, who's a good girl!" Niles says in that special voice reserved specifically for dogs. That gravelly-yet-high-pitched noise people make while it's time for some nice, heavy scritchscratches, languid belly rubs, or—in Niles's case—nuzzling into her familiar fur and rasping his fingers up and down her short, stubby sides. His heart is swollen with relief and a heavy dose of love. "She smells good."

"I had her groomed," Jason says. "She was a mess when I found her."

"Oh my God, I can't thank you enough!" And Niles finally looks up. Jason sits on his couch, a wide sectional in brown leather that curves around in an L shape. He leans into the cushions as if he has no strength left, sporting a nice black eye which he holds a bag of frozen peas over while favoring his left arm. Niles's heart sinks. "What did he do to you?"

Jason shrugs with one shoulder. "A good knock to the face to get me down, a few kicks to my ribs, a real heavy one to my shoulder." He tries to move it and winces a little.

"You could get him arrested," Niles says, a heartsickness creeping in. He doesn't want Tristan to get in trouble, but he doesn't want him to get away with this either.

Jason shrugs again. "It's an Alpha thing."

"Which only matters if he's fighting another Alpha."

The smirk that crosses Jason's face is tight, pulling up to one side, and Niles is immediately sorry for calling out his designation. It's like calling him inferior to his face. But he's not. He's uncomplicated. Sweet. Generous. So, so many things.

"I'm sorry," Niles says.

Jason pats his knee in two sharp *whaps*, and Bee-bee turns her head to push off Niles, tail wagging nonstop. She launches herself toward the man who found her, jumping up and resting on his lap with a happy huff. Seems like someone liked being fed in the wild for weeks by her temporary master.

"Don't be sorry. It was his decision to claim you," Jason says.

"I didn't ask to be claimed!"

Not out loud anyway and certainly not like this.

Now it's Jason who says, "I'm sorry. I feel like I put you in this position."

"I could say the absolute same." Niles scrubs his hands over his face. "This is a mess."

Getting up, he brushes off his pants and looks around again, noticing the nice lamps and the big entertainment center. There isn't a single speck of dust. Either Jason is a neat freak, gets bored a lot, or hires someone to clean.

Shaking his head, he remembers he's here for a purpose. "How can I help?" he asks, hands on his hips and acting much stronger than he really is.

Jason's face falls. "I feel bad asking for anything."

"It's too late for that now. I'm already here."

He nods in agreement, taking down the frozen bag from his face and showing off his purple shiner. That's going to last a while.

"I didn't eat yet. Could you maybe make something? It hurts to stand for a long time."

"Oh. Shit. Absolutely. Of course. Anything special?"

"I know it's late, but wanna do breakfast for dinner? I've got eggs and bacon."

Niles *pffts*. "That can't be all you want."

Jason shrugs on one side again. "It's easy enough."

"Your faith in my cooking skills leaves much to be desired."

That patented Good Boy smile comes back. "Maybe you can make me something more complicated next time."

Next time. Niles hears those words like a tolling bell. Even now, after rejecting him, this man has his hopes set high. Still, sitting there after taking a beating he didn't deserve, Niles will deny him nothing. The Beta deserves a break from reality. Maybe they both do.

"Alright." Niles rolls up his sleeves and works his way to the stainless-steel kitchen. "But you're going to either have to direct me where to find stuff or just allow me to expose all your kitchen-secrets on my own. I hope you don't hide your pornography in your knife drawer."

"Who puts pornography in their knife drawer?"

"You're never allowed in my kitchen with an attitude like that," Niles says, earning a laugh that's followed by a grunt of pain. His heart sinks.

The pots and pans are in predictable places, bowls for mixing, too. It's arranged mostly like his own kitchen, which keeps everything easy.

They exist in a comfortable silence. Jason leans his head back with the bag of frozen peas on his face, scratching Bee-bee absently as Niles bustles around in the background—well, to the extent one has to bustle for bacon and eggs.

"Omelet? Sunny side up? Scrambled?"

"Chef's choice," Jason replies. "I'm not picky. I only know how to make scrambled. Every time I try to make an omelet, I end up with scrambled anyway."

Niles snickers. "Bacon from a frying pan, from the oven, or from the microwave?"

"You can make it in the oven?" Jason asks with wonder. Then, "Microwave's fine. It's faster."

Niles fumbles around in the fridge, deciding someone Jason's size can handle four eggs. If not, he can trash it. Considering the expensive style of this place, it doesn't seem like the man would be worried about the waste.

"You should call out of work tomorrow," Niles says with sympathy.

"I don't work weekends."

"Good. You need to rest up. If you want, I'll make you some stuff you can keep in the fridge and nuke for yourself tomorrow."

"What a good Omega," Jason says with a tone of admiration, not of teasing.

Niles is going to ignore how his cheeks heat at the praise. "Hush, or I'll beat you with this whisk, and you can't take any more violence at the moment. You've reached quota."

Hearing the microwave beep and snagging a fork from a drawer that sadly contains no pornography, Niles brings the meager meal over to the mopey man. Jason tosses down his bag of frost-covered peas, shoos away the dog, and tucks in like he hasn't eaten in days.

"Whoa, boy. Slow down. If you've got cracked ribs, I don't recommend the Heimlich."

Jason seems ashamed of himself suddenly. He slows down but eats in silence, smelling off. Another scent Niles can't put a name to. When he's done, he sets his plate on his coffee table, the legs carved into ornate shapes that coyly show off their finery.

"I hate having you see me like this," Jason says, crossing one arm over to the other and massaging it in soft squeezes. He has a furrow in his brow and a frown on his face.

Niles isn't sure what to say. Inside he wants to scream. At Tristan for doing this, at himself for believing he wouldn't. "Do you really think he might be the one who's stalking me?"

Jason lifts his gaze up but says nothing, and that's confirmation enough.

Niles leans forward, running his hands over his braids and pulling them into a knot behind his head out of nervous habit, winding the tie from his wrist around his hair only to unwind and rewind it again. "I'm so stupid. How could I have thought he'd change? How could I let him trick me like this?"

"Don't blame yourself. You went for a strong Alpha. That's what good Omegas do, right?"

Locking eyes with Jason, Niles scowls. "Then maybe I don't want to be a good Omega." It comes out in a rush of spite, and it feels good to say it. "Maybe I hate being an Omega."

The leather creaks as Jason slides over to perch next to him. He rests a hand on Niles's knee and rubs a thumb back and forth in a soothing pattern, just letting it calm Niles's nerves for a moment.

"I like you just the way you are," he murmurs.

And Niles's heart throbs. It's like it was early in their relationship before Tristan got in the way. The walls he's been putting up to bar this man passage drop slightly, and he lifts his hand, caressing the bruise that rings Jason's eye with tenderness.

"I'm sorry," he says again.

Jason's eyes sink shut as he leans into Niles's touch. "It's not your fault."

"But he—"

Jason catches his hand before it withdraws and holds it firm and fast. He swirls his thumbs over the scent glands at Niles's wrists, making him focus on his pulse point. "I said it's not your fault."

A tingle runs up Niles's back as Jason rocks his face into his cupped palm, dragging his lips over the pale skin there.

"I should—"

"Don't go," Jason says, and it comes out as a command as much as a plea. His cheeks flush as he kisses the heel of Niles's hand. "Stay with me."

Some rational part in Niles's mind shuts down. The part that second guesses. The part that overthinks. The part that worries about future consequences. The part that remembers to *dread.*

"What do you want from me?" Niles asks in a whisper.

Jason's denim eyes darken. "Everything."

Niles had said that once upon a time, back when he was so in love, he thought he would burst.

Jason pulls Niles's wrist in a quick snag, launching him into his lap. Before there is time for second thoughts, Jason's mouth is on his, sinful and hungry. He wastes no time forcing his way in, his tongue laving at Niles's as he moans, a deep rumble of sound that makes Niles's insides clench. A frisson of want crawls its way up Niles's body, unexpected but not unwelcome, and he gives in without complaint. Going limp in Jason's arms, Niles is subservient. Just like instinct tells him to be.

After a heady forever, Jason releases with a gasp, though he doesn't pull an inch away. "Do you know how long I've wanted to do that?" he asks, voice breathy and dripping with desire.

Niles gets no chance to answer because he's pulled into another kiss, this one softer. Slower. Jason's lips are like cushions, and his tongue is slick. His fingertips slide down the side of Niles's neck, a barely-there touch, but those clever digits do yet another sweep, this one over his mating gland, and Niles cries out against his mouth.

"God, that's sexy," Jason says, and repeats the motion, making Niles's slick gather inside him. "That's it, handsome. Make noises for me."

Niles can't help but oblige, mewling and gasping as Jason works his way down his jaw and starts sucking on his mating gland. Resting his forehead on Jason's shoulder, his erection hardens in his pants, and whether Jason's hand brushes it on purpose or by mistake, Niles doesn't know, but he moans either way. It's a sound of encouragement, no matter how unintentional, and Jason splays his hand over Niles's crotch as he keeps sucking, licking, and dragging his teeth over Niles's most holy spot, making every part of him electric and willing.

"Yes, Alpha," he says by mistake, habit more than anything else, but the guttural groan Jason makes is a fiery reward.

"Christ, yes, say it again."

Niles obliges, and Jason leans him down onto his back, hovering over and putting their hard, clothed lengths on top of each other.

"See what you do to me?" Jason says, angling his hips for a dry stroke. "Sometimes I touch myself, thinking about you. Did you know that?"

Cheeks heating, Niles says, "Too blunt" with the smallest of smiles, only to have Jason take another kiss from him, firm and hard.

Niles runs his hands through Jason's hair in soft scrapes that work toward his collared shirt—the kind he always wears. The strands are coarse, almost rough against his fingers, and it makes him remember how soft Tristan's hair is in comparison.

But no. Niles refuses to think of that man right now.

A light pluck of his button grabs his attention, and he realizes it's a silent question. One he nods his head for even as his tongue licks its way over the roof of Jason's mouth. The man needs no further confirmation, undoing it in an easy flick, balancing on his knees precariously to use both hands to ease down the zipper. The crown of Niles's cock is straining beneath his briefs, and Jason slides his hand over it. The broadness of his palm is a thing of wonder, his fingers spanning almost from one side of Niles's hips to the other as they put pressure on him, sending a scorching heat through his groin and making him feel the thrum of his heart in his veins.

The next silent question is a tug at his jeans. Niles is mindless at this point, lifting his rear to have them tugged down while quashing that little niggle that says *slow down* and *this is wrong* and *you need to stop.*

Jason releases Niles's mouth only to work his feverish lips down his shirt. With a rough grab, it's bunched up to his chest so the Blond Beta can take full advantage of his skin. Jason runs his tongue over it in hot kitten licks before he gets to Niles's cock and lays a full, flat-tongued stroke from the root up. Niles lets out a gasp when Jason sucks him in, like in his fantasy, and works him down his throat in tight slides.

Running his hands through Jason's hair again, Niles throbs and aches as his slick starts to trickle out. If this were Tristan, he would smell it. He would praise him.

No, he scolds himself. *Stop it.*

Jason lets out a rough grunt, a sound that zings up Niles's body and settles in his loins, making him bob in Jason's mouth. His brain is floating as he begins to cant his hips, wanting deeper. Wanting faster.

Before he can cough up the courage to say it out loud, he jolts as two fingers come to rest against the pucker at his backside. That, more than anything else, wakes up his brain.

"I-I'm not ready," Niles says.

Jason's hand withdraws immediately even as he rains down nips and suckles on Niles's rigid length. "Okay."

And for some reason, Niles doesn't like that answer. Tristan would have said a confident, "I'll *make* you ready," and suddenly, that's what Niles wants. Even if he's furious at him, even if he hates him a little, he still wants him. He can't change his heart so easily.

Jason pulls back and lifts his shirt off in one go, his forehead furrowed in what might be pain as he works his shoulder. His ribs are a spattering of cherry blossom petals in pinks and purples, mottling his pale, moonlight skin. Niles's eyes linger, tracing their shapes and embedding their reason for existence into his mind. Jason has tried so hard for so long and has received nothing but grief. How can Niles say no to him?

The room becomes alive with Jason's scent, that indefinable sharpness, and his newly revealed expanse of flesh answers all Niles's silent question as to how strong this man is. He's thick and broad, a sweet layer of baby fat over a solid rock wall of muscle. For as pale as he is, his is a rainbow of color, flushed rouges, bruised blues, creamsicle freckles, and lashes so dark they're like dustings of onyx on his cheeks. Jason brings his khakis down to his knees, brandishing his cock's dusky head and leaking tip, looming as both a promise and a threat all at once.

"I said I'm not ready," Niles breathes out, staring at Jason's girth, as impressed as he is intimidated.

"I know," he soothes, bringing his hand to his mouth and running his tongue over it in a wet line. He smooths the saliva down his shaft, making him glisten, and does it again, wetter this time, running it over Niles. "But can I do this?"

He leans his hips down until their cocks rub together, a silky slipping that glances their foreskin off one another, pulling at it ever so lightly. The sensation is nothing but a tease, making Niles want more, even as he wants less. With a hushed sigh, Jason wraps a heavy hand around both of them, pivoting his hips until he slides through the circle of his fingers.

"Come on, handsome. Have mercy."

Those words fill Niles with a rush of lust as he feels the urge again to obey. He plants his feet and tilts his hips until they're both gliding through Jason's fist, the slick slide of them making Niles's balls ache in that perfect way. His jaw drops in a silent cry as they pick up their pace, both fucking the same tight circle and stroking each other. It's Niles who spits on his hand this time, taking over and keeping that friction pulling them toward their precipice.

"I'm not gonna last." Jason moans like he's barely holding on. Little drips and drabbles, little "ahs" and "pleases" fall from him like lustful prayers, heated and desperate. Niles's Omega stands up and takes notice, fascinated by the dynamic between them. Having power like this is a rush that can't be denied. There is something special about being a man's fetish come to life.

"You wanna come on me, Alpha?" Niles bites his bottom lip as the corner of his mouth ticks up in mischief.

"Wanna come down your throat. In your ass. Anywhere you let me."

At the words, Niles's backside clenches, aching to be filled as more slick spills out.

"Please, Niles. Let me have you."

But he doesn't want that. Instead, he works his hand, no longer satisfied to let their hips set the pace. Jason's words stop as his mouth drops into an "O." Electricity is nipping up Niles's spine as he gets closer, closer, but he can't get over the edge. Why can't he get over the edge?

Letting his head fall back on the couch cushions, he lets his mind burst into color. It's Tristan's knot in his hand as his Alpha hisses, "My sweet Omega. Fuck, baby, you're mine. Every part of you is mine. God, you feel so good. I want to swallow you whole. Can I come inside you, baby? Can I leave my seed in my Omega and make him feel good?"

Niles is panting now, Jason above him barely hanging on. "Omega, please come. Come for me."

Niles is so close, he's trembling, but it's not enough.

He needs to focus on the moment. He needs to listen to his lover. But instead, it's only when the fantasy Tristan commands him, "Come for me, baby. Come for me *now!*" that Niles lets out a high-pitched gasp as he lets go, his hand pumping them both for all he's worth.

Jason follows soon after with a growl that keeps Niles leaking in a lasting crescendo, cresting in waves as he drips down his hand in small rushes. The heated beads are proof of his sin, and each tug gets slower, milking them both onto Niles's naked belly. A silky drip runs over the curve of his waist in a telltale line of passion, leaving a cooling stripe behind.

Jason's forehead *thunks* down on Niles's chest as he cages him, panting and nuzzling. "You're so perfect. Better than I ever dreamed."

Niles's euphoria sinks all too quickly, leaving him guilty, wet, and cold. What the fuck has he done?

Jason presses a chaste kiss to the center of his chest, right between his pectorals. "I'll get us something to clean off with. One sec, okay?"

He's up and off in a moment, tucking himself away and getting dish towels from his pretty kitchen. Staring at the splashes of cum on his belly, Niles feels dirty. This isn't just a fling. He can't treat it like one. He can't smile and walk away and never think about this moment again. ...But he'd be lying if he said it was anything more than a pity fuck.

Jason doesn't toss him a towel, no. With a quiet groan of stifled pain, he gets to his knees and gently starts wiping up, nothing but soft concentration on his face, making sure he gets every drop. Clucking his tongue, he dips into Niles's belly button, soaking up the slippery white. When Niles tries to smile and pull up his pants, Jason only tsks.

"Ah, ah," he says, keeping Niles down and producing a fresh

cloth. This one he dips between Niles's legs to clean the slick from his inner thighs and lower. Niles is humiliated. Ashamed. This was so wrong.

"Jason," he tries to start. "I'm sorry, I didn't mean for this to happen."

The man only gleams. "Neither did I. But I'm so glad it did."

Grimacing, Niles lifts up and pulls his pants back on, doing the zipper and button as fast as he can. He's about to start panicking, he can feel it. He tries to find the words, the right apologies, but is coming up empty.

Jason must see his distress because his kind expression wanes. His lifted eyebrows knit and that twinkle fades. His smile dies and becomes a small, tight lipped frown of realization. "You think this was a mistake."

Niles flinches…but he doesn't say no.

"You want to leave," Jason states instead of asks.

Niles opens his mouth to say "I'm sorry" again, but the words falter. They're woefully inadequate for this moment. Instead, he wraps his arms around himself and makes his body small.

There is a heated debate going on in Jason's head. Niles can see his wheels turn and the focus of his pupils go in and out as he spirals. Jason's scent spikes into anger, maybe even fury, and Niles doesn't blame him one bit. He should be yelled at. Scolded. Excommunicated from their friendship—one that can no longer exist.

He sees the exact moment Jason realizes that, too.

"Then that's the way it is," the man says, his voice humorless, dark, and flat. "I'll go upstairs and get Bee-bee's leash."

Niles watches Jason's broad back as he plods away, raking a hand through his blond hair, still favoring one side. Those bruise marks walk their way up his back as well, wrapping his ribcage in terrible tattoos. Niles wonders how much it hurt for Jason to hold his body above him for so long…and yet, he'd done it. This moment had mattered that much to him.

Niles is going to cry. Unmoved, Bee-bee stares at him from a round floor pillow near the stairs with accusation in her eyes, something he's very much earned. She makes no move to help him feel better, as she would have in the past. Maybe she's forgotten him after all this time. Or replaced him.

Taking a sharp breath, he stands up to get his jacket from the kitchen where he'd plopped it on the counter. Habit more than anything else makes him pluck out his phone. Tristan had messaged him…because of course he did.

> Sorry I missed your call. Was running a gaming session. Everything okay?

Niles scowls. The Alpha casually forgot to mention he spent part of his evening beating the crap out of a rival.

Niles wants to call him. He wants to scream at him. This whole situation is his fault; Jason is heartbroken, and Niles is the world's biggest asshole all because one man couldn't keep his Alpha in check!

Angry brown thumbs type out the words:

> I need to talk to you. Now.

He watches the bubbles from Tristan's side form with red rage in his heart, clenching his jaw and ready to burst into a million jagged pieces…

But then a hand clamps over his mouth from behind, hard and unyielding. Instinct makes Niles try to jerk away, but the grip is like iron. Another arm slings around his shoulders and neck, holding him in place no matter how he struggles.

"You want a possessive Alpha, handsome?" Jason snarls. "I'll give you one."

He can't get away. Niles's brain kicks into overdrive as he panics, gagging on the cloth shoved over his face, the scent overwhelming, bitter like rubbing alcohol and making him lightheaded.

…Making…making his eyes roll back.

………Making him…foggy…

………………Making…

…………………making him…

………………………………………………

CHAPTER 12

SURPRISE, SURPRISE

Thud.

Thud-thud.

His brain pulses in time with his heartbeat, throbbing as if trying to outgrow the narrow space behind his sinuses. With a groan, Niles works to open his eyes, but they only flutter instead. His stomach roils like he's about to be sick, and through the groggy haze, Jason's voice calls to him, distant and soft.

"You were out longer than I thought. It's about ten in the morning now. How do you feel?"

His tone oozes a lilt of concern Niles can barely hold onto. "Where…where am I?" he says, the room fading in and out in white blurs.

"Home." The word is shy and soft…and it's also a lie. Niles's ceiling is a popcorn pattern. This is high-end and smooth with exposed beams.

He rolls over, a heavy pound in his head making him curl into fetal position. The light cuts into his vision, giving it sunspots and floating circles of black confetti that block out anything discernable.

Pushing himself up from the floor, he takes a deep breath as the world tries to normalize. Below him, everything is padded, like the hotel room he and Tristan had gone to together. It's a moment in time that feels far away, almost hidden behind the gossamer silk of a spider web. Something tainted with danger but still beautiful.

Niles's fingers sink into the pad, leaving little indents as he orients himself. More white surrounds him than he's ever seen before. Insulated walls dull the sound, leaving an empty hush. There are no windows, but there is a sink and toilet. Both of which look like they cost too much to be put into a room such as this.

"What is this place?" he asks, his mouth filled with cotton.

"I guess you could call it your bedroom."

Niles's head ticks back on his neck as another wave of dizziness hits him. "I see it comes with an ensuite." His giggle is foolish and unlike him, high and girlish, a tittering noise he's never made before. Turning over his shoulder, he finds Jason, hands laced together in front of him and shame on his face as he hunkers…

Directly behind a wall of glass.

Only then does it start to sink in.

Bee-bee pants at Jason's feet, fogging up a little spot that would otherwise be crystal clear. Niles might not have noticed there was glass at all except for that blurry circle in front of his dog's face. To the right of the oversized floor-to-ceiling window is a door with a keypad and a slot below it—not large enough to climb out of but enough to pass something through. In front of the slot lies a metal baking sheet with food on it, a makeshift tray of fruits and veggies. And cream puffs.

His eyes fly to Jason's.

"I thought you might be hungry," he says with a sheepish shrug. Niles notices he's using both shoulders with ease. His voice sounds slightly muffled, the glass dulling the sound. "I grabbed some things you tend to put in your bento boxes, and I saw you like those pastries. I got them from the same shop you did. Their name was on the bag when we were together before. I figured if I replaced the ones you gave away that night…maybe it would, I don't know, sweeten the moment."

A sort of numbness sinks in.

"I hate this room," Jason confesses. "I didn't want to have to use it again. I was going to prove I was a new man. A *better* man. But I can't change."

His voice breaks on the last word. Facing the floor, he wipes his cheeks roughly with the back of his hand. Niles can't breathe. He can't comprehend. His head is rushing so hard, he might pass out again.

"My ex hated this room, too. He looked like you, you know. He even had a similar background. Dead family, foster homes. The more I learned about you, the more I wondered if being with you would be like having him back again. But it's not like that. You're not a replacement, Niles. You're so much more."

His hand presses on the glass between them, the skin flattening and turning white with pressure. The purple line of bruising over his eye and cheek has only worsened overnight, turning his skin the color of dusty wine.

"You make me smile. You make me laugh. You don't lie or try to hide things, even when you could. When I'm with you, I feel like I have a purpose again. A reason for being. I wanted to do that for you, too. I thought I could make you fall in love with me, and I promise you, I tried to do it right. I was understanding and listened and gave you grace when you made a mistake."

"Mistake?" Niles asks.

Jason finally peers up, his eyes red rimmed with sorrow. "I wanted to be with you during your heat. I was heartbroken when it didn't happen. When *he* got to you instead. But next time, you'll be here. I know if I prove I can take care of you, you won't have to be afraid of us anymore."

Niles's voice comes out strangled. "What are you talking about?"

Jason sighs and rests his forehead against the glass. He doesn't sound like crazy people are supposed to sound. His voice isn't high or manic, he's not raging, he has a tone of acceptable regret, sorrow, and longing. That doesn't stop ice from traveling through Niles's veins.

"I can see you through everything, I swear," Jason says. "You'll see. I'll be so good to you. Won't I, girl?" Jason reaches down and pets Niles's dog, who watches him as if nothing's wrong, her cute doggy snout making a cute doggy grin.

"I'm tired. I waited for you to wake up all night. I think I'll take a nap now, okay? But I'll be back, and we can talk more. Just don't scream. If you scream, I'll have to do something about it."

And even though he's not looking at him, even though it's said in something that sounds like complete exhaustion, the threat is so real, it strangles Niles. This time, it's not lust that keeps him compliant. It's not pity. It's not even fear. It's full-blown terror.

———

Socks long discarded, Niles's feet are sweating, sticking to the white floor pads as he paces. He'd checked for his captor no less than twenty-five times before he gave in and relieved himself in the oddly exposed toilet. Even now, his eyes keep snapping up, waiting for the Blond Beta Bastard to show his face again. Bee-bee naps, curled by the glass as if she doesn't want to leave him, which both warms his heart and makes him irrationally angry, as if somehow his tiny, ten-pound dog should be going to get help, telling strangers he's stuck down the proverbial well.

Wanting to make the most of the time when Jason is asleep, Niles tries several combinations on the padlock at the door. There's a problem, though. Since he doesn't know how long the sequence is, the possibilities are innumerable. He gives it up as a bad job.

Next, he tries to test the food slot, worming his hand through and patting it from both sides. The door is metal and heavy, so there's no breaking through, and the best he can do is get his arm in up to his shoulder. There's more space to flop himself around but not enough for his big fat head.

He wants to kick the wide expanse of glass but worries about the sound. He can only imagine his captor won't appreciate his escape attempt if awoken. Even so, he debates forgetting that risk altogether and tearing off the toilet lid, slamming the thing against his transparent cage and trying to shatter it. Much to his chagrin, it seems Jason already thought of that, because there is neither a toilet lid nor seat to be seen. Apparently, the man expects Niles to put his ass in the water if he needs to perform his baser functions. The only other thing he could possibly get his hands on is the sink's faucet, but it's too small to do much damage with, if he can even get the piece off in the first place.

So, he paces.

It's a spacious thirty footfalls lengthwise and twenty in width. The glass takes up almost the entire portion of the wall that faces the hallway, save the leftmost corner and the far right, which houses the heavy door in a padded wall and metal frame. The edge of another door can be seen down the hall when Niles shoves his cheek against the glass, leaving behind a smear from the oils of his skin. He wonders if it's a bathroom or Jason's bedroom. Probably the former, as Jason hadn't turned that way when he went for his nap. If Niles manages to get out, would he have to sneak past the man's bedroom? Silence would be hard to come by with his dog's collar jingling as she wound around his feet. She'd probably yap, too. It's not without irony that Niles solidifies his earlier thought that, yes, she would be a fantastic watchdog. She'd be like a warning bell.

He flops down painlessly on the padding, tossing himself onto his back.

It's alright. Ari will see I've gone dark, and Ben will tell her about my stalker. The text I sent Tristan will get him riled up, and when he can't reach me, he'll know something's wrong, too. Maybe he'll think I came here. If he beat Jason up, he knows where he lives.

Maybe Tristan will show up and demand to know when Jason saw Niles last. Then he'll catch the scent of any of Niles's leftover pheromones, which would scream distress. Or maybe he'll smell the vestiges of Niles's pleasure and slick, get pissed, and turn tail.

The thought pangs Niles with shame. Why had he done something so fickle and stupid?

It was because Tristan is a bad man, and Jason was supposed to be a good one. But it was more than that. It was Niles trying to forget his Alpha in the arms of someone who he thought deserved to be loved. Would Niles still be in here if he'd acted like he liked it, spent the night, and then just never spoken to Jason again? But like Jason said, Niles isn't a liar, although he should probably learn. In this situation, if he wants to escape, he'll have to learn, won't he?

Tristan had been adamant that Jason smelled wrong. He outright accused him of being the one who stalked Niles. But was it because he was truly picking up on something sinister, or was he trying to pass the suspicion onto someone else?

No. His stalker had to be Tristan. If not, how could he have known where Jason's apartment was? He probably followed him home from the café one day.

Somehow, he's not convinced. In the past, when Tristan followed Niles around, he'd always made it very clear, leaving notes or just showing up, letting himself be seen through windows or sitting close by in restaurants, staring at Niles, wanting to intimidate as much as to watch. But has that changed now that he wants to be seen as reformed? How deep does his deception go?

"What the hell is wrong with people?" Niles mutters to himself, furious. Caleb. Tristan. Jason. They're all insane.

Even so, he needs to bet on that insanity. His only chance is his Alpha chasing him down and overcoming the Beta who's holding him against his will. Niles fantasizes about it for a moment. If Tristan does, will Niles forgive him? Will he chalk the whole thing up to instinct? Probably. Apparently, he's a submissive pushover who only makes bad decisions.

He grimaces, hating himself.

He has no idea what time it is, but his stomach rumbles. Looking at the little food tray he'd shoved to the side during his search of the room, he considers. It's flushable. Or maybe he should shove it all back out of the slot, a feeble protest that hurts no one but himself and could potentially get him into trouble.

Trouble.

He's in trouble.

A wave of fear comes over him again and he curls onto his side. In the café, Jason had said the ending with his ex was explosive. That there was no going back. Did the ex escape, or did Jason possibly…kill him?

Niles needs to be very careful. He's in more than just danger of being hurt. He could die, and Jason could make him suffer when it happens.

He's going to be sick.

Niles wants to go home. He wants to go back in time. He wants someone to break down the door and save him.

With nothing else to do, Niles holds himself, breaks down, and sobs.

"You don't have to save it."

The dulled voice startles Niles out of his misery. He was on the verge of dozing, his terrifying imaginings dipping dangerously close to full blown nightmares.

Uncurling from his position, Niles looks over his shoulder. Jason stands with his hands in his pockets and his gaze focused downward, as if afraid to meet Niles's eyes.

"I put that food out for you. As long as you're good, you'll get as much as you want. I'm going to try to make it as nice as I can for you here."

He starts to saunter up and down the corridor, always staying in view and talking to feet. "I know there's no privacy, but if you need me to step away and give you space for whatever reason, I will. You can even earn shower privileges if you prove you can be trusted."

With a heavy sigh, Jason sits in front of the glass and Bee-bee immediately jumps into his lap.

Traitor, Niles's mind hisses.

"There are a few things you and I are going to have to come to terms with, whether we like them or not. Number one, you're here with me. You're staying until I say otherwise. It is what it is, and there's no changing my mind. It's too late to take it back. We can only move forward.

"Two. You're going to lose your job. No call, no show for days, and it's bound to happen. But you don't have to worry. I have more than enough money to support you. I know you'll be able to get a new job easily once we've got everything sorted. You've got the skills, and based on what you've told me, your portfolio speaks for itself.

"Three. Your friends are going to panic when you go radio silent. I completely expect that, and I also expect you're going to wonder if it will ruin your relationships, given how dependent you are on them."

"I'm not dependent," Niles mutters.

"Yes, you are. You're clingy." He has the audacity to smile. "I like that about you. Meeting me for lunch every day was a bit much, but I loved it. Telling me everything I asked as long as I opened up first proves you're needy for any sort of connection. It's...well...adorable. I'm that way, too. That's one of the reasons I know we're perfect for each other."

Niles glares, but Jason is too busy petting his dog to see.

"When you see Ari and Ben again—because once we get sorted, I promise you will—they're going to be angry, and you're going to want to tell them the truth, but you're never going to."

"How? I've disappeared! What else could I possibly say?"

"That I whisked you away on vacation and you left your phone behind. It doesn't even have to be a lie. Once we're sorted, I'll take you anywhere you want. Europe? Caribbean islands? Tour Japan? Anything you like for as long as you like. Consider it a reward for dealing with this. I know it's not ideal."

Niles wants to claw the man's eyes out.

"But while you're feeling insecure about them, wondering if they'll get angry and abandon you, know that I never will. Don't be afraid. One way or another, you'll never have to be alone again."

Funny how those words from Tristan made Niles's heart throb, yet in this moment, they make his skin crawl.

"I've got your keys," Jason continues. "Give me a list of stuff you want from home, and I'll bring it to you."

"You think I want you in my house?" Niles says with a sarcastic laugh. "I'm not telling you where I live."

Jason runs his hands through his messy hair. It looks as if it's been tugged at constantly. "You don't have to. I already know."

Niles's jaw ticks to the side as realization dawns. "It was you following me. It wasn't Tristan at all."

Jason's eyes burn his. "Never mention that name to me again. Once we're settled, you won't even have to *think* it."

"Settled. You keep saying that. What the hell does that mean?"

"I'm putting you into heat and mating you," Jason says, blunt as ever.

Despite the tightening in his chest, Niles scoffs. "How? You're a Beta."

The smile on Jason's face is wry and self-deprecating all at once, a sideways quirk as his eyes roll to the ceiling. "I seem like it, don't I? I take enough suppressants to keep me in check. Triple prescription. My tendencies are a little too on the dangerous side, otherwise."

"You mean you get worse?" Niles says, immediately regretting it. Jason chuckles, and it only serves to infuriate him further. His voice rises. "How can you laugh at this!"

Jason pauses, wringing his hands together. "Because if I don't laugh, I'll cry."

A twinge of sympathy twists something in Niles's chest, and he hates it. "So, I'm stuck in here until I hit my next heat?"

"Don't worry. It will be soon. I want your suppressants to clear out of your system. Mine, too."

Niles grinds his teeth. "Just because I'm off them doesn't mean I'll automatically—"

"No. But I can give you that special medicine again."

Niles's brain hitches, and his face must show it.

Shrugging, Jason actually fucking blushes. "I'm the one who dragged you off cycle. I put something in your coffee. You didn't drink it all, that's why it took a few hours to kick in, but it was supposed to work within thirty minutes. When you didn't have any symptoms, I almost panicked. It took everything to keep a straight face. I held out hope that you would call me, though. I slipped my number in your bento box. I'm guessing you didn't see it."

Niles's head ticks side to side, knowing he tips the box out over the trash as soon as he gets home.

An honest Good Boy smile surfaces on Jason's face. "That actually makes me feel better. Maybe you would have called me, you just didn't have the opportunity."

Niles refuses to correct him.

"Don't worry. I don't blame you for what you did. You don't seem like the kind of guy to go through a dry heat, so when you didn't call, I kind of expected it."

"Well thank you for being so magnanimous," Niles growls. He might be pushing it, but he can't help himself.

Jason only stands again, Bee-bee jumping off his lap with a few short barks, turning a circle at his feet. She needs to go for a walk. It's her tell-tale sign.

"I'm going to grab a notepad, so you can tell me what you need. When I come home, I'll bring up a movie on my laptop or something. You'll have to tell me what you're into." He presses his palm flat on the glass. "Tonight, I'm going to sleep in here with you. If you fight me, you fight me, but I'll win."

"Because you're an Alpha?" Niles says through his teeth.

"And because I'm not hurt."

The surprises keep coming.

Jason gestures to his ribs where the cherry blossom petals bloomed. "Makeup." To his shoulder, he says, "Totally fine." One last upward flourish of his hand toward his face, he says, "And I did this to myself. No more lies between us. I'll tell you everything you ask, okay? You've always been honest with me, and if I want this to be real, it's about time I returned the favor."

He's about to leave, the dog winding her way around him, then stops. Dropping his gaze, he makes one last confession. "And I've had Bee-bee for weeks. Almost since the beginning. She was my trump card. Whether you pulled away or pulled closer, I was going to use her to make you like me more. I thought finding her would make your heart flutter." He huffs a laugh. "And last night, it seemed to work." Looking at Niles with nothing but sincerity on his face, he says, "I'm sorry. I don't want it to be like this. But it will be better once we're mated, okay? Let's just get through this part together. Then, you'll have the rest of your life to forgive me."

Turning again, he slaps his thigh, telling Bee-bee they're going for walksies after daddy does one more thing.

Watching them go, a root of hate twirls its way through Niles's heart. There's no way he could live his life mated to that monster.

Niles pushes his dinner tray out of the slot, putting his empty water glass out second. His mouth swirls with a meal that was far more delicious than it had a right to be, a crisp chicken parmesan with thick, flat linguine. He rubs the back of his arm over his face, cleaning the corners of his mouth and leaving an orange smear on his long sleeve shirt. He frowns. He's been wearing this since yesterday. It reeks of his desire from the night before, his scent sticking to the fabric both here and in his jeans. All he wants to do is get changed, but Jason hasn't given him his new clothes yet. Bastard probably wants him to wallow in it.

"Fucking mind games," Niles whispers.

A movie plays in the hallway, a dark romance Jason said he likes—because of course he does. The voices are dull and distant but still audible as the story chugs along through a racy sex scene, one Niles has no desire to look at. The Alpha is movie star attractive, strong and rough, and the Omega female is hourglass shaped with those perfect, child-bearing hips they're all known for. Niles touches his own, knowing they flare, too.

"We should make pups," Jason had said on the other side of the glass when the last movie had a pregnant male. Niles had only cowered, put his head on his knees, and wrapped his arms around himself.

Tired, he flops down again, nuzzling into his silky pillow. It smells like his apartment and safety. So does the huge blanket he wraps himself in, tucking his head underneath and curling into a ball.

He didn't get everything I asked for, Niles gripes silently. *Either that or he's not giving it over.*

His scalp is dry. He needs to put his oil in between his braids, or he'll start to get flakey. Why he suddenly cares about that, he has no idea, but he wants his routine and normalcy. Perhaps it was the glass bottles the serum came in he's being denied access to? Everything that was actually delivered—all while his back was to the wall on the far side of the room while Jason tossed things in through the open door—

was either comfort items or time wasters, which he doesn't usually indulge in. Now the padded white floor sports an e-reader with a low battery because Niles had no idea where the cord was, a stack of books on the art of cinematography he'd mentioned over lunch once that he never had time to read, and chew toys for Bee-bee for when she gets let in, which Jason had promised would happen tomorrow. It's not even half of the list.

Apparently, Niles had requested items that must be considered contraband, and he mulls over reasons why. He'd asked for sheets. Denied. Maybe to keep him from hanging himself or something. He'd asked for pen and paper, but it seems Jason also doesn't want Niles to have anything he can stabby-stab him with. Niles wanted his laptop too, but Jason had only rolled his eyes when that ask was made. To be fair, it was a stretch.

In all his forethought, there's one thing Jason didn't seem to think of. The police. Between Ari, his work, and Tristan, someone is going to try to put two and two together. The problem—yet another problem—is no one knows Jason's last name, where he works, or where he lives. If Tristan never attacked him, then he's never been here. And he *didn't* attack him. He didn't stalk Niles either. It was all a lie.

I'm a fucking idiot.

The air under the blanket gets hot and thin, but instead of unearthing himself, Niles opens a gap that faces away from the glass window and lets his lips suck in fresh air.

I'm sorry I didn't believe in you, Tris.

In his mind's eye, Tristan lays curled behind him under the blankets, an arm draped over his waist, and his cheek running calming strokes against Niles's mating gland.

"I forgive you," imaginary Tristan says.

I wish I could see you.

"I want to come save you."

Niles wants that with his whole heart. *I didn't trust you, and now I've ruined everything.*

In Niles's imagination, Tristan holds him tighter.

He's going to mate me. Niles cowers, his lips trembling as he struggles to breathe suddenly, a thread of piano wire tightening around his lungs.

"Shh," fake Tristan soothes. "You'll never let that happen."

I'll give in. I'll submit. It's what I do.

"Be better than your biology, baby. I learned that lesson the hard way. Looks like you're about to do the same. What did I tell you to do?"

Niles sniffs back his tears. *You told me to fight and kick and scream.*

"That's right."

But if I fight, he'll hurt me.

"And if you don't, he may kill you."

It feels like utter truth.

"Keep your eyes and ears open, baby. Shut your Omega up and focus on your brain. Play along. Don't cause a fuss, but don't just switch to being okay with this. To loving him. He'll see right through that. If you fake it too hard, he won't trust you, and you need him to trust you. Remember, he thinks you don't lie."

Which might be the most important card Niles has to play.

A metallic knock, a latch unlocking, and a creak rings through the space. Niles flinches.

"Only me," Jason says, as if it could be anyone else. "Didn't like the movie, hm?"

Niles hears silence. He didn't realize it had been shut off.

Footsteps shuffle slowly closer. "Remember what I told you, handsome. You fight me, you lose, and I don't want to hurt you."

"Circumstances speak to the contrary."

The blanket shifts, lifting off him, and Tristan's imaginary body wisps away, a more solid one replacing it, not wrapping around, but lying beside.

"Tomorrow is Sunday," Jason says. "We have the whole day together."

"Great," Niles grumbles. "Let's go to the fucking park."

Jason laughs a little, rocking his hips to the side and nudging Niles. "In no way do I trust you with that, but we'll get there. On Monday, I'm going to put in a leave of absence at work so I don't have to leave you alone, but it might take a few hours. My dad's gonna be pissed."

More sass blooms on Niles's tongue, but he bites it back.

"Will you let me hold you?" Jason asks.

"Do I have a choice?"

That hush of air fills the space as time draws out. "For now."

The light remains hazy-bright in this room with no view of the outside. It's night, Niles knows, but how is he going to sleep like this? Every place where Jason's heat touches him is twitching, and Niles tries his damnedest not to pull away. Still, he starts to quake, and Jason hushes him.

"Just sleep now, handsome. You'll get used to it."

Which is the last thing Niles wants.

CHAPTER 13

SHATTERED GLASS

Niles's muscles are rigid as he sits across from Jason, eating another dinner with the devil. This time, it's chopsticks and General Tso's chicken, the too sweet American Chinese food reminding him of Ari and her love of the stuff, despite the pain in her belly. She'd always assumed she was allergic to MSG, but as she moaned in the bathroom, she'd still say the words "Worth it."

There's no doubt of Jason's true designation now. All too quickly, his suppressants are wearing off, and his Alpha is rearing its ugly head. He stares more intensely. He's more forward and touchy. His presence is all-consuming, taking up all the space in the room. If he wore blockers, those have long flown out the window as well, making his sharp scent borderline overwhelming as it surrounds him like an aura. Even now, Niles can't identify his taste in the air. It's not a rugged, earthy smell like he's used to from other male Alphas. It's one that sets him on edge.

His captor is also tense, but not from the situation. He's brimming with unleashed energy. His scowl shows his constant state of discomfort, and his only solace is Niles's calming Omega scent.

"Like honey," he'd whispered, crawling on his hands and knees toward Niles with a predatory gleam in his eyes.

When he came close enough, he purred a low rumble in his throat, leaned in, and ran his fingers down Niles's skin, marking him and making his Omega respond. Niles waved it off, focusing on his disgust instead. Jason must have smelled it because he backed off, but it took him longer and longer as the day wore on.

"Do you like the food?" Jason asks, mouth slightly full.

"It's not my favorite," Niles says, his mind repeating, *Honest. Stay honest. You can only trick him if you're honest.*

Jason smiles, closing his chopsticks around another bite and chewing slowly. Speaking with his mouth half full, he reminds Niles, "I like you."

"Yeah, well, forgive me if my feelings are mixed at this point."

"Mixed? I'll take it," Jason says, digging back in. "You know…I'm freaking out a little here."

"Gee, I wonder why."

"Not that," Jason says. "Tomorrow, I'm going to tell my dad I'm taking off of work, and he's going to ream me out."

"Apparently, you're an Alpha. You can take it."

"Especially since he's a Beta," Jason agrees, "but it's not just that. I'm…" he clears out his mouth as if taking a moment to search for the right words. "I'm twitchy. Ready to fight. If you aren't there to calm me down, I'm afraid I'll get violent when he argues with me. There's a reason I'm on as many meds as I am."

You don't say, Niles thinks, having the sense not to say that one out loud. Why this man likes to have normal conversations, as if they're a real a couple versus monster and mouse, he has no idea.

Setting his food aside, Jason leans back on his hands and stretches his legs out to either side of Niles, bracketing him and making him want nothing more than to run away.

"Don't run," his inner Tristan reminds. "Alphas like it when they can catch you. And when they catch you…"

Niles doesn't need to be reminded.

Setting down his meal as well, half-finished and glistening with grease, Niles observes his hands. "Tell me about your ex."

The air in the room changes. "I told you. We exploded, and then it was over."

"Believe me, that's been on repeat in my mind, thank you, but that's not what I'm talking about. You said we were similar. Our back-stories and stuff. Tell me more."

Jason tries to play it off with a smile. "Jealous?"

But Niles only narrows his eyes with his brows up.

Legs strewn aside Niles's hips, Jason asks, "Why do you want to know?"

So I can hear what he did to get in trouble and avoid it. I want to see what he did to make you feel good, so I can use it to help me get out of here.

"Morbid curiosity."

Jason lets out a breathy, uncomfortable laugh. "You want the romance of it or the quick summary?"

"Everything. Beginning to the end, explosion and all."

There's a sense of electric fear. Not only does Jason look like it, but he smells like it, too. With his scent amping up, Niles is having an easier time discerning what's going on in the man's mind. Hopefully, it will work to his advantage. Bitch of it is, Jason can smell him, too.

Fiddling his toes back and forth, Jason says, "I met him outside an old train car diner in the rain. He just smelled so sad, I couldn't leave him be. I had to talk to him. It was love at first sight, I think. For both of us. He had this gorgeous dark skin and left his hair natural. Cute and puffy. He'd always pretend to be irritated when I'd pat it, but I know he secretly liked the attention.

"He had nowhere to go. His roommates were vicious and kicked him out after a nasty heat cycle, apparently. My Alpha prodded me, and I needed to protect him, so I brought him home. It was never awkward. We started living together, and it was so easy, you know? Like we'd been doing it for years. He was funny too. Like you but far less cynical and sarcastic." Jason tosses him a smirk.

"Didn't you say you were from western Mass? He was, too. He aged out of the foster system with nothing to his name, so he decided to go someplace where he wasn't the only male Omega in a sea of pretty girls. He figured the city was the best place for it. His one regret was that he left behind his little brother. Their parents had died, and it hurt his brother more than him."

The story hits too close to home.

"Don't get me wrong, my ex was heartbroken about their loss too, but he accepted it. He was good at that. Accepting. Until he wasn't."

"What happened?" Niles asks.

"I got too rough once. I was angry about something. Something that had nothing to do with him, actually. My father was divorcing my mother, and the prenup was leaving her penniless. She'd always been a housewife, so she had no skills, no potential careers on the horizon. She was terrified, but my father told me if I supported her, he'd cut off my trust fund and oust me from the company. I was livid. Out of control. I wanted to hurt him. Make him see how horrible he was. No matter how my ex tried to calm me down, he couldn't." Jason reeks of regret and his breath hitches. "I hit him. I hit him a lot. That, he couldn't forgive. I was sorry after. So, so sorry, but I'd broken something I couldn't fix. I'd always doubled my suppressants since I presented, but I tripled them for him. It wasn't enough, though. Nothing I did was ever enough."

"And so, he left."

"Tried to leave," Jason corrects. "I sensed it coming. Whenever I came near, he smelled like you do now. In fact, he smelled a lot like you in general. Sweet. Sugary. It was more caramel, though."

Something niggles in the back of Niles's mind.

"I don't know if I'll ever be completely over him. He's a part of me. As soon as I met him, he fit. He filled up all the cracks in my heart. That's why I couldn't let him leave. I...I drugged him."

"Like me?"

His voice is quiet when he admits, "Worse. I kept him out for days while I had *this* thing built." He gestures around them. "I called it the Rut Room Plus, trying to be cute, but when he was locked in here, cute was the last thing he saw in me."

"If you know this is a bad place, why use it again?"

"Because it worked for a while. He got sweet again. But he wouldn't sleep with me. Didn't trust me. And the more desperate I got, the angrier I was. But instead of submitting like he did before, he started fighting me. Yelling." He looks at Niles like a kicked puppy. "I hated it when he did that. I had to make it stop."

A pit of black rises from somewhere deep inside of Niles. Flat and cold, he asks, "Did you kill him?"

At first, Jason doesn't answer, then his eyes shimmer. "It was an accident."

Niles's chest hurts, his heart picking up. His fear is a tangible thing, turning his insides to liquid. "Are you going to kill me?"

Jason sits up onto his knees, reaching out to Niles, but everything in him rejects it. His feet paddle, shoving him backwards until he hits the wall, pressed flat and hard. His Omega wants to go belly up and beg, "Alpha, please don't hurt me!" and he can't help it, he really can't, his knees go up to his chest and he presses his hands over his eyes, letting out a sob.

"Shh, I'm not going to! That's why I have to mate you, don't you understand? If I do, you can't leave me! Then you'll be safe! Niles, I want to keep you *safe!*"

"I'm afraid of you!" Niles cries.

"You think I'm not afraid of myself! You think I don't remember what it was like to look into his blue eyes and watch them fade?"

Niles's blood cascades frozen fractals in his veins. "Blue eyes? A black Omega with blue eyes?"

Jason nods, a sharp bob of his head with an exhale to match.

Something terrible rises within Niles, a horror unlike he's ever felt. His mouth opens and closes again, begging for it not to be true. "Tell me his name."

"Why?"

"Tell me his name!" Niles shouts.

Jason leans back on his heels, his shoulders rounded. "Trey."

And the floor drops from beneath Niles. His head lightens, and his lips go numb as he starts to hyperventilate. Any intake of breath seems to sear him from inside and he can't see through his misty eyes. Reeling, he pitches to the side, catching himself on his palms.

"Niles?" Jason asks, sounding on the edge of panic. "What's happening?"

So soft, small, and airy he can barely hear himself, Niles whimpers, "That was my brother."

"What?"

"THAT WAS MY BROTHER!" he screams, baring his teeth. "He left me! He left me, and he never came back again!"

The smell in the air turns acrid, and suddenly, Niles knows without a shadow of a doubt what Jason's sharp scent is.

It's blood.

"Oh God," Jason lets out, high pitched and reedy, covering his mouth. Wet lines flow down his face in slow rivers. "Christ, I'm sorry. I'm so, so sorry. I didn't mean it! I swear I didn't! He was fighting me in the bathroom, and he—"

"I don't wanna know!" Niles wails. "I don't wanna know how you killed him! I don't want to see it in my mind! I don't want to picture him like that!"

Jason flinches. His words come out in a rush, tumbling over themselves. "It was quick! He didn't feel it. I know!"

But Niles can only gasp and try to hold onto his consciousness. He wants to scream, *I hate you. I FUCKING HATE YOU!* But the Tristan inside him holds him back. He can't say those words. He's doomed if he says those words.

"I'm so sorry! Don't tell me this can't happen," Jason pleads. "I need you and me more than I can say. Tell me you can forgive me. I need it. I need to hear those words."

You think I give a fuck!?

But Niles says nothing. Jason rears up, starting to pace, thrusting his hands through his hair and chanting, "I didn't mean it. I didn't mean it." He finally sounds like the crazy person he is. "I'm so sorry. For that and for the fact that I love you. I'd do anything for you."

Niles bites out, "Except let me go."

"Something's wrong with me!" Jason insists, anger replacing his desperation, the scent wafting off him as he walks back and forth across the padded white room, his feet making little slaps and sticking rips when they lift.

Everything in Niles is on high alert. Even so, *Honesty. He needs honesty.*

And he takes a risk. "I don't care. It's not my fault and it sure as hell isn't my problem."

And Jason freezes. The scent of anger kicks up to fury. He whips around and takes Niles's jaw in his hands, lifting it painfully upward, straining his neck. "Are you sure about that? You know, all true Alphas walk a razor thin line between being a foe and being a felon. Which side do you think I'll land on tonight?"

Niles doesn't pull away, but his eyes plead, round and wet. "Please don't hurt me. Don't hurt me like you did him."

Jason's head drops. He sniffs back his tears. "I don't want to."

Which isn't the same as "I won't."

He steps back, burying his face in his hands, his breath stuttering behind cupped palms. "I can't do this."

He turns on his heels and punches in the keypad. Eight digits. That's too long.

Storming out, he pauses behind the glass and leans against it, his chest heaving. "I'm going to leave you alone for a while. I don't know how long. I just can't. It's too much."

Something Niles can absolutely agree with.

Detaching, calming, and seeming far away, Jason says, "Be good. Remember. Don't scream. I don't like it when you scream. I don't like a lot of fucking things right now."

With that, Jason moves on, slamming a door stage left and leaving Niles alone to suffocate in silence.

***

Fifteen-year-old Trey had sat on a knotted, low hanging tree branch tossing stones into the creek. Wearing his favorite green shirt, twelve-year-old Niles had stood with his hands on his hips, watching the clouds and seeing the shapes of his enemies. He'd wanted to punch holes in them.

Trey told him, "The thing about stopping bullies is this: Never let them get away with it. Bullies are cowards deep down. If you show them you're not afraid to stand up and get scrappy, ten to one says they'll back off."

"But how do you do it?" Niles asked his brother. "It's like you're not scared."

"Oh, believe me, I am. But do you know what being brave is? It's being scared and doing it anyway."

"Sounds more like being stupid to me."

Trey laughed. "And that's why life is hard. You have to figure out what's stupid-brave and what's safe-brave."

"Safe? What if the bully beats me to death or something?"

Trey ticked his head to the side, humming in thought. "Nah. Worse comes to worst, you come back with a black eye and be brave again."

"And what if they gang up on me all together?" Niles asked, tossing his hands up.

With a soft grunt, Trey hopped down from the tree. "Then you keep your head up. It's not 'they win, and you lose.' It's 'even if they win the fight, you can still win the war.'"

The marbled rock was heavy and smooth against Niles's fingers as he picked it up and tossed it, trying hard to make it skip. Instead, it *plunked*, a plop that sent splashes and ripples all the way to the shoreline. He sucked at this. Story of his life.

"I don't wanna fight a war. I just want someone to take care of me."

"Welp," Trey said, lobbing a stone and getting a good two skips out of it. "I'm not going to be able to protect you forever. Eventually, you're going to have to stand up for yourself."

"Pfft. Yeah, right. Even when you're out of high school, I want you to visit and freak out all the people who pick on me."

"With my buffness?"

"You're not that buff."

"Nah," Trey admitted. "And now that I'm an Omega, I never will be."

"What will you be instead?"

Trey winked at him. "Sexy."

"Ew!" Niles squawked. "Nope. Nope. Nope!"

There was a crunch of footsteps as Trey came over to headlock Niles, the pressure against his throat non-existent as Trey noogied his head. It felt good more than anything else, warm and familiar.

"I don't wanna go home," he grumbled in the crook of his brother's arm as he began to drag him off in that direction.

"Me neither. I hate it there. I don't want to stay anymore."

"You're stuck until you're eighteen." Niles struggled to pull himself from his brother's grip, but he only held him tighter.

"Who knows? Maybe life will surprise me."

"I don't like surprises," Niles said.

Trey released only to grab him again, bringing him in for a rough hug as he walked him backwards. "Too bad, kiddo. It's part of life."

Sitting in this place is both terrifying and boring; he almost wants Jason to come back, if only to have something to do. Hating someone and fighting with them is better than this never-ending moratorium. Niles misses the winter cold, of all things. He wants to get up off his ass and go for a walk. He hasn't been fed in what must be days, but his stomach has given up complaining. He can get water from the faucet at least. Every now and then, he hears the noises of Jason being alive. Coming up and down the stairs, shutting himself up in his room, clunking pots and pans around in the kitchen downstairs, but he never comes to the window.

Bee-bee does, though.

She jingles up now, panting with her tiny tail wagging. Niles works his way over to the glass, stiff and slow, leaning backwards to crack his spine along the way.

"Hey there. Who's a good girl, huh? Is it you?"

She barks her standard yips and yaps as she stands on her back legs and puts her paws on the wall between them. Her nails make little clicking sounds, and she starts licking its flat surface, her pink tongue leaving slurpy marks behind.

Niles smirks. "How does it taste?"

She just keeps licking.

"You like that?"

Her tail goes crazy.

"Well, at least one of us is enjoying themselves."

Done with him for now, Bee-bee trots off to the left. That's where the stairs are, past Jason's bedroom. She's working her way down, collar jingling, no muss no fuss as she goes to play with his captor. He's of mixed feelings about it, happy to have his dog safe and sound, happy to have her here, but horribly betrayed that she dares to like that man as much as him.

He hears Jason downstairs talking to her, but barely. Niles spends way too much time envisioning what's going on. Jason taking her out for walks and cuddling on the couch. Him feeding her kibble or bites of his dinner. Sleeping with her in his bed or during naps while he watches TV all day.

"I wish you'd trusted me," imaginary Tristan says.

I wish a lot of things.

"I wish your brother never died."

Niles's heart aches. He's cried so many tears at this point, there are none left to give. He's imagined what must have happened over and over again to the point where he's numb to it. It's like a silent movie playing out in black and white, surreal and unreal all at once.

I want to go home, he thinks. And Tristan agrees.

Niles jumps when he hears the door, his body jerking up from his pillow and blanket, his braids mussed and coming unwoven. Jason enters holding a tray, one of those same baking sheets he'd been serving Niles on back when he actually fed him. A glass of wine, a pale yellow Chardonnay or a Riesling maybe, sits in a high stemmed glass, making Niles's mouth water. So does something else. There is a rich, meaty smell coming from a jaw droppingly large bowl, and Niles's stomach wakes up with a rumble.

Jason chuckles. "Hungry, are we?"

"Is water wet?"

"Yes?"

"Then yes," Niles says all too quickly, wanting what's in that bowl more than he'd ever wanted any food in his life.

There are no conditions, Niles has to do no song and dance, Jason simply sets it down in front of him and sits across, smiling. Niles's hands are on the bowl in a blur, and he starts spooning hunks of meat into his mouth in a thick red broth that tastes both sweet and salty all at once.

"It's Belgian stew," Jason says. "My grandma used to make it. I make it special though. High end meat that I cook over a few days to get it nice and tender. I skim the fat off, too. It's got—don't laugh—prunes and beer. And bay leaves. A ridiculous amount of bay leaves."

"Don't they say if you get a full leaf in your food, you can't go outside?" Niles asks offhand. If the superstition has any merit, he probably has a lot of bay leaves.

Jason rests his elbows on his knees, propping his fists under his jaw and watching. "I'm sorry for staying away so long. I was…pretty depressed. If it makes you feel better, I haven't really eaten over the past few days, either."

Snarfing up his meal, Niles keeps his voice monotone. "I highly recommend the special on the menu tonight. Compliments to the chef."

Those words earn him that patented Good Boy smile. The one he'd like to tear off this man's face. Swallowing roughly, he picks up his wine glass and takes a swig. It's Moscato. Chilled, syrupy, and delicious.

"Sorry it's not a red wine to go with the beef. I'm not a fan of red, myself."

"In this place, wine is wine," Niles says, and it's the goddamn truth. Maybe if he could have been drunk this whole time, it would have made things easier.

Jason's gaze goes soft. "I missed you."

Could have fooled me.

"I'm happier today," he says. "I feel, I dunno, hopeful."

Bowl half empty at this point, Niles dips in some crusty bread that had been set off to the side. "And why's that?"

"Because I just gave you your medicine."

The red of the stew sinks into the bread, turning it soft as the white fibers absorb the juice in a veining pattern. The aroma of the dish is heady, the savory bits swimming in the pool of the bowl, innocuous and delicious even as they contain Niles's doom. Looking at Jason, Niles's eyes are wide as the moment stretches.

Jason blushes. "I tested it so many times to make sure you wouldn't taste it. I guess I got it right. I can't tell you how many batches I threw away."

The shaking clatter as Niles sets the bowl on the tray is the loudest thing he has ever heard.

"Not going to finish?" Jason asks, picking up the dish for himself and taking a bite. "It's okay. We can do it in half portions. It will just take longer."

"Y-you're taking it too?"

The smile on Jason's face is boyish. "A rut and a heat together, like it was supposed to be in the first place. Kind of romantic, isn't it?"

Niles's fingertips sink into his thighs.

"Now we can walk out of here mated. I'll spend my life showing you how sorry I am, and proving how good I can be to you. Then, you'll forgive me. Then, you'll love me back."

Jaw clenching, Niles holds his tongue, brain on high alert. His body is now the enemy.

"And once you're my Omega, you'll be able to soothe me like a good Omega should. You'll keep us both safe and happy. We can tell people I spirited you away, but it was the beginning of our future. It will be worth it all for the life we'll have together."

The spoon clinks against the ceramic as Jason finishes eating, dragging a finger along the inside of the bowl to catch every last drop.

"How long do we have?" Niles asks, his voice hauntingly quiet.

"I'd say about an hour." Jason picks up Niles's wine glass and sets it in his hand. "This might help calm your nerves."

"Give me privacy," Niles blurts. When Jason blinks at him, he rushes on, "You promised you'd give me privacy when I asked for it."

The most startling thing is the soft look of love that falls over

Jason's face, the lines in his forehead fading, his lips curling up at the sides. "Yeah, I did."

He stands up and dusts his hands. "Finish your bread. I'm going to stockpile a few things we'll need. We'll be in here for a few days, I expect." He winks and Niles's gut churns. "I can't wait to hear you call me Alpha again."

He dips down and places a kiss on Niles's forehead, and where they touch, his skin burns.

It hurts. Niles holds his lower belly as another cramp rolls through him. A bead of sweat cascades down his back, not the first and certainly not the last.

"You can't let this happen," his inner Tristan says.

He's going to mate me, and then, it will be all over.

Niles's slick starts to trickle into his already dirty pants. His body is on fire. He wants to be touched. His skin yearns for it.

"No. You tell your Omega to go fuck itself," fake Tristan hisses. "Escape plan, baby, *think!*"

But all he can think about is how his body is a ticking time bomb. Eyes flicking down to his bedding, he already wants to make a nest. A good nest, a nice nest. *Please Alpha, like me. Be proud of me.*

"No," Niles growls.

If he fights Jason, he will lose. Comparing their bodies would tell anyone that much. Niles is slim and trim while Jason is broad and meaty. Thick everywhere. Especially the silky length between his thighs.

"No," Niles snarls this time, keeping his budding lust in its place.

What if he didn't need to fight hand to hand? What if he could...

His chin dips down as he looks at the metal baking sheet. If he could stun him...

"With that thing?" fake Tristan scoffs. "And what then? How are you going to get out afterward?"

And that's the crux of it. Without Jason's code, there's no way out.

Niles rocks, arms wrapped around himself. The air is stifling now, as if the oxygen has been zapped out and replaced with muggy heat. His chest rises and falls in a rough rhythm as he heads to the faucet to douse himself with another handful of cold water. It's the only thing keeping him in the moment instead of off in his vivid, hyper-sexual imagination. That ancient ache is taking over his insides, his body begging for aid and succor…but he'll give in when hell freezes over.

But how not to fall victim to the man who killed his brother? If Trey couldn't get out, Niles doesn't stand a chance. Trey was the bravest person he ever knew, much stronger than he got credit for, whereas Niles is a coward and always has been. Even so, necessity is the mother of invention. Maybe it's also what inspires death defying hero- ics, no matter how self-serving they may be.

Jaw clenched, his gaze roams the room left and right. Porcelain toilet. Too fine marble sink. Locked door with its uncrackable code. Glass wall. Blinding white padded floor. Time-wasting books. Disheveled blanket. Silky pillow. Makeshift meal tray. That's when his eyes fall on it, and all the puzzle pieces click into place.

"There we go," fake Tristan whispers, infecting Niles with a thrill of hope—perhaps false hope, but hope nonetheless.

Niles swallows nothing, his throat sticking to itself. *And it can't be just a threat, either.*

"It has to be real," fake Tristan agrees. "If you don't do this right, there's no escape."

He shudders, and this time, it has nothing to do with his heat.

"It's time to lie, Niles."

It absolutely is.

The sensation of stripping his clothes is sensual, the fabric sticking to the sheen of moisture that dapples his pores. His jeans are too rough, scraping over the sensitive semi-erection he can't control no matter how hard he tries to concentrate on other things. Naked, the dense air caresses him with its heated breath as he hovers over his blanket, calculating with narrowed eyes. He weighs his actions like sacks of gold and poison; what will pay off and what will get him killed?

His decision is made.

He doesn't need to do this yet, but he will. Rooting around, he presses the crest of one hip to the floor and rolls on his side, using his nose and cheeks to scoot his blanket, pillow, and dirty clothes just so. He scrubs as much of himself on it as possible, making sure he's leaving his heat-scent behind. It's not strong enough yet, he's not quite there, so all he can do is keep writhing against everything, hoping that quantity makes up for quality.

Though his slick is a thin stripe along his inner thighs, it's not enough, so he tries to gather it from inside, smearing it around and dragging it to the backs of his knees in shiny, glistening lines. This is like that sexy picture he took of himself for his online profile. He has to be every Alpha's wet dream. It's the only way he's going to get away with this.

Lies.

Perfect, believable lies.

He arranges the rest of what he needs a few inches outside the nest he's made, within arm's reach but not too close. This is the biggest trick of all. Without this, all is lost.

The next part is more difficult. It shouldn't be, not when he's like this, but his mind-space is wrong. Still, Niles takes his semi-hard length in his hand and begins to pump. The glide of it makes him gasp, and his toes curl despite everything. It's too good, the tingles glowing bright inside him with an alluring, heady plea for more. He needs Jason to come back now before this feeling becomes all that exists, and he loses his mind.

Be better than my biology, Niles repeats like a mantra, stroking himself from half-mast to full, letting himself—*making* himself—moan.

That sound must be a siren's call because Jason is at the window in record time. Both palms stutter along the glass as the Blond Bastard's eyes gleam. He wastes no time. His clothes are shucked off without hesitation, his muscles flexing as he does so, and the door to the room flings open with a bang.

Niles focuses on what he's doing. He slams his eyes closed and imagines Tristan again, making himself whimper, "Alpha..."

The voice that comes back is filled with nothing but low-toned possessiveness. "Look at you." Jason hums appreciatively. He gets down on his knees, crawling closer and taking in Niles's scent, crude inhales that hiss in through his nostrils. "I've waited a long time for this, handsome. Seeing you in a nest you made for me means every second of heartache was worth it. Are you ready for your Alpha?"

Focused, Niles channels every heat he's ever had as he keeps his hand working. "Need you. Please. It hurts."

And it does. That part, at least, is honest.

Jason flips him to his back and presses a hand on his lower belly, the warmth of his palm lessening Niles's cramps ever so slightly. "Will Alpha's seed make it all better?"

Niles lets his mouth drop wide as he nods. "Please."

A rumbling purr echoes from Jason's chest as he leans down to nuzzle the crook of Niles's neck.

He won't bite me yet, will he? Please don't let him bite me.

He doesn't. Instead, he licks a long trail over Niles's mating gland. Niles rocks his head to the side with a cry of unfortunate pleasure, offering more access and a terrifying amount of trust as his captor sucks him like candy.

"You like this?"

"Yes, Alpha."

"Christ, I love it when you say that. Can I kiss you?"

Niles nods, pressing his face into Jason's shoulder with a needy mewl.

"That makes me happy." Jason kisses his temple. "*You* make me happy." The space between his eyebrows. "And after today, you always will." The tip of his nose this time. One cheek, then the other, landing gently on his lips.

Eyes cinched, Niles conjures his Alpha. His real Alpha. The one who didn't trick him after all. Who knew this man was trouble. Who tried to protect him. The one so embedded in Niles's heart, he wants no one else. With that picture held firmly in place, he opens his lips and lets Jason's tongue in, meeting it in gentle strokes.

"I want to taste you, Alpha," Niles's whispers over his lips. "Will you taste me, too?"

His chest is a tight coil as Jason's nose caresses his in little nudges.

"Really?" Jason asks.

Another nod. He has to do this, and he has to do it better than he's ever done before. He needs Jason to let go of him first, though. If not, Niles is in for a world of hurt.

Jason kisses down Niles's body, large hands gripping his flesh in slight squeezes. They would feel good if not for the man giving them, but Niles brings his mind back. If he can't keep up this charade, Jason will smell it on him. He has to keep his mind on task and his body willing. His slick begins to trickle thicker, his thighs gliding one over the other, and Jason grabs around his hips, snapping his body close in a rough gesture as he swallows him in one gulp.

With a grunt, Niles's forehead hits Jason's thighs as the sensation of heat and sinful pressure seeps up through his belly. The evil Alpha's legs spread expectantly, and Niles complies, wrapping a hand around that impressive girth and taking his first taste. Jason's precum has the familiar flavor of salt and he smells like unbridled need. No blockers and no suppressants make this man an open book of scents. Jason lets out a high-pitched whine through his nose as Niles sucks. He responds to every tongue flick with a little twitch. Every hot gust of air with a muffled whimper. He's so hard. So sensitive.

This should be easy, then.

And it is. Blowing Jason seems to blow his mind. He releases Niles quickly, keeping him close as he moans beside Niles's cock, managing little licks and sloppy kisses, but not much else as Niles does what he's best at. Hands, tongue, and teeth. Twists of wrists and sloppy suckles. Cupping hands and clamping throats while Jason gasps against Niles, holding on for dear life.

It's when Niles feels that thickness begin at Jason's base that the world seems to both slow and go too fast all at once. His knot thickening, Jason is on the edge, distracted, blissed out, and Niles knows, if he doesn't do it now, he might not get another chance.

Tipping Jason onto his rear, Niles hovers high, his face and action blocking Jason's view of what's to come. The Blond's denim eyes roll back in his head as he flushes pretty pinks and ruddy rouges, offering loud pleas to every God in the pantheon.

Unseen, Niles's free hand inches forward in agonizing millimeters.

After what seems like hours, eons, epochs, his fingers brush against a cool edge, and it brings back that twinge of hope. The bevels of the smooth metal fill him with an exultant flash of power as he wraps his fingertips around them. Snagging the metal tray, he lifts, smashing the left-behind wine glass with a crunching shatter. Jason's head draws up, but it's already too late. Niles's fingers bleed as he gets a tight grip on a large, curved shard and brings it in lightning fast. The skin of Jason's inner thigh makes a sickening *pop* when the glass digs in in a deep jab, and ripping open the man's flesh is like opening a zipper. The blood is immediate, red and gushing as Jason pulls back with a scream, but Niles is already up and at the door, brandishing the spattered glass before him, mixing his blood with his captor's on the floor.

Jason flops to his side, trying to get up, but his eyes shutter and he goes down. The blood is trailing out in ravine-like rivulets, and its loss must be making his head spin. Another thing the Blond Bastard must not have thought of. Niles is smart. Niles is wily. And he knows exactly where the femoral artery is.

"Tell me the code!" Niles shouts, one hand on the door.

Jason clutches his bleeding gash, paler than ever, his chest heaving.

"Tell me the code right now or we both die in here!"

Of all the things to happen, Jason smiles…but followed quickly by a cry of pain and a widening of the red puddle beneath him.

Niles's heart is in his throat. "Don't move! Don't make it worse! Just let me out, and I can save you! I'll get help!"

"You'll…you'll leave."

Niles's lower lip trembles. His eyes well with tears as he begins to quiver, adrenaline pumping him full of what feels like insanity. "If you don't want me to die like he did, you will tell me how to save us."

"Us?" Jason murmurs.

"Us," Niles repeats firmly, nodding. "I don't want you to die, either."

That Good Boy smile comes back, fading into pain and grit teeth. The eight digits he gives—weak, feeble, and trailing—make up a date. The day he and Jason first met.

Of course.

The door is flung open, and the plush texture of carpet is disorienting as Niles breaks into a run, stumbling down the steps and barely catching himself against the wall, leaving red smears in the shapes of his fingers. Bee-bee barks from above, likely locked in Jason's bedroom, but Niles can't think about that now. On the end table, two phones charge side by side as if they belonged together, a pair of electronic lovers, and Niles snatches his own.

There is a number he's supposed to call. An emergency number for police and safety and doctors. Instead, he rams buttons and dials for the first voice he wants to hear. The voice he's imagined. The voice that means home. Tristan picks up in a clear panic, but Niles barely hears him. Instead, filled with a frisson of panic that keeps his shoulders tight and his muscles coiled, he sobs four simple words.

"Please, I need help."

CHAPTER 14

AFTERMATH

LIGHTS FLASH BLUE AND RED, slashing pain through Niles's skull. His heat is in full swing now, his stomach cramping into a fist, closing on nothing and leaking slick in a slippery mess. It collects in the blanket under Niles's naked body in a puddle of scent, his body's vain attempt to beckon other Alphas to his rescue. His heart is a whirlpool of emotions. Fear. Relief. Horror. Triumph. Shame. Justification. Need. Revulsion. It's a mire of muck he can't wade through.

When he called 911, he didn't know where to tell them to go, and Jason was too busy dying upstairs to ask. The first few minutes of that call were a stream of chest pummeling anxiety, Niles's brain spiraling into question after question. Can they come? Will they come? If they come, can they get here in time?

In the end, they tracked his phone. Niles had run out into the winter night, naked as the day he was born and covered in blood. His arm was a streak of color from his own wounded hand, stained from palm to elbow, and his chest was scarlet from the slice he opened up in his unwanted Alpha.

Manic, frantic, and blood-spattered as he was, they'd made him get down on his knees at gunpoint, but that was over before it began, a female Omega cop throwing herself in front of him and snarling at her Beta companions. Now Niles sits in ambulance number two, number one having zoomed far and away to try and save the life of a man who doesn't deserve it. He's a murderer. He should be six feet underground. And yet...

"I'm type O," Niles tells the EMT, shaking so hard his teeth chatter. "I-I'll donate, if you need me to."

The Beta male adjusts the blanket on Niles's sweating skin, another heat-thrill swimming through him even as his palm weeps crimson into the gauze the EMT presses against it.

"Just focus on yourself right now," the stranger says, soft and delicate, as if Niles would shatter at any moment. He might.

The EMT shushes and pets him, not realizing he's making it worse instead of better. Niles wants to say something but can't put words together right now. His mouth is clamped shut as he tries not to beg for something, anything, to stave off the pain of his induced affliction.

"Where is he?!" cries out in the din of milling cops in pitch black with silver badges. Tristan's face is like a beacon in the crowd, and as soon as he sets sights on Niles, his eyes widen into large, wet circles.

Tristan only needs five strides to get to him, elbowing and shoving innocents out of the way. The EMT gives space and the Alpha's hands are all over Niles in frantic jerks, his cheeks, his shoulders, his arms. Tristan's knuckles run over his forehead in a sweep.

"He's burning up. Jesus, can't you give him anything?"

With his one good hand, Niles grasps onto the forearm of the man before him, fingers embedding in the softness of his tan-colored jacket. Tristan fogs in and out of view as Niles holds his dizziness at bay. Wetting his lips, he asks, "Alpha, are you real this time?"

Tristan lunges in, squashing their bodies together in an inelegant embrace. When his nose hits Niles's neck and swollen mating gland, Niles cries out, only to hear Tristan's resounding growl when he breathes in the scent of him, overwhelming at this point. He knows what's happening without needing to be told.

"How? It's too soon! What did that fucker do to you?"

Niles digs deeper into the scent of fall leaves, clenching and hurting. His voice cracks as his face crumbles. "I think I killed him, Tris... I...I'm..."

Those arms wrap around so tight, they steal Niles's breath. "It's self-defense. Whatever you did, he deserved it."

And Niles finally gives in to the Omega inside, bawling, "Alpha, I'm so sorry! I didn't mean for it to happen! He tricked me!"

Kisses rain down on the top of his head as those comforting hands grab tighter. To the EMT, Tristan asks, "Can I take him home?"

"I'll ask the detective. Will you see him through his heat?"

"No," Niles chokes. "I'll do it on my own."

Tristan smells as if the words physically wounded him.

"It's not you. I...I have to prove to myself that I can do this. That I can b-be strong...I don't want—"

"I get it. Shh, shh, I understand." And those kisses come again, making warm spots pepper the crown of his head in this bliss of open-air winter. "But can I take you home? I can still feed you and be there for you, even if I never touch you. Okay?"

Niles sags into his Alpha's arms, taking every tiny comfort he can as he nods with a sniffle. "You can help walk my dog."

With a soft, sad huff of laughter, Tristan says, "Of course."

Rigid and tense, Tristan straightens the collar of Niles's polo shirt, keeping the lines crisp.

"You don't have to do this," Ari says. "You saw him enough in court."

"Seeing him isn't the same as talking to him," Niles replies.

"And what's the point in fucking talking to him?" Ben gripes, parking the newly acquired, used as hell minivan in one of the prison's vast array of empty spaces, choosing one up close in front of the facility's main door. A cop saunters by and considers them, but Ben flicks his fingers rudely against the blue handicapped placard hanging from his rearview mirror in a clear gesture that makes the other man turn on his heels and saunter in the opposite direction.

"Asshole," Ben mutters.

Niles eyes the building. It's rooted to the ground in a way no other building has ever been—full, sprawling, and heavy. Concrete slabs are embedded in the haphazardly mowed grass, brick after brick laid with an expertise that makes them look like one solid expanse of wall. The place casts a shadow on everything in front of it and sends a prickle down Niles's back.

"I have to say my piece," he says.

Ari twists in her seat, her wide belly making it almost impossible as she reaches into the middle row where Niles sits, taking his hand and squeezing it. She of all people knows how important such things are. Tristan lays his palm over Ari's and, with a sarcastic groan, Ben reaches back and lays a heavy hand on top of them all, a sandwich of colorful fingers knitting together.

"Is this where we chant something that summons demons?" Ben asks.

"No," Tristan says. "This is where we engage our superpowers and perform the ultimate team attack."

"You nerds." Niles snickers, a weight lifting. How can these people make him laugh in the most inopportune of times?

"We can come with you," Ari says, but Niles shakes his head.

"I can do this."

Ari's understanding smile makes Niles swell with an affection so deep, he can feel it in his every cell. This is what true love is like, four people holding hands like idiots outside of a prison to help one of their crew fight the last battle against his personal boogeyman. Never mind holding his hair back when he throws up, this is the new stick to measure any future friends by.

With a grunt and a shove, Ari opens her door and hefts herself out, mostly consisting of a slide from the high seat to the ground, and yanks Niles's door open. No matter what they do, they can't seem to get the child safety locks off.

"Then go and be free," she says, placing both hands on the small of her back and leaning into a heavy S-curve, balancing her belly.

Hopping out, Niles rubs her broad tummy, and one of the triplets kicks him for his trouble. "Only one more week," he reassures.

"For the sake of my poor body, please," she answers.

And with that, Niles takes a huge breath of muggy, summer air and walks toward the oppressive building. The barbed wire atop the fenced areas gives this place an other-worldly feeling, like he's stepped onto a movie set. This can't be real life. But it is. It's Jason's real life. Niles is just an approved visitor. He didn't even have to apply for it. The not-so-Beta had made an assumption and listed him. That, in and of itself, is terribly sad.

Inside, a set of Labradors sniff Niles in wet snuffles. If they catch a whiff of Bee-bee, they don't show it, merely nosing him up and down and doing their jobs. The person handling their leashes nods curtly at Niles, as if saying "Routine" though Niles has rarely had his hackles up so high. What if he smells like B.O. and B.O. smells like drugs or something?

Released from inspection, Niles takes his driver's license out. He approaches a desk where a crotchety old woman scrutinizes him and his little plastic card as if everything was fake. As if Niles's nose was prosthetic and his identification was pirated from some nefarious ne'er-do-well on the internet. He assumes it's his scent more than anything else that makes her wipe off her stern expression and unlock a set of heavy jail bars with a dislikeable buzz, like cicadas, bees, and party favor horns had a threesome baby.

The next door is through a length of gray hallway in dire need of a paint job and the final door at the end seems thigh-thick. The rectangular glass panel window is a viewport to the myriad of convicts where Jason sits all in orange, disheveled and barely shaven, stubble skirting around his cheeks in a fine five o'clock shadow. His hands are cuffed to the table with a length of chain that allows for movement, though not much, and a wave of bitter satisfaction fills Niles's chest with heat.

He sits with little fanfare, staring Jason down. "You look worse than I remember."

The Good Boy smile has dimmed to a flicker of what it once was.

"How's your leg?" Niles asks, perhaps out of spite. He's not sure.

"Scarred. You got me in an unfortunate location, by the way. You know how hard it was to walk or do anything with stitches holding my inseam together?"

"My heart bleeds for you." Niles plays the world's smallest violin, his fingers rubbing together.

Jason only gazes at his lap. The big bear of a man has diminished over time. He's thinner. His shoulders are rounder. His cheekbones are more hollow. His lips turn downward at the corners naturally without him having to frown.

Jason's denim blue eyes are soft when he asks, "Did your friends leave you behind? You always seemed worried they would. This"—he points a finger upwards and twirls it in a circle facing the ceiling—"must have been quite the ordeal for them to see you through."

Somehow, even being asked such a backhanded question, Niles smiles. "If there was any doubt in my mind as to who would be there for me, it's gone now. I couldn't have done this without them."

"It won't last. Do you think Ari will actually have time for you? She'll give birth, and they'll get busy. Then, all you'll have left is me, locked up in here and unable to save you."

Niles squints his eyes, lips pursing. "You really are fucking crazy, aren't you?"

"Are you avoiding the question?"

Niles sits forward, steepling his fingers under his chin, his expression as placid as he can make it. "If they get busy, I'll be the one to reach out. I'm not going to be afraid of her drifting away. If she does, I'll be there when she has time or needs a friend. And she'll be there when I need a friend. Besides, I'm not alone anymore."

"The ex?" Jason cocks his eyebrow.

"Is no longer an ex."

The Blond not-so-Beta leans back in his chair, sighing through his nose. "Yet another person who will disappoint you."

Niles pushes his chin down onto his fingertips, their pressure grounding him. This is like a pointed version of one of their coffee shop talks, but the words fill the air with cool candor as opposed to the friendly warmth they once held. Yet there is a familiarity to it. A tête-à-tête of two people who once toyed with love.

"You know," Niles says. "I think I must be growing as a person."

"How so?"

"I realized I was never abandoned. My parents died. Who can blame them for that? I pushed Tristan away because I was afraid of him. I never gave him a chance to prove himself, and I never bothered to consider what he was going through. And Trey…" Niles's eyes lock onto Jason's. "You took him from me. This whole time, I was making myself out to be the victim when it was really the others who suffered. They didn't want to leave. Not one of them. I've been angry all this time when I should have just been grateful to have had them in my life at all. They made me who I am today. And I like myself more now than I ever have."

The question that's burned Niles rides the tip of his tongue, but hovers there, afraid to come out. Afraid the answer might hurt him. Or worse, make him forgive in some way. Still, this is what he came for.

"Why did you confess to Trey's murder? You were only on trial for me. There was no evidence for anything else. So, why?"

Jason is stiff as stone, staring at the table with such intensity Niles isn't sure he'll answer. He can hear the ticking of an old-fashioned clock on the wall, arcane, like the rest of this place.

With a sharp breath, Jason says, "It was the least I could do for him."

A fine tipped needle slides, deep and hard, into Niles's heart.

"I loved him, and I hurt him. And I hurt you…" Jason puts his face in his hands, the chains clacking roughly as they bounce over the metallic tabletop. "I need to be here. Believe me when I say I know I can never make it up to you. But I can't promise I'd never do it again if I had the chance. Even now, I need you. I hate that other people are taking my place. I hate knowing you're sleeping beside someone else."

Digging the knife in, Niles adds, "And falling in love."

Jason folds into himself, resting his forehead on the table and thumping it once. "It was supposed to be me. But I ruined it. I'm so sorry."

"I know you are," Niles says. "But I don't think I care anymore."

Arms slide up defensively over Jason's head, as if he's trying to block out Niles's words. "You're never coming back, are you?"

"No."

"Will you at least write me letters?"

"No. I'm going to do my best to forget everything about you."

Jason shudders and makes a heavy, wet sigh. "Please don't say that. I'm all alone here. I'll miss you. I'll always be thinking about you."

"Of course, you will." Niles pushes back his chair with a loud scrape and stares down. "Because I'm the one who put you in here."

He turns away from the broken man, irredeemable before Niles ever met him and irreparable now. He refuses to feel pity. Instead, he walks wordlessly out the way he came, nodding at guards and others who are doing their jobs, not knowing each step away is both freeing and painful for the Omega before them.

The sun is bright, and he squints his eyes, holding a hand up as the summer heat wraps around him once more. It's over. It's all over.

Fall is coming soon, the best time of the year. His best friend will give birth to three new family members, her mate will do his best to be a father to his pups, and Tristan—beloved Tristan—will be by Niles's side, plying him with everything pumpkin spiced, finding couples costumes, and diving into fall leaves that smell like him.

With a smile, Niles looks over to those who wait for him, who will always wait for him, and walks on toward his future.

It's sure to be a good one.

ACKNOWLEDGMENTS

So many "thank yous" go to the *321…Write!* Discord group, where we authors coalesce and beg each other for support of all kinds, whether that be talking each other down from throwing ourselves off a cliff, inspiring each other to write one more word, brainstorming when we've painted ourselves into the proverbial corner, or editing one another's stories.

Huge love to my beta readers: Emme Cordeiro, Ashley Hawthorne, and Christina D. Ambrose, and especially to Kirsten Blacketer for diving in, even though life got hard.

Thank you all. I love you.

AUTHOR'S NOTES

When I first wrote *All's Fair in Ruts and Heats,* I thought it was a clear single novel. One and done. Then, a few fans of the book asked me to make a sequel based on Niles, the best friend character. At first, I didn't know how keep the same dark romance tone (Niles was so funny and supportive throughout the entire first book), but as soon as I realized that the darkness and threat could come from outside him and his bubble of safety with Ari, it clicked.

This book became about so much more than just a love triangle, hot guy sex, and overcoming personal trauma. In that way, it was more complex and challenging to write than I'd originally imagined. There were several times where Niles had to experience racist behavior, but I also took a look at how Alphas, Betas, and Omegas might see each other and their role in the world. It had its own kind of racism feel to it. Designation-ism (which isn't a word). Additionally, with Ben being handicapped, there was that to think about. I didn't want to be ableist, but I wanted him to have difficulty with this change in his body. He fell into a coma at the height of his strength and woke up weak and unable to walk. It's a huge life change that one doesn't just accept with no qualms. That being said, I didn't want to have him outright give up and say he couldn't do things, either. He was virile, he was funny, he was sexy and successful. All of those things could be true in the same space with his internal struggle to accept his new reality.

It was easy to give Niles a backstory, though. Both he and Ari had grown up in foster care after all, so the base of it was already written for me. I loved the idea of a mother whose aim was to come back for her kids but couldn't. There was potential for it to be more heartbreaking than stories of parents who never planned to come back at all, as it would have given the kids a tangible hope, perhaps even a cockiness or a confidence at first—a sort of "I'm not like you, because my mama is coming back!"—but then it would all fall apart. I thought it would help set up Trey and Niles's early relationships in the foster home to be antagonistic. There would need to be some damage control on Trey's part after their mother died, helping to make him mature even further at an early age as well as continue that thread of needing to protect his brother from adversaries. There was so much written about their life in the home that couldn't make it into the book (otherwise this would have been a completely different story), but it's there in my heart.

With Ari and Ben, it was a little trickier. They needed to have a concise, loving relationship that was stained with grief. Ben had to be the more complex of the two in my mind, as he'd gone through so much and, unlike Ari, could rightfully blame himself for parts of it. He also has a bit of an old mindset, having not quite adjusted to the new world he woke up into, which affected some of his language choices.

While this book wasn't about Ari and Ben, I wanted them to still have their moments come to life on the page. I knew readers of the first book would have loved to have seen more of that, and this was my chance to give it to them. Even so, I couldn't let Caleb fade into nothing. He was pivotal. I knew Ben would look at Caleb through rose-colored glasses so thick Ari would keep a good portion of what happened to herself. And being the good person she is, she would focus more on her sympathy for her first mate than spend time blaming him for his deplorable actions. After all, if she wasn't that kind of person, how could she come to love Ben beyond his scent?

There's no such thing as a clean, wholesome relationship without baggage in this Omegaverse world I've created—and isn't that always the way? Someone always has something to overcome, otherwise there's no story. Niles had to find his courage and let go of his hurt. In the end, I think that he was able to do that. I'm proud of him.

BOOK TRIVIA

- **Jason was almost named Noah.** I had to change it because, in scenes, Noah and Niles's names bled together and it became hard to read. I said to myself, "What's an everyday, not crazy sexy, unassuming male name?" Voila. (Apologies to all Jasons for this assessment.)
- **In the initial outline, Trey had a much smaller role to play.** I was writing the end of the story and my brain said, "Ooh, what if Jason's ex-boyfriend was Niles's brother!?" It sounded cool but was also sort of random. I had to go back and write a whole ton in about Trey and Niles growing up to make sure you would care about the big reveal.
- **I had a pen-and-paper list of scenes we spent with Jason and Tristan.** I wanted to balance them, so we got enough time with each potential love interest…but then I realized Niles's heat ruined that whole prospect, since there is an entire chapter dedicated to their…ahem…affection. C'est le vie.
- **I almost had Jason shave Niles's braids off as a punishment for bad behavior.** To me, this would have been the most ultimate devastation, ruining Niles's sense of self. Very Sampson and Delilah. That being said, it was too horribly traumatic, and I couldn't imagine Niles enduring that without completely shutting down and giving in.
- **I did a lot of work deciding how to present the flashbacks.** "Do I make them a little part of every chapter? Do I chunk them up into one?" The deciding factor was the pacing. My next book deals heavily in flashbacks as well, but that is treated differently. I'm interested to see which approach fans like more!

It's inevitable that I'm going to write fluffy short stories about Niles and Tristan and their life together, just like I did for Ari and Ben. Alas, my blog will be the only place to put those words out into the world. Feel free to check out: nixcomix.com/blog to see what I come up with or subscribe to my newsletter. I'm sure it will be a cute, sweet, sexy read.

Thank you for coming along on this journey. I'll see you next time.

ALL'S FAIR IN RUTS & HEATS

AFTER DEFENSE ATTORNEY CALEB REED IS TROUNCED IN COURT BY A ROOKIE LAWYER - AN OMEGA NO LESS - HE KNOWS ONE THING AND ONE THING ONLY. ARI JACOBSON WAS MEANT TO BE HIS MATE...WHETHER SHE WANTS TO BE OR NOT.

WITH EVERYTHING HE'S DONE, CAN CALEB GO FROM ENEMY TO LOVER, OR WILL HIS BLIND OBSESSION DESTROY THEM BOTH?

TAGS: RAPE/NON-CON ELEMENTS, ALPHA/BETA/OMEGA DYNAMICS, EMOTIONAL MANIPULATION, STALKING, PRAISE KINK, VIOLENCE, SUICIDE, ANGST, BITTERSWEET HEA.

WHITE WITCH, DARK MOON

The war is never-ending. Morale is non-existent and magic stains the sky as dragon riders spiral, trying to take down the raging soldiers of the Dominion. The people are exhausted. The battles need to end. But how? The hate between the factions is just too strong. Unless...

When Reyanne, the White Mage of the Separatist movement, goes head-to-head with her arch nemesis Zanthrand, the Dark Moon of the Dominion, many choices abound. You, dear reader, hold their fates in your hand. Choose your path and choose wisely. Can you end the forever-conflict? Can you bring these soul-bound sorcerers from enemies to lovers? Or will your choices doom them both?

Good luck, my friend. It's all up to you.

THE RETELLING OF FAIRY TALES

Prepare to be surprised

THE RETELLING OF FAIRY TALES is a reimagining of some of our most beloved childhood stories for an adult audience, adding twists and turns that bring them into fantasy worlds, modern day settings, alien planets, and may even take the point of view of the villain.

Fully illustrated, this collection will make you laugh, pull your heartstrings, and let you fall in love. Come with us and enjoy the call of destiny, the sizzle of romance, the ache of tragedy, and the timelessness of magic, all wrapped together in this one unforgettable collection of short stories.

ABOUT THE AUTHOR

Known for her weirdness and general snarkasm, Nichol works to engage her audience in several mediums. Many stick to one favorite genre, but she can't seem to make up her mind. You will see her dipping into everything from graphic horror, graphic novels, to graphic romance. Trust the descriptions, mind the tags and just know that, if you like her writing, you're in for a good ride.

Visit her at nixcomix.com to read exclusive short stories, see more about what books are coming out next, watch author interviews and more.

Find her on social media:
Twitter / TikTok / YouTube – **Nixcomix**
Tumblr / Instagram – **Nixcomix1**

www.ingramcontent.com/pod-product-compliance
Lightning Source LLC
Chambersburg PA
CBHW070458300726
48975CB00007B/2227